DUSTY

A boy, a pony and a dream…

CRAIG RYDER

www.craigryder.co.uk

"There are times when you need the silence of animals to recover from the noise of humans."

Cover Art by Craig Ryder.

Proofread by Julie Stark.

For Macsen and Cybi –

Caru Chi, Dad x

The wild Carneddau ponies roam the higher reaches of the Conwy Valley, a living link to the history of the ancient landscape. I last encountered them on a windy autumn afternoon, high above Rowen. They seemed timeless and otherworldly, a reminder of nature's enduring strength. Watching them I wondered: how is it that horses form such profound connections with humans, even as they remain animals with natural instinct?

The bond between humans and horses is unique, forged over centuries of companionship and cooperation. Today, this bond is being explored and understood in way that may have seemed mystical in the past; horses are increasingly recognised as having the power to heal, their sensitivity and presence is now at the heart of 'equine-assisted therapy' programmes designed to help individuals navigate challenges and life-changing circumstances.

At the heart of this power is the horse's ability to connect. A horse's senses allow them to pick up on the subtlest of human emotions – fear, sadness, anxiety or joy – and respond in ways that can feel intuitive. Scientific research now tells us that horses can synchronise their heart rates with ours, and create a physiological connection that can bring about trust and calm. It is a phenomenon that can be seen in equine therapy sessions where a horse and a human both experience an alignment that has the ability to create a sense of mutual understanding and safety – that for some humans (and horses) has been all too rare.

The mirroring of emotions can appear uncanny; a person who is nervous may find that their horse becomes restless, whereas a switch to a calmer aura in a human often leads to a more relaxed horse. The mirroring is not just a reflection of a horse's sensitivity but an amazing tool for therapy, that offers people the chance to recognise their own emotions and to start to be able to regulate those motions alongside a horse giving them real time, non-verbal feedback.

Perhaps most remarkable is how horses adapt to the needs of the people they work with. Their ability to sense vulnerability – whether that is physical or emotional – enables them to respond with apparent patience and a soothing gentleness. For individuals who have disabilities, life-altering injuries, psychological trauma and other challenges, the responsiveness of a horse can be transformative, creating a space where barriers no longer exist and possibilities emerge.

Recent research shows the impact of equine assisted therapies on mental health and wellbeing. Interactions with horses have been shown to lead to significant improvements in emotional regulation and social functioning in both adults and children. Horses don't judge us, which is probably a big thing for people who need support.

It was the 2024 Nature-Based Interventions and Equine Therapy for Uniformed Public Services Symposium held at Anglia Ruskin University in Chelmsford that really convinced me that I need not doubt what is written above. Fellow speakers, including Mary Jo Beckman, an American specialist in Equine Assisted Therapy, talked about the benefits of equine therapy in diverse communities, including those affected by suicide, trauma and limb loss. Demonstrations and videos reinforced the message with testimonies of the enduring power of horses to bridge and heal, to create hope and empower people to bring about change and reframe their challenges.

I wrote to Craig not long afterwards, knowing he was writing 'Dusty'.

Nature is a powerful force, whether it is horses we turn to in times of need or walking in the wind. There is something for everyone if we reach out to connect.

Dr Ailsa Snaith

(Neuroscientist, nerd and advocate of nature therapy – ex pupil of Ysgol Dyffryn Conwy.)

1

Leaving Henryd.

Ten-year-old Dylan Evans watched silently from his bedroom window as his dad hurled black bin bags into the back of the van. He wondered, not for the first time, whether this would be the final time that they moved house. He let out a deep sigh and slumped against the grubby wall, his back accidentally flicking the light switch. The room stayed dark – no bulb, just like there had never been one since the day they moved in. He'd asked countless times but nothing ever changed.

At the age of ten, Dylan had already lived in more houses than he could count on his fingers. Henryd, though, had felt different. It was a beautiful Welsh village tucked neatly into the side of a hill, with fifty-two houses, a tiny chapel, and a little village shop. More importantly, there were no pubs. It felt safe, like a community full of hope and kindness. Neighbours watched out for one another, and Welsh was the only language spoken from dawn until dusk. Henryd had made him feel like he belonged somewhere, for once in his life.

'Maes Refail' hadn't felt like any other council estate. It felt posh, at least to Dylan, with its neat rows of houses and well-kept gardens. His next-door neighbours, Mr. and Mrs. Pierce, had made it their personal mission to ensure Dylan spoke Welsh fluently. They'd invite him over on Sunday afternoons, feeding him cake and biscuits while testing his Welsh vocabulary, eager to help him thrive in school. Henryd had been where Dylan found his roots, where he discovered his Welshness. It was also the place that would later evoke the deep longing of *hiraeth*; that untranslatable Welsh word for the homesickness he was sure he would carry for the rest of his life, but as he watched his mam stuffing the last bags into the van, he knew that Henryd was just another stop along the way. No matter how much he wished it were different, this would be his last night here. His friends, Michelle and Claire, would wake up tomorrow and wonder why he wasn't banging on their door to walk to school.

Dylan could see a warm light glowing from Michelle's bedroom across the road. For a moment, he wished he could run over and tell her he was leaving the village. He knew she'd be surprised; no one ever knew when Dylan was going to disappear from their lives. It always happened like this, suddenly and quietly, with no chance for goodbyes.

He thought of Michelle's house – how it always smelled so clean, like freshly washed clothes and Mr Sheen polish. Her curly-haired mam, Helen, was a whirlwind of energy constantly bouncing around the house, tidying up even when there was nothing out of place. Michelle's world was orderly, safe. She played the piano every day, forced to practise to a timer, tapping out gentle notes with her stubby fingers. Dylan sat quietly beside her, wishing he could pound the piano keys and release the emotions he kept bottled up inside.

Claire's house was the complete opposite. Her liberal parents smoked weed and filled Claire's head with all sorts of information she didn't need to know yet. Dylan liked both girls though, and for once, he had felt like he belonged somewhere.

Now, as he stood in his nearly empty bedroom, watching the soft light from Michelle's window, he wondered what she'd think when he didn't show up tomorrow. Would she miss him? Would anyone?

Dylan's thoughts turned to his favourite person ever – Jill, the local teenage babysitter, who often looked after him, even though she was rarely paid. Jill initiated Dylan's addiction to horses at Bwlch Mawr riding stables. There, Dylan had met Guinness, a patient little black pony with a kind heart. It had been love at first sight. Each weekend, Jill would walk with Dylan up the winding hills to the stables, the sweet smell of horses hitting him long before they arrived.

Wendy, the riding instructor, (who was more of an adoptive mother to the 20-odd feral little horse-lovers) was kind but strict, and what she didn't have in height she more than made up for in voice. Standing at barely 4 feet 10 inches, she had a way of commanding respect that could make even the most unruly of kids snap to attention.

Her booming instructions echoed across the arena, and every child – whether seasoned rider or complete beginner – covered in horse shit and sweat, was eager to impress her.

Wendy's love for horses was undeniable and contagious, as if she carried some kind of equine magic in her words. No matter how chaotic things got, Wendy had eyes on every child, every horse, and every detail, ensuring the young riders followed her orders to the letter.

"Sit up straight, Dylan!" she barked, her signature sibilant 's' cutting through the air. "Up, down, up, down... Don't let Guinness canter yet! You need to *feel* the trot first!"

Dylan tried to focus, fighting the urge to rush ahead, even though Guinness seemed more than happy to pick up speed. Wendy's piercing voice kept him in line, but it was the warmth underneath her bark that kept him coming back. When he managed to rise to the trot correctly, Wendy's face would soften into a smile that felt like winning first place in a competition.

"Well done, Dylan," she would say, her usual sharp tone turning into something that felt like pride. "You've come a long way in a short time."

Bwlch Mawr was paradise, a world far removed from his troubled home life. His dad's gruff voice jolted him back to reality, yanking him out of his daydream. 'Come on, Dylan! Fuckin' hurry up!'" he snapped. "Whatever is left will just have to stay. There's no more room in the van!"

Dylan felt his eyes begin to leak.

The thought of the new flat tugged at his heart – no garden; no space for his dog, Prince, to run; no more riding stables. The idea of never seeing Guinness again made his eyes fill with tears. It was like all the things that made life bearable were slipping away. Why did they always have to move house at night? Like they were sneaking away, slipping out of one life into another.

"If I have to come up those fuckin' stairs…" his dad threatened.

Dylan quickly grabbed his riding hat and boots – his most prized possessions. He glanced at the wooden domino toy box his taid had made him for his birthday. A pile of toys still sat in the corner, abandoned and forgotten in the rush to pack.

He sighed, feeling the familiar weight of disappointment settle in his chest.

"Never mind" he whispered to himself. "It's a new start…again."

****

2

Innocence Lost.

Sunlight glared harshly through the curtainless windows. The constant roar of the river outside was deafening, so different from the gentle stillness of the quiet village nestled in the mountains. Dylan stirred on the floor, pulling himself up from the makeshift bed of blankets where he had slept. His body ached, unused to the hard surface. He rubbed his eyes and took in his new surroundings.

The view outside was nothing like the rural life he'd known in Henryd. Welcome to Llanrwst!

Kids screamed in the distance and Dylan could see teenagers hanging from monkey bars, some of them smoking cigarettes. Girls strutted by, dressed as though they were playing adults, their bright lipstick out of place in the cold morning light. He pressed his nose to the window, trying to make sense of this strange new world.

What the hell was this place? Glanrafon Flats.

The estate shimmered under the Autumn sunlight, its bleak grey buildings somehow catching the light like a cheap 1980s soap set. Dylan pulled away from the window and scanned the room. His gaze landed on a small horse-head plaque left behind on the wall by the previous tenant. A faint smile tugged at his lips. Maybe, just maybe, things would be okay here.

He hurried downstairs, his heart heavy with uncertainty. The moment he reached the living room, a thick cloud of cigarette smoke hit him. Barry, his dad – but not really his dad – sat at the table, shovelling down cornflakes from a chipped bowl. Kwik Save cornflakes, of course. Kellogg's was too posh for Glanrafon Flats.

"Take Prince out for a shit, Dyl," Barry grumbled, barely glancing up from his bowl. "He's not used to the flat yet."

Dylan looked down at Prince, his brown-and-white Springer Spaniel, who was already wagging his tail, eager to explore. Prince was more than just a dog; he was Dylan's best friend, his only constant in a life of endless change. No matter where they ended up, Prince was there, always ready with a wag of his tail and an endless supply of love.

Dylan slipped on his worn shell-suit jacket and his favourite fluorescent green shorts, dodging the empty bottles of Country Manor wine and Stella cans piled near the door.

"Come on, Prince."

Prince shot outside, down the stairs from the first floor maisonette, ahead of Dylan, racing towards the patch of grass out front. He didn't hesitate, squatting to relieve himself immediately. Dylan rubbed the back of his neck, glancing around at the grey walls that loomed over them.

"Good boy, Prince," he muttered. "Do you like it here?"

Prince cocked his head, as if to say he was just as confused by this new place. The two of them looked around at their strange new home, feeling as though they'd landed in a foreign country. The grim, unfamiliar estate made Dylan uneasy as he and Prince trudged back up the stairs.

"There wasn't much milk," Barry called out when Dylan re-entered the flat, "but you can have the bit left over from my cornflakes. Pour it over yours."

Dylan peered into the bowl his dad was offering. The leftover milk was tinged yellow, bits of Golden Virginia tobacco floating on the surface. Dylan grimaced. There was no way he was drinking that. Instead, he made a beeline for the kitchen, where he pocketed the last two custard creams from the almost-empty pack before anyone else could claim them.

"Survival of the quickest," he whispered to himself.

Barry grunted, barely looking up. "I'm heading to town. Mam's taken Ela and Baby J to the post office. Don't go wandering off, you're babysitting later."

"OK, T'ra," Dylan mumbled, already tuning him out.

The door slammed shut behind Barry, the noise vibrating through the thin walls of the flat. Dylan looked around. Unlike their last place, this one actually had light bulbs in every room. He flicked the kitchen light on. Then the living room. Both worked. A small thrill of excitement sparked in his chest – something worked here, at least.

Dylan ran back upstairs, with Prince bounding after him, the dog's tail wagging as if nothing had changed. He unpacked his things slowly, carefully setting aside his riding hat. The sight of it made his chest tighten. His thoughts drifted back to Henryd, to Jill, to Bwlch Mawr. A tear slid down his cheek, but Prince, always there when Dylan needed him, nuzzled it away with a soft, comforting lick.

"We'll be ok, Prince. We have to be." Dylan whispered, his voice shaky. "We just need to find some horses and some riding stables, then we'll be fine."

He dug through his bag, pulling out his crumpled poster of John Whittaker and Milton, his prized possession. He smoothed it out carefully. There was just enough Blu Tack on the back to be able to press it on the wall. He stood back, staring at it for a moment before glancing out of the window at the bleak view of the flats.

"One day, I'll get out of here," he whispered to himself. "I'll have a big white horse. I'm not meant to live here."

Next, he unrolled his Bros poster and hung it beside John Whittaker. The familiar song lyrics about wanting to be famous floated into his mind, and before he could stop himself, he started singing quietly to the empty room.

His voice filled the small room, surprising even himself. Dylan had a good voice – something he'd discovered at the local Eisteddfod in Henryd.

"I can't answer, I can't answer that," came his mam's finely-tuned soprano voice from the hallway, laughing.

Dylan jumped, spinning around.

"Maaaaam! You gave me a fright!"

Magi chuckled as she leaned against the doorframe, her bright blue eyeliner and blue eyeshadow lit up by the piercing sunshine.

"Alright, boy?" she asked, her voice softer than usual. "So what do you think? D' ya like it here?"

Dylan hesitated, glancing around the room. "Erm, not really. Will I still be going to Llangelynnin school?"

"No, I told you. You're starting a new school tomorrow."

His chest tightened. "But what about my horse riding?" he asked, the hope in his voice fading fast.

Magi's eyes softened, but only for a moment. "Did you see? The little girl who lived here before left that behind for you." She gestured to the horse head plaque on the wall.

Dylan nodded. "Yeah, I love it. But do you think I can still go riding with Jill?"

His mam sighed. "No, Dyl. You can't go to Wendy's any more. The last two cheques bounced, and we can't afford it. Besides, it's too far away. You'll just have to find a new hobby. There's a swimming pool in this town, you know."

"But I can't swim."

"Well, you'll have to bloody learn then, won't you?"

Dylan blinked back the sting of tears. "What about my friends?"

Magi gave him a weak smile. "Forget them now, Dyl. You'll make new friends here. Jamie, the boy next door, seems nice enough. I've just spoken to his mam. He's going to be your best friend."

"But what if we don't like each other?" Dylan asked, his voice barely above a whisper.

"You will," she said, her tone final.

And just like that, it was another school, another life. His old friends faded into distant memories, like faces in a dream he couldn't quite recall any more. Forget them. Forget Henryd. Move on. But the one thing he couldn't leave behind was his love for horses.

Dylan slipped on his battered orange headphones and pressed play on his Walkman, escaping into his tape of last week's Top 40. The music was his escape, a way to drown out everything else. Dylan took great pride in his ability to stop taping when the presenter was talking and then to start taping again just as the next song was starting. He considered it one of his many skills – as well as knowing all the words to every Bros, Madonna and randomly, Shirley Bassey song. Dylan closed his eyes, swaying as he hummed along to the familiar tune of 'La Isla Bonita' under his breath. His voice picked up as he sang words about dreaming of distant places, imagining himself far away, dancing on a tropical island where everything felt alive and free.

Dylan was startled as he felt a hand on his leg. It was his five-year-old sister Ela. "Mam is shouting you to come downstairs," she said, smiling. "Prince has just been sick." She squirmed through the sides of her dummy.

Dylan ran downstairs to find Prince in the living room, wagging his tail, eating up what was left of his sick on the bare wooden floors.

"Dylan, I've been fuckin' shouting you to come and help me," came the cries of his mam from inside one of the little cupboards in the kitchen, her legs hanging out like little matchsticks. This was the usual procedure when they moved houses. Magi would hacksaw the padlocks off the electric and gas meters and the family would live like kings for the first few months, with free electric and gas.

"Woooohooooo" came the joyful sound of Magi's voice as she slid out of the cupboard. "The meter man hasn't been to empty it. We can have some chips and ice-cream tonight, kids!"

It was like they had won the lottery, when in reality there was probably no more than twenty pounds in each meter. But that was a lot of money in 1986.

"Right, I've got a job for you.' She said, smiling.

"I know, I know…" he responded playfully, before going on to mimic his mam's voice. "Run this 50p through both meters and then you can keep the 50p afterwards to buy sweets." This wasn't Dylan's first rodeo!

Dylan snatched the fifty pence piece with glee, knowing he was going to be able to buy his favourite sweets and not have to share them with his siblings.

Dylan knelt to check the meters, but before he could insert the 50p, Ela leapt onto his back with a giggle. "Horsey, Dyl, horsey!" He smiled, with his nose pressed to the electric meter. "Yes, horsey… Dylan is a horsey… Do you want to trot?" he asked in a fake posh voice, as he placed the 50p in the meter, wound the dial and then caught it again at the bottom. "Up, down… up, down…" he instructed as Ela bounced around on his back, giggling. Dylan was always good at entertaining the kids. On many an occasion he would be left alone to babysit his five-year-old sister and two-year-old brother.

The electric meter dial was turned as high as it could go, so Dylan moved on to the gas meter. A sudden knock on the door made Magi freeze. Her hands darted for Baby J, pulling him close as her eyes flicked nervously towards the door.

"Sssshhhhh…" she hissed, her voice low and urgent. "Ela, get off Dylan's back now." She hurriedly dragged Ela and Baby J into the living room.

"Dylan," she whispered, "go answer the door and tell them nobody's home… and don't let anyone in the house."

Another knock came, louder this time, more insistent. Dylan stood hesitantly for a moment, his heart pounding. Lying wasn't something he liked to do, but when Mam asked, he didn't question it. As he made his way to the door, Prince was already there, bouncing excitedly, his tail wagging furiously.

Dylan cracked the door open to find two men who looked like the Chuckle Brothers standing on the doorstep.

The taller of the two men smiled down at him. "Hiya, boy. Is your mam or dad there?"

"No," Dylan replied, trying to keep his voice steady while holding back Prince. "They've gone out."

"Ah, alright then. We've got the new television your mam ordered last week. Can we leave it in the hallway?"

Dylan blinked in surprise. "Yeah, that'll be fine."

The men carried the large TV into the hallway, gently placing it down.

"Does your mam know how to work the meter on the back, or should we show you?" one of them asked.

Dylan shook his head, grinning confidently. "Nah, she'll just pull the lock off."

The two men burst into laughter. "Helluva joker, eh, boy?"

Dylan found himself laughing too, even though he wasn't sure what was so funny as he was only telling the truth. He shut the door behind them, still chuckling as he turned around, only to find Prince lifting his leg and relieving himself against the brand-new television.

"Prince!" he shouted, horrified. "Not on the new telly!"

****

3.

The New Boy.

Being the new boy in school had become second nature to Dylan by now. He'd had plenty of practice – this was his fifth school. But there was something about *Bro Gwydir* school that felt different; something bigger, colder, and harsher than any school he'd walked into before. The corridors seemed endless, stretching out like the tunnels of some factory where everyone moved in perfect lines, their footsteps echoing off the tiled floors. The strict, regimented feel of the place unnerved him. At his old school in Henryd, things were more relaxed, more personal. There were only three teachers in the whole school, and the creaky floorboards always warned you when someone was coming.

Here, it was like entering a new world – a world that wasn't his.

"Blwyddyn Pump, Dyma Dylan," Mrs. Jones announced to the Year 5 class in Welsh, her voice husky and formal. "He's from a little village called Henryd. Make sure you speak Welsh to him."

With that, he was thrust into this new environment, halfway through the school term, given no more than a passing introduction. Dylan could feel the eyes of his classmates scanning him, assessing him. He was a stranger in their world, and he could sense it immediately – the wariness, the sizing up.

Mrs. Jones pointed to a desk at the back of the room, where he was to sit with three neanderthal boys who looked more suited to a cave than a classroom. Aled, Gareth, and Iwan resembled caricatures out of *Spitting Image*. Rough, rubber-faced inbreds.

"So, why do you move around so much? Is your dad in the army or something?" Gareth asked, his voice deep for a ten-year-old, his question more of an accusation than an inquiry.

Dylan hesitated, the weight of his reality pressing down on him. How could he explain the truth? His dad wasn't in the army, unless you counted the battle to find the next drink. His father's only strategy was moving from pub to pub, dragging the family along whenever he couldn't afford the rent. But Dylan wasn't about to say all that. Not here.

"Just moved a lot for my mam's work," Dylan mumbled, keeping his eyes low.

"Wyt ti'n hoyw?" Aled asked, his voice dropping into a conspiratorial whisper, his expression sly.

Dylan blinked, unfamiliar with the word. He hadn't heard it before, but the tone and the sniggers from the other boys, told him enough. He looked at Aled, confusion twisting in his stomach.

"What? You don't know what that means?" Aled's fat grin widened, and he leaned closer, his eyes gleaming with mischief. "It means, are you a queer?"

The laughter from Gareth and Iwan followed, sharp and cruel. Dylan's throat tightened. He didn't know how to respond. His brain scrambled for something to say, but nothing came. Not in Welsh, not in English. He dropped his eyes to the desk, hoping the conversation would end if he just stayed quiet.

Mrs. Jones, oblivious to the low hum of bullying brewing in her classroom, droned on about some local history – the old bridge that connected the town to the rest of the neighbouring villages. Dylan wasn't listening. His thoughts were somewhere else, anywhere but here.

In a desperate attempt to change the subject, he asked, "Do any of you ride horses?"

He felt the weight of his own voice, awkward and too hopeful. His heart reached back to Henryd, where he could lose hours riding horses, feeling the world shrink beneath him as he soared across fields. It was one of the few things that made him feel grounded, in control.

Aled snorted. "Horses? Horse riding is for girls." He wiped his nose with the back of his hand, train tracks of bright green snot reappearing almost straight away.

Dylan's cheeks flushed with embarrassment. He should've known better. This wasn't Henryd. The boys here were harder, meaner. He wasn't going to find any kindred spirits in them.

"Are you a girl, then?" Iwan piped up, his eyes narrowing like a predator locking onto prey. "Should we start calling you Delyth instead of Dylan?"

The laughter that followed was sharp, cutting into him like shards of glass. Dylan clenched his fists under the desk, knuckles turning white, but he kept his head down. He knew better than to fight back. They'd only come after him harder if he did.

He tried to disappear into himself, letting his thoughts drift back to Henryd, to the village where everything had been simpler. He could see Michelle and Claire, his two closest friends. They never teased him like this. They understood him, or at least they never made him feel like he didn't belong. Their world had been gentler, safer. He missed that world.

"Hey, Delyth!" Iwan's voice cut through his memories, followed by more mocking laughter.

Dylan shot him a look but stayed silent. What was the point? He wasn't going to win here, not today. The bell rang and he let out a quiet breath of relief, pushing himself out of his seat. The boys continued to snigger as they packed up, their cruel words still hanging in the air, like cigarette smoke, clinging to him.

As Dylan walked out of the classroom, he felt the familiar ache of loneliness settle in his chest. He'd felt it before, every time he was the new kid, but this time it felt heavier, more suffocating. Surviving *Bro Gwydir* wasn't going to be easy. He wasn't sure if he had the energy for it.

Just then, Jamie, his neighbour, appeared at his side, offering a faint smile. "Follow me, Dylan. We've got to get our dinner tickets."

"Dinner tickets?" Dylan repeated, confused.

"Yeah, for free meals. Most kids from the flats get them. Do you get free meals?"

"I—I don't know," Dylan stammered.

Jamie nodded sympathetically. "Don't worry, Aunty Bev will sort you out."

The two boys hurried towards the canteen, where the infamous Aunty Bev – the school's no-nonsense dinner lady—stood at the doorway, her arms folded over her apron. She was a short, stout woman with bobbed hair and a booming laugh that could fill a room.

"Hiya, boys! And I know who you are," she greeted Dylan warmly. "Ew you look like your mam, ynai del? Remind me of your name, boy?"

"Dylan Evans, Miss," he replied politely.

Aunty Bev's eyes crinkled as she smiled. "No need for 'Miss,' Dylan. You can call me Aunty Bev. Now, let's get you sorted with a dinner ticket, eh?"

Dylan felt his stomach twist, embarrassed at not knowing the routine. But Aunty Bev's kindness soothed him, and Jamie gave him a reassuring nudge.

Outside, the lines for lunch were forming. There were three: one for the packed-lunch kids – the ones Dylan always thought were lucky because their mums made them food every day. Then there was the line for kids who paid cash, the 'rich' kids, the ones who went on ski trips and always had new shoes. And finally, there was the third line, the one Dylan found himself standing in now – the line for the 'free-school-meals' kids, the ones with hand-me-down clothes and scuffed-up trainers. The ones who, like him, were just trying to make it through another day.

As Dylan stood in the free-meals line, he couldn't help but feel like this was exactly where he belonged – whether he liked it or not. The jumble of emotions – nerves, embarrassment, loneliness – was softened only slightly by the chatter around him. At least here, no one was openly mocking him like earlier in the classroom.

"This is Dylan; he's my next-door neighbour," Jamie said proudly, nudging Dylan towards the group.

"Hi Dylan! You can thit by me if you want to. I alwayth end up on the end of the table with no one thitting by me," came the chirpy voice of one of the boys. His lisp was immediately noticeable. "My name ith George, but they call me Lithpy," he added, smiling wide and without any self-consciousness.

Dylan's lips twitched into a small smile. George, it seemed, had the IQ of a crayon, but Dylan took an instant liking to him.

Jamie, however, leaned in with a playful whisper, "I wouldn't sit by Lispy. There's a reason he always sits by himself – he robs everyone's food, and he sometimes shits himself."

Despite the teasing, George didn't seem to mind. He just kept grinning, as if used to it, or maybe just happy to have someone new to talk to. Dylan found his own tension easing slightly. The mocking was still there, but it felt different – less cruel, more like a game among kids who'd known each other forever.

One by one, the other pupils introduced themselves. There was Rhys, who had an eye patch and looked like he'd combed his hair with a pork chop.

"Without that patch he's got one eye looking at you and one eye looking for you… but he'll be normal soon." whispered Jamie.

"Fuck off Jamie, or I'll tell Miss you're taking the piss." warned Rhys.

"I'm just saying you'll have normal eyes soon. I wasn't taking the piss," Jamie responded, "sorry Rhys."

"I only have to wear this patch for another few weeks," Rhys stated proudly, "then my eyes will be laser-strong, like ET's. That's what my mam says."

Owen, who was the tallest of the group, with a huge forehead and a small tuft of ginger hair on the top of his head, earning him the nickname 'Sloth', smiled and nodded in agreement. But it was Caroline who stood out most.

Caroline, with her blonde hair, a natural tan, and a face that was constantly flushed pink, smiled at Dylan. She had a warmth about her, like the kind of person who made everyone feel welcome. "Hiya boy, nice to meet you, Dylan," she said brightly. "Are you liking the school?"

She reminded Dylan of Michelle, his friend back in Henryd. Caroline had that same motherly vibe, looking after everyone else, even if she didn't have to. She didn't belong in the 'free meals' line – everyone knew that. Her parents owned a café in town, and she helped out there on weekends.

"I get this flushed face from all the steam when I empty the dishwasher," she explained casually, wiping her rosy cheeks. It was like she always had to justify why her face was red. She grinned, clearly used to teasing about it.

As they neared the front of the line, a booming voice of Aunty Bev called out, "Caroline, get in the other queue please."

Caroline just rolled her eyes with a smile. "That's Aunty Bev. She always yells at me for being in this line. But this is where my friends are, so…" she shrugged. "I don't like queuing with the joskins, talking about their dad's new Volvos."

The others laughed as Caroline reluctantly stepped out of the line and moved to the cash-payers' queue. It was a routine everyone seemed familiar with. A daily ritual.

For a moment, Dylan felt his shoulders ease, as if a heavy weight had lifted. There was something about this group-an oddball mix of characters-that reminded him of *The Goonies*. Despite the teasing and the quirky dynamics, there was a strange sense of belonging that hovered just out of reach. He still felt out of place, like a puzzle piece that didn't quite fit, but the edges were starting to align. It wasn't perfect, but it wasn't as unbearable as it had been earlier. Maybe, just maybe, he could survive here after all.

****

4

The Council Estate Jungle.

The autumn days slipped by as the sunlight hours shortened. One rainy Saturday afternoon, Barry and Magi were in the kitchen, clinking bottles and muttering over their rocket-fuel homebrew. In six to eight weeks, Dylan knew, this loopy-juice would lead to arguments and fights, regular as clockwork.

"Add more sugar, will you?" Barry slurred, already half-drunk.

Magi rolled her eyes, stirring the murky liquid in the plastic barrel. "This stuff doesn't need more sugar. It's already strong enough to knock out a horse."

"If you don't add more, it'll taste like horse-piss. Just put it in."

Dylan sat perched on the back of the tatty burgundy sofa, Shirley Bassey's dramatic 'I Who Have Nothing' pumping through his battered orange sponge headphones.

Even as Shirley's voice filled his ears, he couldn't block out the hum of Barry and Magi's bickering in the kitchen or the loud, relentless noise of *Tom and Jerry* blaring from the TV. Ela and Baby J sat huddled under a stained bobbly blanket, slurping blue slush puppies from plastic cups.

The rain streaked down the window as Dylan's thoughts drifted. How the hell had he ended up here, in Glanrafon? Was this grim estate what Mam would have dreamed of when she was a kid? Even at the age of ten, Dylan wanted better. He needed better.

Not that the people here were all bad. He'd learned in just a few weeks how kind his neighbours could be. 'Gwen next door' – always called by her full title – was a constant presence. Day or night she was always there, ready with a cup of sugar or a bit of washing powder. She even took in kids when fists started flying in the middle of the night. Then there was Mrs. Jones from number 20, always saving her 50p pieces to make sure the electric meter stayed on for families like Dylan's. She knew that without those coins, they'd be sitting in the dark more nights than not.

And Muriel from number 2. She was like the queen of Glanrafon. First person on the estate to get SKY TV, and she'd often invite the little flat-rats – like him and the other estate kids – into her sitting room to stare wide-eyed at the flashy, otherworldly programmes. Everyone played their part in keeping the community tight. What little they had, they shared. Granted, like any estate, there were a few who looked like they brushed their teeth with *Pedigree Chum*, but their hearts were big.

A thud came from the kitchen, followed by Magi's shouting.

"Barry, for fuck's sake, watch what you're doing! You nearly knocked the whole bloody demijohn over."

"Fine, do it yourself then," Barry retorted bitingly, "you're a miserable cow."

"Miserable?" Magi spun on him, wiping her hands on a towel, her voice rising. "It's alright for you, spending all afternoon at the pub while I'm left here with no money for these kids. You're a selfish bastard."

"It's not my fault we were rained off today." Barry retorted.

"Rained off. A bit of fuckin' drizzle and you can't build a fuckin' wall? Is this how it's going to be now you can walk to the pubs? Is it?"

Dylan tensed. The fights had already started, earlier than usual this time.

Ela glanced at Dylan and rolled her eyes. Baby J kept slurping his slush puppy, oblivious.

The door clicked open, and 'Gwen next door' breezed in without knocking, as usual. "Picked up a few bits from Spar for you," she said, waving away the tension like it was nothing. "Just to keep you going."

Magi, caught mid-argument, softened. "Thanks, Gwen. You didn't have to."

'Gwen next door' glanced between Barry and Magi, her eyes flicking to Dylan with a knowing look. "That homebrew again, isn't it? I've told you both, it'll be the death of you."

Barry huffed. "It's tradition, Gwen. Cheaper than the shops. Just a bit of fun."

"Fun, right…" Gwen shot back, with her hands on her hips. "Until someone ends up sleeping outside the front door!" She turned to Dylan, lightening up her voice, "Hiya, Dylan. You alright, boy?"

Dylan shrugged. "Yeah."

But the weight of the scene pressed on him. In six weeks, when the homebrew was ready, the fights would be worse. The adults always claimed things were fine, but their voices betrayed them.

Gwen lingered by the door. Before leaving, she reassured Dylan. "Hey Dyl, if you need anything, you knock, okay? You and the little ones are always welcome."

He nodded, but 'Gwen next door's' kindness only reminded him how trapped he felt. It was all fine – until it wasn't. In Glanrafon, things could turn bad really fast. He looked at Baby J, eyes wide and fixed on the TV, and wondered if his little brother would ever know anything different.

"Dylan, grab us a bottle opener," Barry called from the kitchen.

Dylan didn't move.

"Dylan!" Barry shouted. "Oi! Don't ignore me, you little prick. Get over here."

Dylan felt his pulse quicken, heat rising in his chest. He wanted to shout back, to tell Barry where to go, but his throat tightened. His voice stayed stuck somewhere deep inside him.

The sound of 'Gwen next door's footsteps echoed faintly down the stairs outside, and for a moment, he wished she hadn't left.

He grabbed the bottle opener and handed it to Barry.

"Hey, come here," Barry said, his voice suddenly affectionate.

Dylan hesitated, dragging his feet towards him. Barry took a long drag of his rollie, cupped Dylan's face tightly between his hands, and blew the smoke right into his face. Dylan coughed, almost choking on the thick cloud of tobacco.

"Don't ignore me again you little prick" Barry laughed, giving him a hard shove against the wall.

Tears filled Dylan's eyes, but he wouldn't let them fall. He clenched his fists. *Fuck you, Dad*, he thought to himself.

Shoving his headphones back on, he fast forwarded his tape to hear Madonna's soft voice flooding his ears with the lyrics of 'Live to Tell'. Dylan made his way into the living room, undefeated, singing to himself as the drizzling rain cleaned away the dirt on the windows. His fingers traced invisible patterns on the windowsill as the melody poured out of him. The words weren't just Madonna's – they felt like they belonged to him, each one striking a chord deep within.

Dylan quickly pressed stop on his Walkman. He blinked and rubbed his eyes. Was he dreaming, or was there really a pony outside his window? His small nose pressed against the cold, misted glass, as he squinted into the grey light of the drizzly afternoon. Wiping away the fog left by his breath, he saw it – clear as day – a little black pony, trotting leisurely along the pavement wearing a bright red head collar.

He couldn't believe his eyes. Excitement surged through him and without a second thought, Dylan sprinted to the door with Prince trailing right at his heels, tail wagging eagerly.

"No, Prince. You stay there. Good boy," Dylan commanded, holding the dog back.

Prince sat down obediently, though his eyes stayed locked on the door, brimming with curiosity. Dylan shoved his feet into his trainers, pressing the backs down in his rush, half hopping and half stumbling around as he tried to pull them on properly. The thrill of the moment made his heart race.

Down the stairs and out into the council estate he ran, spotting the pony again just ahead, now being led away by a girl in a bright yellow shell suit. Her pace was slow and casual, as if walking a pony through a council estate was the most normal thing in the world.

"Hey... hey! 'Scuse me! Hello!" Dylan called out, his small legs pumping furiously, trying to close the distance. He was panting by the time he caught up, but the sight and smell of the pony made his exhaustion vanish. He could smell the familiar, comforting scent of damp horsehair, and suddenly his mind flashed back to Bwlch Mawr riding stables. This pony, with its glossy black coat and bouncy walk, reminded him so much of Guinness, the pony he used to ride before moving here.

"Hi," Dylan panted, introducing himself between breaths, "I'm Dylan."

The girl, taken aback, stopped and turned around, giving Dylan a puzzled look. She had a tall, gangly frame, with soaked ginger hair sticking to her forehead from the drizzling rain, her cheeks red from the cold. For a moment, she seemed to wonder why this boy was chasing after her and her pony, but then her expression softened.

"I really love horses," Dylan added quickly, sensing her hesitation. "I haven't seen one for ages. Can I please stroke her?"

The girl's face lit up with a smile. "Of course! Her name's Dusty."

Dusty. It was love at first sight. The pony stood there calmly, her big, gentle eyes blinking at Dylan as he approached her cautiously. He extended his hand slowly, careful not to startle her, and began stroking her neck. The pony's coat was soft and slightly damp from the rain, and Dylan spoke to her in a low, soothing voice.

"Good girl, Dusty. Good girl," he whispered, moving his hand to her forehead, gently tracing the white star that adorned her brow. Dusty nuzzled into his hand, then licked his palm with her warm, velvety tongue.

"She likes you!" the girl said with a laugh. "She usually bites."

Dylan grinned from ear to ear. "She's lovely! She reminds me of a pony I used to ride called Guinness," he said, "but he was a gelding." He added, to demonstrate his equine knowledge.

The girl, who looked a few years older than Dylan in her yellow shell suit, extended her hand confidently. "I'm Dawn. Do you live around here?"

Dylan nodded shyly. "Yeah... we moved here a few weeks ago," he said, feeling a little embarrassed about the run-down estate he now called home. "Do you know if there are any riding stables around here?"

Dawn wiped a strand of wet hair from her forehead and nodded. "There's a stables up the valley, but it's pretty far – like miles away."

Dusty, growing bored of standing still, tugged at the lead rope. Dawn smiled apologetically. "I should get her back to her field before it gets dark. You can walk with us if you want."

Dylan's heart raced. "Is it far?"

"About twenty minutes if we walk fast," Dawn replied.

Dylan hesitated for a moment, his mind racing as he thought about his mam calling him back to babysit his siblings. But the sight of Dusty, the little black pony, was too irresistible. The idea of walking beside her, of getting to know her better, was far more tempting than staying at home. "Okay," he said, trying to sound casual, though inside, his heart was racing with excitement.

"I'm just looking after her for a week or two while my cousin's on holiday," Dawn explained, her hand firm on the lead-rope as Dusty tugged her, eager to keep moving. Dawn glanced at Dylan, who was still beaming, his small hand resting on Dusty's neck as though he couldn't quite believe she was real. "Do you want to help me look after her?"

Dawn didn't have to ask twice. Dylan's face lit up like a Christmas tree, his eyes wide with excitement. "Yes! Definitely! I'd love to!" His voice was practically shaking with enthusiasm. "Do you go to see her before school?" He asked, hopeful that he could spend as much time as possible with the pony.

"We can do," Dawn replied, clearly amused by his eagerness. "If you can get up early enough."

"I can!" Dylan blurted out, his face flushing slightly as he corrected himself. "I mean, I don't... but I will! Just tell me when and I'll be there. Promise."

Dawn chuckled, impressed by his determination. "Alright, it's a deal," she said with a nod, her grin growing wider.

Dusty, as if understanding the excitement between the two new friends, nuzzled Dylan's hand again, her breath warm and soft. Dylan could hardly contain his joy, his mind racing with the thought of early mornings spent with the pony, maybe even riding her one day. It felt like a dream he didn't want to wake up from.

The three of them – Dylan, Dawn, and Dusty – walked briskly as the daylight began to fade, eager to reach the field before it got too dark. They wound through the market town, past rows of shops, and then down the one-way system that led towards the town's most cherished landmark – Pont Fawr, the Big Bridge.

Dusty's hooves clacked against the concrete as they approached the narrow, ancient bridge, which was just about wide enough for a car to pass over. Dylan, full of excitement, ran ahead with Dawn, pulling Dusty into a quick trot to avoid the traffic that was already beginning to pile up on the other side.

"The traffic light system here never works," Dawn explained, slightly out of breath. "There's always arguments in the summer with tourists – bloody English people can't reverse for the life of them."

"I bet Dusty could reverse," Dylan joked, grinning.

Dawn laughed, the sound echoing off the stone walls of the bridge. "You could teach her!"

On the other side of the bridge, the trio made their way briskly down the long stretch of road. Dawn slowed down as they reached a gate. "Here's her field," she announced, her voice filled with pride. "If you can open the gate for me, I'll get her in."

Dylan quickly obeyed, fumbling with the latch before swinging the gate open. Dawn led Dusty into the field, expertly removing her head collar and hooking it on to the gate as she explained, "We never leave her head collar on, just in case she gets stuck on something. Better safe than sorry."

Dylan nodded, his eyes wide as he watched her work. He stepped forward to give Dusty one last gentle hug before Dawn pulled a carrot from her pocket and offered it to the pony. Dusty munched on the treat happily, her soft eyes closing in contentment. Once the carrot was gone, she gave a playful whinny and trotted off up the field, calling out to the other horses in the distance.

"Are there other horses up there?" Dylan asked, straining to see through the growing darkness.

"Yes, a few," Dawn replied, "but it's getting dark now, so you'll have to meet them tomorrow."

And with that, the two of them headed back towards home, the sky quickly turning to dusk. The streetlights flickered on as they approached, casting a warm, golden glow over the town.

As they reached the bridge again, they found themselves caught in a small traffic jam. A farmer in a tractor was refusing to reverse, causing a long line of cars to stretch out behind him, their headlights glowing dimly in the evening haze.

"See?" Dawn said, gesturing to the scene with a smirk. "This is what I mean. Big Bridge drama. I'll meet you here tomorrow at 7:30 a.m., and we'll check on Dusty before school, alright?

"My house is that way," Dawn pointed right, "and you need to go that way," she pointed left. "See you tomorrow!"

"See you tomorrow!" Dylan chirped back, his voice filled with a new kind of energy.

For the first time since moving to Llanrwst, Dylan felt truly warm inside. He had a new friend in Dawn, and most importantly, he had Dusty. His life had changed in a single evening, though he didn't yet fully know just how much.

Full of excitement, Dylan hurried through the town, his heart still racing from the thrill of his new friendship and encounter with Dusty the pony. However, as he glanced at the darkening sky, panic set in. He'd been gone longer than he realised. Picking up his pace, he sprinted through the wet streets, his trainers splashing through puddles, knowing what was coming. Before he even reached the flats, he could already hear it – his mam's shrill voice cutting through the evening air.

"Dyyyy-laaaaaaan!" Magi's high-pitched scream rang out from the flat window. As she spotted him in the distance, her frustration only seemed to grow. "Dylan, get in... now!"

The bubble of excitement that had carried him since meeting Dawn and Dusty popped in an instant. Dylan's shoulders sagged as he trudged up the slippery stairs, his once-joyful energy now drained away. Pushing open the door to the flat, he braced himself for the inevitable.

"Where the hell have you been?" Magi's voice was a fierce wall of sound as she paced the room, pulling on her cardigan with hurried, angry movements. "I'm late for Bingo now, and it's your fault! I've told you not to bloody wander far!"

Dylan tried to soften her anger, hoping the news of his exciting day would ease the tension. "I've just made a new friend called Dawn," he said, his voice still carrying a trace of excitement. "She's got a pony called Dusty, and she—"

"I don't care about a bloody pony!" Magi cut him off, nastily. "And don't be expecting any money for riding. We haven't got it. Baby J needs his nappy changing and there's only a little bit of milk for his bottle so put some water in it too. Don't stay up late. T'ra."

With that, Magi slammed the door, her heels echoing in the stairwell as she strutted away in her blue denim mini skirt and black mohair cardi, her eyes set on bingo in 'The Club'. Dylan watched her through the window as she disappeared over the little bridge, her brisk walk punctuated by the click-clack of her heels. He sighed, his excitement from earlier evaporating like mist.

Turning back to his younger siblings, Baby J and Ela, who were sitting on the worn-out burgundy sofa, he forced a smile. "Right then, what are we going to do with you two?" he asked with exaggerated cheerfulness. "Tom and Jerry? Or..." He paused dramatically, trying to inject some excitement into the situation, "I think I've taped Button Moon! Shall we watch that?"

Ela's face lit up, and Baby J clapped his pudgy hands, both of them bursting into song with the familiar tune, their faces full of joy as Dylan rummaged for the video tape. He carefully changed Baby J's heavy nappy then dressed them both in their pyjamas, their little arms reaching out to him trustingly. Once they were settled on the sofa, Dylan plopped himself between them, the comforting warmth of their small bodies on either side of him.

"Alright, Ela, you're in charge. Press play on the remote," Dylan instructed with a grin. He loved giving Ela little responsibilities – it always made her feel important.

Ela leaned forward eagerly, her small finger hovering over the button. But just as the opening scene flickered on, the television screen went dark.

Ela's hopeful face fell instantly. "The pound's gone," she said quietly, her voice carrying a weight of resignation that no child her age should know.

Dylan's stomach twisted with worry. "Don't worry," he said, trying to sound confident, even though his heart was pounding. "There's no lock on it any more. I just need to run the pound through the meter."

Rummaging through the small coin box on the back of the television, Dylan felt a wave of relief when his fingers closed around a pound coin. He turned to his siblings with a playful grin, holding it up triumphantly. "Look what I found!" he said, pretending to pull it from behind his ear.

Ela's face lit up again, her earlier disappointment forgotten. "Do mine!" she giggled, leaning in close, her little face glowing with anticipation.

Dylan repeated the trick, pretending to pull another coin from behind her ear. Ela laughed, her worries washed away by the simple magic of the moment. Little jokes like these had a way of easing the heaviness in their world, if only for a while.

Dylan ran the coin through the meter and the screen flickered to life again, the familiar sights and sounds of *Button Moon* filled the room. As the three of them snuggled together on the sofa, Dylan couldn't help but feel a small sense of pride. Despite everything – the stress, the yelling, the constant pressure of looking after his siblings – he could still make them laugh, still bring a little joy to their world. And for now, that was enough.

****

5

A New Beginning.

"Open this fuckin' door NOW, Magi!" Barry's voice echoed through the hallway, raw and full of menace. "Or I'm going to kick the door in!"

Dylan jolted upright in his bed, his heart racing. He fumbled in the darkness, pressing the button on his small Casio watch to check the time: 1:26 a.m. The shrill scream of Magi's name, followed by a loud, desperate thud against the door, sent a jolt of panic through him. Dylan had hoped they had left all this behind in Henryd and that Llanrwst would be a new beginning for them all.

Another round of ferocious banging shook the door as Barry's voice erupted again, filled with venom. "Fuckin' let me in, Magi! I swear, I'll kick this fuckin' door in!"

Dylan's gaze darted to Baby J, fast asleep next to him. His chubby cheeks were flushed, his little forehead slick with sweat, oblivious to the chaos unfolding downstairs. Dylan's stomach twisted with dread. He couldn't let Barry wake up the others. The door rattled again, followed by a furious kick. Dylan slid quietly out of bed, careful not to disturb Baby J or Ela, who lay snuggled under her thin blanket in the corner of the room.

He tiptoed down the stairs, each creak of the floorboards making his heart race faster. His mam's door was half-open as he passed and, through the crack, he saw her sprawled across the bed, starfish-like, dead to the world. A bottle of cheap wine next to her bed told him she wasn't waking up anytime soon.

The pounding on the front door grew more intense, as if Barry was trying to smash it down with his bare fists. Dylan hesitated, knowing what was coming but not knowing how to stop it. His hands shook as he reached for the cold metal of the door handle. Opening it a crack, he barely had time to react before Barry shoved it wide open, knocking him off balance and sending him flying onto the floor.

"What the fuck are you doing up? Get to bed, you little bastard!" Barry snarled, his words slurred and soaked with alcohol. He staggered into the living room, barely keeping his balance as he kicked his boots off and crashed onto the sofa. "Always fuckin' interfering, aren't you?"

Dylan stayed on the floor for a second, his cheek pressed against the cold linoleum. His shoulder throbbed from where he'd hit the ground, but he didn't cry. He wouldn't give Barry the satisfaction. There was no point in explaining that if he hadn't come down to open the door, Barry would still be outside. Barry didn't care. He never cared.

Quietly, Dylan got to his feet, rubbing the sore spot on his arm. He stole a glance at Barry, who had already slumped back into the couch, his head lolling to one side as he fumbled for the remote. The room reeked of cigarette smoke and booze. Dylan's nose wrinkled at the familiar stench that had become part of their life.

Without a word, Dylan slipped quietly back upstairs, his bare feet barely making a sound on the creaky wooden stairs. As he reached his room, he gently closed the door behind him, careful not to make a noise that would wake Baby J or Ela. The weight of the night's tension settled deep in his chest, but he pushed it aside as he climbed into bed, curling protectively around his baby brother. Baby J shifted slightly but stayed sound asleep, his tiny hand resting against Dylan's arm.

Dylan lay there in the darkness, the pounding of his own heartbeat loud in his ears, yet somehow it harmonised with the soft, rhythmic breathing of his siblings. The comforting sound made the room feel safer, like a quiet lullaby in the middle of a storm.

There was just one thing missing.

A soft sniffing came from under the door, followed by a gentle nudge as it creaked open. Dylan smiled. Right on cue.

"Come on, Prince," Dylan whispered, his voice barely above a breath, "there's room for one more."

His loyal companion padded into the room, the soft thud of his paws on the floor barely audible in the stillness of the night. Prince, with a nose for sensing when things weren't right, nudged his way onto the bed with practised ease. He wriggled under the duvet, settling into the familiar spot behind the crook of Dylan's bent legs, curling up as if he were made to fit there.

Dylan reached down, running his hand over Prince's soft fur, feeling the steady rise and fall of the protective dog's breathing against him. It brought him a sense of calm, like having a warm, comforting presence that understood him without a word. In this small world – just him, Baby J, Ela, and Prince – he felt a moment of peace.

He smiled to himself, eyes growing heavy as he lay there, trying to quiet his mind enough to sleep. Despite the chaos downstairs, despite everything that had happened tonight, Dylan's thoughts drifted to tomorrow. His heart fluttered with excitement, the memory of Dusty still fresh in his mind. He could almost smell the damp, earthy smell of the little pony, hear the soft clop of her hooves on the wet pavement.

Morning couldn't come soon enough. Tomorrow was all about Dusty. And maybe, just maybe, things would get a little better.

With that thought, Dylan's eyes finally fluttered shut. Four souls, safely connected in their sleep.

****

Beep-beep. Beep-beep. The alarm on his Casio watch pulled Dylan from a restless sleep… 6:45 a.m. The piercing sunlight streamed through the bare window, warming the chilly room. *There is one good thing about not having curtains,* Dylan thought.

He looked over at Baby J and Ela, both still somehow fast asleep, curled up in the tangled blankets. Sliding out of bed like an SAS commando on a covert mission, he carefully avoided disturbing them. Prince, their loyal dog, wagged his tail slightly but remained sleepy with the little ones, as if knowing it was his job to keep watch over them.

Dylan pulled on his worn, slightly dirty school uniform, then crept to the bathroom. Splashing his face with cold water, he eyed the empty tube of Castell toothpaste – one of the freebies from school. He squeezed out the last pitiful bit onto his toothbrush. *Just a quick brush today. I've got more important things to do.*

He tiptoed to the kitchen and opened the fridge. There wasn't much; considering that Baby J and Ela would need milk for breakfast, he thought there would be just enough for him to have a small bowl of Rice Krispies too. As he shovelled the cereal into his mouth, he thought ahead to the day – his first official morning with Dusty. A solitary carrot, slightly wilted but still good enough, caught his eye in the veg rack, and he grabbed it, tossing it into his school bag. He glanced at the shiny 20p coin on the table and pocketed it, hoping it was meant for him.

Before stepping out, Dylan checked the living room through the crack of the door. Barry was still sprawled out on the sofa, one leg hanging over the edge, clearly not up in time for work again. Dylan sighed inwardly. *More arguments tonight then,* Dylan thought, but shrugged it off. Right now, he didn't care; today was about Dusty and nothing else.

He quietly shut the door behind him and sprinted down the stairs. Running through the sleepy streets of the market town, Dylan couldn't contain his excitement. The crisp autumn air stung his cheeks, and his breath formed little clouds as he rushed along, his trainers slapping the wet pavement. By the time he reached Big Bridge, it was 7:22 a.m.

Dylan gazed across the river at the little café, its walls dressed in vibrant red and gold autumnal leaves; it was almost like looking at a postcard and the bright sunshine reflected off the full fast-flowing river below.

Dylan paused for a moment, taking it all in. He'd learned about this place in school. He felt a small burst of pride for finally connecting something from the classroom to the real world.

"Ty Hwnt i'r Bont," Dylan muttered to himself, smiling.

"What are you mumbling about?" Dawn's voice rang out, appearing as if from nowhere.

"Errrr….nothing," responded Dylan with slight embarrassment, "I was just talking to myself."

"Come on then," said Dawn enthusiastically. "Let's go and say good morning to Dusty."

Dawn appeared older in her school uniform, with her tall, lean frame and confident demeanour. At first glance, you'd have thought she was at least a few years older than Dylan. But in reality, at just 12 years old and with him having just turned ten, she was only two school years ahead of him, though her maturity and street-wise attitude seemed to set her apart. They walked side by side, their conversation flowing easily; the excitement of their shared love for horses binding them together.

The crisp autumn air carried the scent of damp earth and fallen leaves as they made their way up the road towards the field. The morning sun hung low, casting long shadows, but its golden rays cut through the mist in a way that made everything feel warm and alive. They didn't stop talking the entire way, chatting about everything from school to Dusty's quirks, like how she sometimes nipped at her lead rope when she was impatient.

As they approached the field, they could hear the faint whinny of Dusty before they even saw her. There she was, right by the gate, pawing the ground as if she had been waiting for them all morning. The sight of her made Dylan's big blue eyes light up with pure joy.

"I've got a carrot in my bag," Dylan said, practically bouncing on the spot with excitement. "Am I okay to give it to her?" His voice was filled with hope, his hands already fumbling with his backpack.

"Of course," Dawn replied, a knowing smile on her face. "I think you've got a friend for life there." She watched with amusement as Dylan's face broke into the widest grin.

Dylan, without a second thought, climbed over the gate, slipping down into the muddy patch on the other side. "Watch you don't get your uniform dirty, Dylan!" Dawn warned with a laugh. "You don't want to be a walking mess when you get to school!"

But Dylan didn't care. His school uniform, already a bit worn, was the last thing on his mind. He slowly approached Dusty, who was eyeing the carrot in his hand with eager anticipation. As he held out the carrot, Dusty nuzzled his hand before gently taking it and crunching it contentedly. Dylan beamed, patting her on the neck affectionately. He leaned in closer, burying his face in her mane and inhaling that comforting "horsey smell" he had missed so much. The scent filled him with a deep sense of happiness, despite the fact that his uniform was now streaked with horse hair.

"How do you feel about checking on her in the mornings for me?" Dawn asked suddenly, her tone casual but with a hint of seriousness. "I can then do the afternoons."

Dylan's eyes widened. "Really? You mean, check on her... on my own?" His voice faltered slightly, but the excitement quickly overtook any hesitation.

Dawn nodded, adjusting her school bag on her shoulder. "Yeah, I'm starting a paper round tomorrow, so I won't have time to come up here *before* school every day. If you could do the mornings, it'd be a big help."

Dylan couldn't believe what he was hearing. His heart raced with the thrill of being given such responsibility. "I'd love that! I mean... I'll have to ask my mam, just in case she needs me for Baby J and Ela, but I'm sure it'll be fine. Do you want me to start tomorrow?"

"That'd be perfect," Dawn replied, looking relieved. "And then maybe we can both come up here on Saturday, spend more time with her?"

"Yes!" Dylan practically shouted, hardly able to contain himself. "Will we be able to ride her?"

"Yep, we can take her up to the forest. She loves it there," Dawn said, smiling. "But for now, let's get her sorted. Pull that bramble from her tail, will you?"

Dylan walked around to Dusty's hind quarters, his small hands gentle but sure as he tugged the bramble from her tail, being extra careful not to hurt her. Dusty stood still, her tail flicking slightly, but she seemed to trust him completely.

"Good girl, Dusty... good girl," Dylan whispered, his voice soft and full of affection. After removing the last of the bramble, he gave her one final pat on the neck. "See you tomorrow, Dusty!" he added, his voice almost a secret between them.

Dusty gave a soft whinny, almost as if she understood, and trotted off towards the other horses at the top of the field. Dylan watched her go, his heart swelling with happiness.

"We should get going," Dawn said, glancing at her watch. "Don't want to be late for school."

The two of them power-walked down the road, their footsteps creating a steady rhythm on the wet pavement, the soft squelch of their shoes echoing in the otherwise quiet morning. Their breath puffing visibly in the cool autumn air.

When they reached Big Bridge, the point where they had to go their separate ways, they exchanged quick goodbyes. "See you Saturday then, meet me here at 10 o'clock." Dawn said with a grin before darting off towards her school.

Dylan's heart swelled with warmth as he waved her off, his chest tight with anticipation. "See you Saturday!" he called after her, his voice laced with joy. Thoughts of Dusty, and the responsibility that had been placed on him, danced in his mind. It was a feeling of pride, mixed with the eager thrill of adventure.

He practically floated into school, his steps light and carefree. For once, the weight of home felt miles away. As he stepped through the school gates, he was greeted by Caroline, who approached him with a concerned look.

"Hi Dylan, do you know you're covered in animal hair?" she asked, her tone teasing but kind. "Do you want me to rub it off for you?"

Dylan looked down at his sleeves, now realising they were streaked with Dusty's hair. "Yes, please," he replied with a grateful smile, feeling a little embarrassed but mostly appreciative of her help.

As Caroline brushed the hairs from his uniform, she continued speaking. "I'm supposed to be singing in assembly tomorrow with Deiniol, but he's off sick with tonsillitis. I remember seeing you at the Eisteddfod in Conwy – you've got a hell of a good voice. Do you want to duet with me?"

Dylan's stomach flipped at the unexpected request. He hadn't sung in front of others in a while, and the idea both excited and terrified him. "Erm, I don't know," he mumbled, "What song are you singing?"

"'Dod ar fy Mhen,'" Caroline responded confidently, her eyes brightening. "Do you know it?"

Dylan's face softened as he nodded. "Yes, we used to sing it in chapel. I know the soprano line," he said, his lips curling into a smile.

"Great!" Caroline beamed. "I'll sing the alto part. Shall I ask Mrs Jones if we can practise at lunchtime?"

Dylan hesitated for a second before nodding. "Yes, okay." A quiet confidence began to bloom inside him as the day ahead seemed to open up with new possibilities.

The morning classes were a blur of lessons on local history and folklore. They had been learning about the legendary Dafydd Ap Siencyn, but Dylan's mind kept wandering. He rested his chin on his hand and, catching the faint smell of Dusty's coat on his sleeve, smiled to himself. His thoughts drifted to the hills beyond the school, where Dusty would be grazing under the autumn sun, free and happy.

His daydream was interrupted by a sneering voice. "Oi, Dylan," called Iwan from across the classroom, his tone dripping with mockery. "Why does your hair look like pubes?"

The other boys burst into laughter, but Dylan, unfazed, shot back quickly. "Probably for the same reason your ears look like the handles of the FA Cup – genetics."

The room erupted in laughter, but this time at Iwan's expense. Mrs Jones quickly shushed them all, bringing the lesson to a natural end and announcing that tomorrow, some of Year 5 were going to be selected for leading roles in the school nativity play this year.

Caroline, not missing a beat, raised her hand. "Miss, Dylan's going to sing with me tomorrow in assembly. Could we have a practice with you, please?"

Mrs Jones looked up in mild surprise, her brow arching at the thought of Dylan singing with Caroline.

"Let me just put the kettle on, and I'll play through it with you," Mrs Jones replied warmly, her smile encouraging.

As the two students walked towards the piano, a few other children sniggered behind their hands as they were leaving the classroom. The thought of Dylan, the new boy from Henryd, singing alongside someone like Caroline, seemed amusing to them. Dylan's stomach twisted with nerves, but he kept his head up. He wouldn't let them get to him.

Mrs Jones glanced between them as they stood by the piano. "Right," she said, flipping through the sheet music. "Who's on the soprano line? Caroline?"

"No, me," Dylan answered, his voice steady and proud.

Mrs Jones blinked in surprise but smiled, nodding. "Well, this is going to be interesting."

They began to sing, their voices blending together beautifully:

"Dod ar fy mhen dy sanctaidd law,
O dyner fab y dyn…"

Their harmonies filled the room, and soon, even the students who were still packing their bags stood still and listened quietly, mesmerised by the performance. Mrs Jones' face lit up with approval, her fingers still hovering over the piano keys.

"Hyfryd," she said softly. "Absolutely beautiful."

At that moment, Dylan wasn't just the lost boy from Henryd any more. There was a newfound potential within him, something that had caught the attention of not just his classmates, but his teachers too. And with the promise of tomorrow's assembly – and Saturday afternoon with Dawn and Dusty – his world was slowly beginning to feel a little brighter.

****

6

The Birth of the Opportunist.

Walking home from school, Dylan stopped to gaze into the window of 'Toys and Games' – his favourite shop to spend some time day-dreaming. The brightly lit display caught his eye, showcasing the latest My Little Pony figures, their colours gleaming under the soft glow of the cabinet lights. He stood for a moment, lost in thought, already planning to drop a few subtle hints to his mam about them being the perfect Christmas present for his sister. Of course, he had his own motives too – he could already picture himself spending hours with the ponies, creating elaborate stories and adventures.

As Dylan daydreamed, a voice broke through his thoughts. "Do you like the new Action Man figures?" Jamie's familiar tone was friendly, as always. "I've asked for them for Christmas," he added excitedly, pointing towards a row of action figures in the corner of the display.

Dylan glanced at the figures, but he didn't want to lie to Jamie. "Hmmmm… yeah… I just want horse riding stuff. I'm not really interested in Action Man." Dylan admitted truthfully, turning to Jamie with a smile. It was nice to be honest with him – Jamie was one of the few people Dylan felt comfortable enough around to share his real interests, knowing there'd be little judgement.

Jamie grinned. "Fair enough," he replied, unfazed. "I'm a bit scared of horses!"

Just then, a loud, booming voice echoed down the street. "Jaaaaamieeeee!" came the unmistakable call of Bill, Jamie's dad. He appeared a moment later, lugging a bulging bag of groceries.

"Carry this bag home for me while I pop to the Pen y Bryn for a quick pint," Bill said, thrusting the heavy bag into Jamie's hands with a grin. He gave Dylan a nod of acknowledgment, then added, "Hey, Jamie, why don't you show Dylan what I just bought you?"

"Yeah, I will," Jamie responded, struggling with the heavy shopping bag, "T'ra Dad. Come on Dyl, come to my house."

Dylan watched as Jamie struggled with the oversized shopping bag, his arms straining to hold it up. "Let me help you," Dylan offered quickly, stepping forward. "I'll take one of the handles."

Using a handle each, the two boys shared the burden of the grocery-filled bag and made their way to the flats.

At that moment, Dylan noticed Prince sitting by the corner of the library. The loyal dog's ears perked up the second he spotted Dylan and Jamie, and within a heartbeat Prince was bounding towards them with his tail wagging furiously, his excitement palpable after a long day of wandering around the flats on his own. His tongue lolled out of his mouth, and he danced around Dylan, as if greeting an old friend after years apart.

"Hello, boy!" Dylan exclaimed, kneeling down to meet the enthusiastic dog, rubbing Prince's head affectionately. "I've missed you," he added, his voice soft and full of warmth. Prince responded with a happy bark, his tail swishing even faster as Dylan continued to shower him with attention.

Jamie chuckled as Prince darted between the two boys, nudging Dylan playfully with his wet nose before trotting back over to Jamie for his turn. "I bet he's been waiting for you all day," Jamie said, giving Prince a friendly pat on the side.

Dylan smiled, watching as Prince wagged his tail and circled around them, still bursting with energy. "He's the best," Dylan said, standing up. "He never forgets where I am, even after a whole day in school."

As they started walking again, Prince happily trotted along beside them, his tail wagging in rhythm with their steps.

Dylan stepped into his flat and threw his school bag into the hallway.

The familiar scent of stale smoke hit him immediately, filling the quiet air. As usual, no one was home. He gently guided Prince into the living room, giving him a gentle pat before closing the door behind him. Prince would be fine there for a bit.

Outside, Jamie waited patiently. Dylan joined him, and the two boys made their way next-door, to Jamie's flat.

"Hello, boys," Jamie's mam greeted them warmly as they entered. "Did you have a good day at school?"

"Yes, thank you," Dylan responded with a polite smile, his voice upbeat.

"It was okay," Jamie shrugged. "Dylan's coming to play for a bit. Is that alright?"

"Of course," Jamie's mam replied, giving them both a kind smile. "Go on then, show him your new toy!"

"I will!" Jamie's voice echoed from halfway up the stairs, already darting up with Dylan close behind, eager to see what the surprise might be.

Dylan felt a sense of familiarity as he entered Jamie's house. The faint smell of stale smoke lingered here too, just like in his own home. Their lives weren't all that different – both had one sister, both lived in small flats, and both had parents who were always at the pub. Yet, there was something unique about Jamie's family. His mam, Zabette, was French, and his dad, Bill, was from Essex, a combination that stood out in their small Welsh town of Llanrwst. But they had somehow blended seamlessly into the Glanrafon community with their quirky ways. Bill was known for his knack of getting his hands on just about anything – from car engines to the latest shell suits. If you needed something, Bill could find it... for a price.

As they stepped into Jamie's bedroom, Dylan's eyes widened in disbelief. It was unlike anything he'd ever seen.

"It was my birthday present," Jamie said, beaming with pride. "Not many people have one of these in their bedroom. My dad says I'm spoilt."

Dylan couldn't stop staring. Standing in the corner, with bright flashing lights and gleaming chrome, was an old gambling slot machine. The sight of it was mesmerizing, completely out of place in a child's bedroom but fascinating all the same.

"It's ten pence a go, but I've got some tokens," Jamie said, handing Dylan a small stack of tokens. "Go on, have a go!"

Dylan let out a laugh, reaching up to insert one of the tokens into the towering machine. "I've never seen a gambling machine in a bedroom before," he remarked, his curiosity piqued.

Jamie grinned. "Yeah, my dad invites all his mates around on Friday nights and they all play it. He fixes it so there's only one win for the night, and then he keeps all the money."

Dylan's eyes lit up. Even at a young age, the idea of making money like that thrilled him. Jamie's dad seemed to know all the tricks.

Jamie's bedroom was small and grubby. A single bed took up most of the space, and the bedside cabinet, propped up by an old block of wood, leaned slightly. The wallpaper was peeling in the corners, and above Jamie's headboard, a curled-up poster of Ian Rush – a football legend – clung to the wall. Despite the dreariness of the room, the slot machine gave it a strange sense of excitement, as if the flashing lights and buzzing sounds transported them somewhere else entirely.

The lights on the machine blinked furiously as the loud, cheerful music blared. Dylan paused, studying the screen as he tried to figure out how to use the nudging option. He had never played a slot machine before, but he was determined to figure it out.

"Nudge the first one twice!" Jamie shouted, his voice full of excitement. "Do it! Nudge the first one twice, and you've got the bloody jackpot!"

Dylan's heart raced as he followed Jamie's instructions. With one more nudge, the machine erupted into a frenzy of flashing lights and booming celebratory music. Jamie's shout of excitement rang out.

"Oh my god! You've got the fucking jackpot!" Jamie yelled, unable to contain his joy.

The slot machine spat out ten-pence pieces at lightning speed, the coins clattering into the tray below, like a rush of rain hitting the pavement. Dylan stood there in awe, watching the steady stream of coins pour out of the machine, as if he had just discovered treasure. Jamie was jumping around the small room, ecstatic, while Dylan laughed, amazed at how a simple machine could bring so much joy.

"Help me count it!" Dylan shouted, "There's loads here!"

"It's ten pounds," Jamie laughed, "The jackpot is ten pounds. Some of it might be in tokens though. Just put them back in or my dad will kill me." Jamie warned.

Dylan counted the coins with excitement. "One pound eighty, one pound ninety, two pound... there's two pounds worth of tokens. Shall we put them back in?" Dylan asked.

"Yeah, it won't pay out again. Just put them back in" Jamie instructed.

"So can I keep this money?" Dylan asked, with a feeling like he had just robbed a bank.

"Erm... Yes..." Jamie replied, hesitantly.

"Well, let's share it," said Dylan generously, counting out the ten pence pieces. "There's four pounds for you and four pounds for me. Shall we go and get some sweets?"

The two boys, buzzing with excitement and still dressed in their scruffy school uniforms, dashed down the stairs and headed out towards town to spend their winnings. The coins jingled in their pockets, and the anticipation of what they could buy filled them with energy. As they entered *Toys and Games*, Dylan felt a wave of pure joy wash over him. For the first time in his life, he could choose any sweets he wanted without having to beg his mam for spare change. But it wasn't just the excitement of the sweets – he couldn't help but think of Bill's crafty money-making schemes. That thought sparked something in Dylan, a sense of possibility.

This was where Dylan's entrepreneurial spark first flickered into life.

Jamie was quick to spend his share, grabbing a *Teenage Mutant Hero Turtles* figure and a bag full of crisps, sweets and chocolates. His £4 vanished in the blink of an eye, and he looked thrilled. Dylan, however, took a more thoughtful approach, eyeing the shelves and counters with a plan forming in his mind.

"Can I please have ten 10p mixes?" Dylan asked politely, approaching the counter where Rose, the shopkeeper, stood.

Rose raised her eyebrows in surprise. "Ten separate mixes?" she asked, smiling as she pulled out the small pre-packed bags from the basket. "Are you buying some for your friends?"

Dylan's eyes twinkled with a cheeky glint. "Sort of," he replied with a grin, his mind already working out how he could turn this little investment into something more.

Rose chuckled, handing over the ten bags of sweets, each filled with a colourful assortment of treats. Dylan then turned his attention to the little display of glow-in-the-dark animals near the counter. He picked out four, each costing 50p.

"One for Ela, one for Baby J, two for me..." he muttered to himself, placing the glowing creatures on the counter. He quickly did the math in his head. "And I'll still have £1 left to buy Dusty some carrots tomorrow," he finished with a satisfied smile.

While Jamie had spent all his money in a flash, Dylan walked out of the shop not only with sweets and toys but also with a few coins left in his pocket. He felt a sense of pride swelling in his chest. This was more than just a trip to the shop – it was the start of something. Dylan didn't want to just spend his money, he wanted to make it last, maybe even make more of it, just like Bill.

As the boys strolled back towards the flats, their pockets heavier with sweets but their spirits even lighter, Dylan knew this wouldn't be the last time he thought about how to make a little bit of money go a long way. He wasn't just having fun, he was learning how to think ahead. It was the birth of *Dylan the opportunist*.

Sitting by the river in the flats, the two boys stuffed their faces with sweets. High on sugar, Dylan heard the unmistakeable sound of his large living room window being swiped open.

"Dyyyyyy-laaaaan," his mother shouted, "IN... NOW!"

"See you tomorrow, Jamie. Don't tell my mam I didn't spend all my winnings, or she'll take it off me!" Dylan pleaded.

"Don't worry, I won't. Actually don't even say you won on the bandit or my dad will batter me." Jamie responded, with genuine concern in his voice.

"Our secret..." Dylan winked, hoping that this could become a regular way of making money for him. "See you tomorrow," he waved as he stuffed the sweets and toys into his pockets.

Dylan ran through the estate and burst through the front door of his flat, dodging Prince who was chewing on one of Ela's dolls in the hallway. He barely slowed his pace as he made a beeline for his school bag which lay crumpled by the staircase. Scooping it up in one swift motion, he dashed upstairs to his bedroom. His mind was racing with excitement; he needed to hide the sweets he'd bought before anyone could ask questions. Quickly, he buried the goodies in the school bag, carefully concealing the stash under some old towels. He gave the cupboard door one last glance, satisfied that his treasure was safe for now.

With his secret safely tucked away, Dylan headed back downstairs and into the kitchen. "Mam, can I have my dinner on a tray in the living room?" he asked, hoping for some relaxation time in front of the TV.

His mother, Magi, sat at the kitchen table with a glass of wine in hand, her gaze distant as if her mind was already out of the house. "Just sit at the table, please," she replied, taking a long sip from her glass. Then, as though remembering something important, she added, "I need you to look after Ela and Baby J tonight. I'm heading out in a minute, so you'll need to get them ready for bed, okay? Be a good boy."

Dylan's heart sank. The idea of babysitting again wasn't appealing – he longed for freedom like his friends, to run outside and play without a care, not having to change nappies or worry about bedtime routines every single night. But just as the frustration began to rise, he caught Ela's smile from across the kitchen. Her sweet, innocent grin melted away his irritation in an instant. Even when he wanted to be mad, his little sister had a way of making him feel responsible and protective. He loved them, even if it was tough sometimes.

Magi stood up, moving towards the door, grabbing her bag and coat in a rush. "I'm meeting your dad straight from work at the Red Lion," she announced, her voice suddenly more animated. "He's started a new job today, so we're going out to celebrate! Don't stay up too late, alright? I want everyone asleep by half past nine. No messing around."

Before Dylan could even respond, Magi leaned down, planting a quick kiss on each of their heads. "Na-night," she said with a hurried smile before heading out the door. The slam echoed through the house as she left. He stood there for a moment, knowing full well that now, with his mam gone, the evening was his to manage.

With a sigh, he turned to Baby J, who sat in his high chair making a mess of his food. "Right, Baby J," Dylan said, his tone playful despite the situation, "looks like you're done with dinner. Let's get you out of that nappy – you stink!"

Ela giggled from her seat at the table, her eyes twinkling. "He does stink," she said, wrinkling her nose in exaggerated disgust. "He's been stinking since I got home from school!"

Dylan couldn't help but laugh. Moments like these, with their banter and little inside jokes, made it easier to handle the responsibility. He quickly scooped up Baby J and lay him on the floor, where the smell hit him full force. "Poooo, Ela wasn't lying!" Dylan teased, making a face as Baby J squirmed. "Let's get you cleaned up, stink bomb."

Once Baby J was changed and in his pyjamas, Dylan turned his attention to Ela. "Alright, your turn now, missy. Let's get you ready for bed too," he said, his tone more gentle. He gave her a flannel wash across her face, wiping away the day's dirt and grime with the same care he always did. As the eldest, it was his job to make sure everyone was taken care of – and tonight was no different.

After settling both of them into their cosy pyjamas, Dylan led his siblings into the living room. The rain outside had picked up, drizzling steadily against the windows, making the world beyond seem grey and cold. But inside, the house was warm, and the three of them were snug on the sofa. The lack of curtains made the rain seem harsher as it splattered against the glass, but they were safe here, cocooned in their little world. Dylan smiled to himself as he tucked Ela under a blanket and handed Baby J his favourite teddy.

For now, everything was okay. The kids were fed, warm, and wrapped up in the safety of Dylan's care. He glanced out at the rain, towards the mountain where Dusty would be in her field. He worried for a second that she might be cold… that she might be hungry. The sooner they all went to bed, the sooner he would see Dusty.

"Shit, I've got to sing tomorrow with Caroline." Dylan muttered to himself. "I need to make sure my uniform is clean."

With that thought in mind, Dylan left the two little ones watching Fraggle Rock on the video player and he rushed around the house to make sure he had clean uniform.

Ironing his shirt and jumper, a skill he had proudly learnt from watching his mam, he sang through the words to the song… "Dod ar fy mhen, dy sanctaidd law…" perfecting his tone and tuning. "Shit, why the hell have I agreed to this?" he said to himself.

****

7

Hymns and Hoof Prints.

The next morning, Dylan sprang out of bed with a burst of excitement, barely able to contain his energy. He pulled on his well-worn jodhpurs, the fabric snug and familiar against his legs, then carefully placed his neatly folded school uniform into a plastic bag. The uniform would need to stay clean for later, and he had a big plan for the day.

As Dylan moved about the room, the sound of rustling from under the blankets caught his attention. Prince's head poked out from beneath the covers. Dylan grinned, watching as his dog's tail began to wag eagerly under the blankets, thumping against the bed in a gentle rhythm.

"Go back to sleep," Dylan whispered with a soft chuckle, giving Prince a quick pat on the head. Prince, ever obedient and trusting, gave one more wag before resting his head back down, content to sleep a little longer. Dylan tiptoed across the room and snuck quietly into the airing cupboard, where he had hidden his school bag the night before, carefully packed with small bags of sweets. His secret stash for later. Without making a sound, he slung the bag over his shoulder and crept out of the bedroom, careful not to wake his siblings.

As he reached the front door, Dylan paused for a moment, thinking ahead. He quickly swapped his school shoes for his sturdy wellies, knowing that he would need to be clean to perform later in the school assembly.

Dylan stepped outside into the cold early morning air, the town still quiet, bathed in the soft glow of dawn. The sun was only just beginning to rise, casting long shadows across the street. He hadn't bothered to check the time before leaving, but a quick glance at his watch revealed it was just 7:03 a.m. Perfect. He'd have plenty of time to spend with Dusty before school started. His heart raced with anticipation, knowing how much Dusty would love the surprise he had for her.

Stopping by the Spar on his way, Dylan pushed open the door, the familiar jingle of the bell above the entrance ringing in his ears. He used the money he had won the night before to buy a bunch of fresh carrots, Dusty's favourite treat. As Vanessa, the cashier with the finest coiffed hair, handed him the carrots, he pocketed the 70p he had saved for himself, feeling proud of his thriftiness.

"T'ra del," Vanessa shouted after him, "you be bloody careful around those horses, ynai boy? They can be bloody dangerous you know!"

Dylan responded with a wave through the window. With the carrots in hand and nobody around to monitor how fast he was going, Dylan took off at a run. The wellies, though practical, weren't ideal for sprinting, and he soon realised his mistake as his legs grew tired from the effort. Still, he pressed on, determined to reach Dusty's field as quickly as possible. By the time he reached Big Bridge, his lungs were burning, and his breath came in sharp gasps. He leaned against the wall, taking a moment to catch his breath, then reached into his school bag for a quick snack. He unwrapped one of the sweets he had packed, the sugar giving him a burst of energy. Today was going to be a big day – he could feel it.

After a few minutes of resting and munching on sweets, Dylan pushed on, the Gwydir stretch ahead now familiar and comforting. Arriving by Gwydir castle, the faint outlines of the larger horses came into view, their shadows stretching across the field. Dylan's heart leapt with excitement when he heard a familiar sound – a soft, high-pitched whinny that could only belong to one horse.

"Dusty!" Dylan called out, his voice full of excitement and affection. "Come on, girl!"

As if on cue, Dusty's head popped up from behind the hill, and a second later she was galloping down the slope at full speed. Her small, sturdy frame moved gracefully as her tail arched high in the air, a display of her energy and joy. The morning light reflected off her shiny coat, making her look almost magical as she approached.

Dylan's heart swelled with affection at the sight of his beloved pony charging towards him. He could feel the bond between them growing stronger with every visit. A grin spread across his face as Dusty came to a skidding halt at the gate, dirt and gravel kicking up around her hooves. She nuzzled his outstretched hand without hesitation, her warm breath tickling his fingers as she greeted him with enthusiasm.

"I've got something for you," Dylan murmured, pulling out a bundle of fresh carrots from his bag. Dusty's ears twitched in anticipation, and she nudged him eagerly with her soft muzzle, her large eyes bright with expectation. She knew exactly what he had brought for her, and the excitement in her body was almost palpable. Dylan chuckled as he offered her the first carrot, watching her crunch it down with noisy satisfaction.

He could feel their natural bond in that moment – an unspoken understanding between horse and boy, built on trust and mutual affection.

Before Dusty could finish all the carrots, Dylan walked around her, remembering the instructions Dawn had given him. He crouched down in front of her, checking her front legs for any cuts or scrapes. "No cuts," he said softly, speaking to her as if she understood every word. Dusty, however, was far too focused on her treat, her nose still buried in the pile of carrots.

Dylan moved to her back legs, pushing against her hindquarters with more force than usual, trying to turn her around to inspect her hind legs. "Move over, Dusty!" he said with a hint of playful impatience. But Dusty, stubborn and completely absorbed in her snack, refused to budge.

Determined, Dylan gave her a firmer push. Suddenly, without warning, Dusty let out an almighty squeal and kicked out, her back hoof catching Dylan square in the leg. The force of it sent him flying backward, landing flat on the ground with a thud. Dylan blinked in shock, sitting up to inspect his leg. There, imprinted on his jodhpurs, was a perfect little muddy hoof print. He stared at it for a moment before bursting into laughter, the surprise of it all making him shake his head in disbelief.

"Well, I guess that's you telling me, Dusty!" Dylan said, still laughing as he rubbed his sore leg. "Sorry, girl. I shouldn't have pushed you."

Dusty turned her head towards him, giving a soft, almost apologetic roll of her lips, her big brown eyes blinking as if to say she hadn't meant to hurt him. She nodded her head, the gesture so human-like that it made Dylan grin even wider. He stood up, brushing the dirt from his clothes, as he remembered Wendy from Bwlch Mawr's wise words: *"You can tell a gelding, but you must ask a mare."* Wendy was always right, and today had proven that yet again.

Dylan stepped back towards Dusty, reaching out to gently stroke her neck, his hand moving softly over her smooth coat. She leaned into his touch, her muscles relaxing under his hand as if she, too, felt the comfort of their connection. He moved his hand up to scratch her withers, his fingers finding the spot where he knew she liked it best. Dusty's head shot up in the air, her top lip curling in delight as the sensation tickled her in just the right way. She leaned into Dylan, her weight pressing against him, asking for more pressure.

"Oh, you like that, do you?" Dylan laughed, his voice full of affection. "You're a good girl, Dusty. My good girl."

As Dusty continued munching on her carrots, Dylan leaned across her back, resting comfortably against her warm body. The rhythmic sound of her crunching and the soft birdsong in the distance combined to create a peaceful atmosphere around them. The gentle rise and fall of Dusty's breathing, along with the warmth radiating from her, lulled Dylan into a state of calm. It felt like time had slowed down, and for those precious moments, nothing else mattered.

That was until Dylan glanced at his watch. His heart sank. *Shit.* Time had passed faster than he realised – it was already 8:21 a.m.

With a wry smile, Dylan quickly slid off Dusty's back and swapped his wellies for his school trainers. "Right, Dusty, I've got to go – I'm singing in assembly this morning. Wish me luck," he said, his voice tinged with affection. He placed his muddy wellies into a plastic bag, gathered his things, and gave Dusty a quick kiss on her soft nose. Climbing over the gate, he began the long walk to school, glancing back at her one last time.

"Byyyyyye, Dusty!" he shouted. Dusty raised her head and trotted off towards the other horses in the field, who remained blissfully unaware of the extra treats she'd just devoured.

Dylan hurried down the Gwydir Stretch towards the town, making a quick stop at the public toilets to change into his school uniform. As he stripped off his jodhpurs, he noticed the small hoof print Dusty had left on them and smiled. He pulled out his crisply-ironed uniform from his bag and quickly gathered up his things – stuffing it into his school bag. As he ran some water through his curly hair to flatten it, humming the harmony line he'd been practising for assembly, he caught his reflection in the mirror and grinned. The smell of Dusty still lingered in his nostrils, a comforting reminder of his morning with her. He felt happy – confident, even.

Arriving at school, as Dylan looked down at his school shoes, his grin faded. He realised he'd forgotten to put on black socks, and his white-socked big toe was poking through a hole in one of his trainers. "Shit," he muttered under his breath. He rushed to the classroom, dumping his bag by his desk before scrambling over to the crafts corner in search of a solution.

Scurrying around, Dylan's eyes landed on a black permanent marker pen on Mrs Jones' desk. Quickly slipping off his trainer, he coloured the exposed part of his white sock with the heavy black ink, trying to mask the hole. He slipped his trainer back on and examined his handiwork, chuckling to himself. "Perfect – you can hardly see the hole now."

Just then, a familiar voice piped up from across the room. "I thought I'd find you in here," Caroline said with a chirpy tone. "Shall we have a quick practice?"

Dylan grinned, sneaking the marker back into Miss Jones' pen holder. "Yes, come on then. I've been practising," he replied, feeling more ready than ever.

As the time for assembly drew closer, the smell of the school hall always made Dylan's stomach do a little flip – stale sweat mixed with the lingering odour of yesterday's fish pie. It wasn't the most pleasant smell, but today, Dylan's focus was elsewhere. He was determined to give a good performance.

Singing hymns during assembly was one of Dylan's favourite things. It gave him a chance to let out his energy before being confined to a desk for the rest of the day. Today, the whole school was in fine form, belting out a rousing rendition of *"Sing Hosannah"* in Welsh. Mrs. Jones pounded the piano keys with her usual ferocity, while Mrs. Selway and her music students energetically shook their tambourines.

"Can Hosana, Can Hosana, Can Hosan i'r Frenin Nêf…" the voices rang out in harmony.

Dylan lived for the duetted part, the section of the song that not many kids had the courage to sing. Back in Henryd, the whole school would split in half to sing it gloriously, but here in Llanrwst, most shied away from that challenge. Dylan, though, considered it the best part of the song, and he wasn't going to miss his chance.

"Caaaaaaaaan…. Caaaaaaaan…. Caaaaaaaan…. Caaaaaaaan…" Dylan sang out at the top of his voice, his enthusiasm infectious. Soon, some of the other kids around him joined in, drawn to the fun he seemed to be having, as if they couldn't resist the joy radiating from him.

As the final note of the song echoed through the assembly hall, Mr. Williams, the headmaster, stepped forward and called for Caroline and Dylan to take centre stage. Dylan's stomach flipped with nervous energy, but this was his moment – his big chance to show the school what he was made of. He'd always dreamt of being better than Aled Jones, the famous boy soprano with his floppy hair and angelic voice.

Taking a deep breath, Dylan looked out over the sea of faces in the audience, feeling the weight of every eye on him. For a moment, he hesitated, but as the melody started in his mind, he lost himself in the song. His voice rang out clear and strong. A few boys sniggered from the back rows, but for the most part, the hall fell into an attentive hush; you could hear a pin drop. The teachers at the back of the room exchanged proud smiles as they watched the unlikely duo pour their hearts into the song.

When the performance ended, rapturous applause erupted – not because the pupils particularly loved the song, but because applause was always an excuse to let off some energy and make noise. Still, for Dylan, it felt like a victory.

Scanning the audience, his eyes caught Jamie clapping wildly, his big smile only partially hiding a black eye and a bruised cheek. The sight made Dylan's stomach drop, and his smile faltered. What had happened to Jamie?

As the assembly ended, Dylan tried to push through the crowd to reach Jamie, but he was momentarily stopped by a group of girls. Eirian, the tallest of the group, her curly hair a wild halo around her head, called out, "Dylan, that was amazing! You and Caroline sounded so good together." She pointed to her friend, a short girl with bright ginger hair and thick rimmed glasses. "By the way, Catrin fancies you!" Catrin's face matched the colour of her hair as she shouted "No I don't. Fuck off Eirian."

The girls burst into laughter, their teasing playful but loud. Dylan, caught off guard, blushed but couldn't help smiling. The praise felt good, but he was still distracted by Jamie's bruised face. He needed to find him.

"Jamie!" Dylan called as he hurried down the hallway. He finally caught up to him, noticing the tension in Jamie's posture. "What happened to your face?"

Jamie avoided eye contact, keeping his pace brisk. "You were so good, Dylan. Seriously, you've got a hell of a good voice," he said, clearly trying to change the subject.

"Ahh, not really," Dylan replied, his cheeks flushing with modesty. "But what happened to your face? It looks really sore."

"I fell down the stairs last night," Jamie answered quickly, still not meeting Dylan's eyes. "I'm fine," he added in a whisper, trying to brush it off as he kept walking.

Dylan's worry deepened. "How did you fall?" he asked, his voice soft but insistent.

Jamie's response was hurried and unconvincing. "Oh, I just tripped over the dog and fell down the stairs. I'm okay, it doesn't hurt."

Dylan knew he was lying, but Jamie's tone made it clear he didn't want to talk about it. "I'll see you later, I'm going to be late for PE," Jamie murmured before hurrying off, leaving Dylan standing alone in the hallway.

Dylan's stomach churned with unease. This was the first time he truly felt empathy for someone outside of his family, and it shook him. His chest tightened as he guessed what might have really happened but, with no time to dwell on it, he shook himself off and rushed to class. He was going to be late too.

"Da iawn, Dylan! Very well done!" Mrs. Jones beamed as he entered the classroom. "What a fantastic voice you have," she added, her smile wide and approving.

Before Dylan could respond, Iwan piped up from the back of the room with a sneer. "You sounded like a girl."

Without missing a beat, Dylan shot back, "And you sound really thick Iwan."

The room erupted in laughter. Iwan's face flushed with anger. "Oh yeah? Say that out on the yard and I'll batter you," Iwan threatened, his voice low and menacing.

Dylan's confidence was riding high today, though. He wasn't scared of Iwan or his empty threats. "Yeah, yeah, yeah. Who's going to batter me? Your mam?" Dylan jibed, grinning as more laughter erupted from the other boys. He didn't need their friendship, and today, he didn't fear their teasing.

"Settle down, class!" Mrs. Jones called, trying to regain order. "Today's theme is 'Under the Sea.'"

But as Mrs. Jones began the lesson, Dylan's mind wandered. His thoughts drifted far away from the classroom, back to the open fields and long beaches where he imagined galloping on Dusty, free as the wind. The crashing waves, the soft sand under hooves – it was a far cry from the stuffy classroom and dull lesson.

"Dylan Evans, are you listening?" Mrs. Jones' abrupt voice snapped him back to reality.

"Sorry, Miss! I wasn't, but I am now. Sorry," Dylan apologised quickly, his cheeks tinged pink with embarrassment.

The morning dragged on. Dylan couldn't focus. The subject didn't interest him, and his mind kept circling back to Jamie and the black eye. Something wasn't right, and the feeling gnawed at Dylan for the rest of the morning.

At lunchtime, Dylan scanned the playground for Jamie, but he was nowhere to be found. He wasn't in the 'free school meals' queue, and he wasn't out on the football field where he usually hung out. A slight worry nagged at Dylan, but he pushed it aside, deciding to focus on his plan instead.

Gathering a few of his friends around, he cleared his throat and launched into his announcement. "Right, listen up," Dylan said with a determined grin. "I know you lot who live on farms don't have sweet shops in your villages, so I've decided to start selling sweets here. If you want some, I'll be selling them every breaktime!"

The group stared at him, a mix of curiosity and excitement in their faces. By the end of the day, word had spread around the school: Dylan was selling sweets, and he had better deals than the tuck shop. He sold all nine bags he'd packed, each for 20p – double the price he'd paid for them. By the time the bell rang to end the day, Dylan had made a tidy profit and couldn't wait to tell Jamie. He felt a surge of pride; this little business idea was off to a promising start.

As the children streamed out of the school, Dylan stood by the gate, scanning the crowd for his friend. But Jamie was still nowhere to be seen. Gradually, the crowd thinned until Dylan was one of the last remaining students. He shifted from foot to foot, debating whether to wait any longer. Just as he was about to give up and head home, Jamie appeared around the corner, his head down, hands stuffed deep in his pockets. He seemed startled, almost embarrassed, to see Dylan still waiting.

"Are you alright, Jamie?" Dylan asked gently, noting the strain on his friend's face.

Jamie brushed him off, though his eyes glistened. "Yes, I'm fine, Dylan. Stop asking," he mumbled, trying to hurry past Dylan without meeting his gaze.

Not wanting to push, Dylan decided to shift the focus. "I just wanted to tell you something," he said, trying to sound cheerful. "I started my own little shop!"

Jamie stopped, curiosity momentarily breaking through his sadness. "What? You're taking the piss!" he said with a small laugh.

"No, really! You remember all those sweets I bought in *Toys and Games*?" Dylan explained, grinning. "I sold them! Siôn and Iwan bought some, and even the Year 6 boys from Llanddoged – they don't have any shops up there!"

Jamie couldn't help but chuckle at Dylan's boldness. "I can't believe you actually sold them. How much did you make?"

"£1.80," Dylan replied proudly, digging into his pocket. "Here, take it. Go put it back in the gambling machine. If that will help."

But Jamie's smile faded. He looked down, his voice dropping to a near-whisper. "He... he battered me, Dyl. He said I emptied the machine."

Taking in the bruises on Jamie's little face, Dylan felt a knot form in his stomach, a pang of empathy hitting him hard. He could sense Jamie's shame and embarrassment, the way he avoided eye contact and wiped away a tear that escaped despite his best efforts.

"I told him I didn't touch it, but he wouldn't believe me," Jamie continued, his voice trembling slightly. "And I didn't say a word about you. But now he's rigged the machine so it won't pay out for a while."

Dylan clenched his fists, anger bubbling inside him, but he kept his voice steady. "Look, why don't I come over now and put the £1.80 back in the machine?" he offered gently. "If that'll make him happy, then we'll do it. Or... I could even tell him it was me who won the jackpot. I can sell more sweets tomorrow and get all the money back."

Jamie glanced up, surprise softening his face. The kindness in Dylan's offer caught him off guard. He'd never had anyone go out of their way like this for him before. A small smile tugged at the corners of his mouth, and he stood a bit straighter, as if a weight had lifted from his shoulders.

"You know you won't win again, right?" Jamie said, a hint of his usual energy returning.

Dylan shrugged. "Doesn't matter. At least your dad will know you weren't lying."

Jamie's smile widened, and for the first time that day, he looked almost cheerful. "Thanks, Dylan." The gratitude was written clearly across his face. "I think we're going to be best friends aren't we? Jamie smiled.

"I hope so." Dylan smiled. "And business partners too," he laughed.

Together, the two little boys started walking towards Glanrafon, side by side, ready to take on the world.

****

8

The Gift of Dusty.

Saturday, 10:04 a.m.

Dylan sat patiently by Big Bridge, with Prince loyally by his side. They'd been there since 9:42 a.m. and still, there was no sign of Dawn. Dylan glanced at his watch, then looked up the road, wondering if she'd already gone up to Dusty's field without him. He didn't want to miss out on a single moment with Dusty, so he debated whether to head up on his own or check Dawn's house first. Deciding on the latter, he turned to Prince.

"Come on, Prince, let's go see if Dawn's coming with us," he said enthusiastically.

Prince jumped down off the wall and walked by Dylan's side, serving as his protective bodyguard. They made their way back through the town to the posh estate – Trem Afon – where they reached Dawn's house, its front door adorned with "Jesus is Alive" and "God Will Save Us" stickers. Dylan knocked several times, the sound echoing on the quiet street.

Finally, the door opened slowly to reveal a sleepy-eyed Dawn, still dressed in her pyjamas, her greasy hair sticking up everywhere. Dylan's face lit up with excitement, a grin spreading across his face like a golden retriever ready for a game of fetch.

"Morning, Dawn!" he greeted her brightly. "Did you forget we were going to see Dusty today?"

"Erm... no. Yes. Kind of," Dawn stammered, blinking as she registered his words. "My brother was sick all night and kept me up," she added, rubbing her eyes. "Give me a minute, I'll go and get dressed."

Dylan settled down on the doorstep, absent-mindedly brushing the dirt from his jodhpurs, his fingers tracing the faint hoof print Dusty had left on them – a badge of honour, as far as he was concerned. He glanced at Prince, who seemed just as eager as he was, and gave him a kiss. Dawn reappeared, now dressed and looking more awake.

"How'd you know where I lived?" she asked, a note of surprise in her voice.

"You told me it was the house with the red door," Dylan replied confidently.

Dawn's brows furrowed. "I didn't tell you where I lived," she said, her voice laced with a hint of suspicion.

Dylan paused, momentarily caught off guard. "Erm, oh... maybe Jamie told me? I was talking to him about you and Dusty," he said, scratching his head shyly.

Dawn's expression softened, and a smile crept onto her face. "Ah, okay. And who's this handsome boy?" she asked, bending down to pet Prince, who leaned into her touch, his tail wagging happily.

"This is Prince. He doesn't get to go out much, so I thought I'd bring him along. He just started following me this morning," Dylan explained without taking a breath. "Do you think Dusty will like him?"

Dawn chuckled, giving Prince an affectionate scratch behind the ears. "Well, there's only one way to find out, isn't there, boy?" she replied with a smile. "I'm sure Dusty will be fine!"

The three amigos set off under the morning sunshine, their spirits high as they made their way up to the fields. As they came to the end of Gwydir stretch, a small black dot appeared at the top of the pasture, soon growing into the unmistakable shape of Dusty. Both Dawn and Dylan called out together, "Duuuuuu-styyyyyy" their voices harmonising and echoing across the field.

At the sound of their voices, Dusty's head shot up, and within seconds, she was galloping down the slope. Prince bounced with excitement at the gate, his eyes wide, watching as Dusty thundered towards them. He'd never been this close to a horse before, and his eagerness was matched only by Dylan's joy.

"Good morning, Dusty," Dylan cooed as she reached them, nuzzling her nose into his hand. "And how's my favourite girl?"

Dusty's nostrils flared as she sniffed around Prince, before catching the scent of carrots hidden in Dylan's pocket. Unbothered by Dusty, Prince's nose was equally active, sniffing eagerly at Dylan's hand.

"Oh, you both want one of these, do you?" Dylan teased, pulling a carrot from his pocket. He held one out to Dusty, who took it gently, crunching it with satisfaction, and then handed a second one to Prince, who munched it down with equal delight.

The sound of two happy animals chewing on fresh carrots filled the air, bringing an enormous sense of contentment to Dylan's heart. He couldn't remember a better Saturday since moving to Llanrwst.

Dawn reached into her bag, pulling out two brushes, and handed one to Dylan. "Come on, let's get her looking nice and tidy," she said with a smile. "Then we can take her for a walk up through Gwydir Forest."

Dylan set to work, brushing the mud from Dusty's coat with gentle, even strokes, making sure to be careful not to tug or hurt her. As he worked his way towards her hind legs, Dusty's tail began to swish, lightly whipping his arm in a playful warning.

"Watch out, Dyl," Dawn laughed, her eyes sparkling. "I think you've found her tickle spot. She might kick if she's in the mood!"

Dylan grinned, giving Dusty an apologetic pat. "Sorry, Dusty. I'm ticklish too," he said tenderly. "We'll skip that spot for now, won't we?" He proudly pointed to the faint hoof mark on his jodhpurs. "She's already kicked me once, see? The mark's still here."

Dawn chuckled, clearly impressed. "Did it hurt?" she asked, raising an eyebrow.

"Nah, not really," Dylan replied with a laugh. "It was my own fault for being rough. She was just putting me in my place, that's all."

As they finished brushing Dusty, Dylan reached into his bag and pulled out his little navy blue velvet riding hat, slipping it on with a proud grin. The hat had a tiny ribbon at the back, and every time he wore it, he couldn't help but feel like a winner.

"Right," Dawn said with a smile, "I think we should head towards Geirionydd Lake. Dusty might enjoy a little paddle!"

With Dusty brushed and prepped, and Prince looking relaxed and content beside her, the four of them set off together along the forest path.

As they reached a clearing, the big moment came…

"Do you want to get on her, Dyl?" Dawn asked. "I haven't ridden her yet because she's a bit too small for me, but you'd be just the right size. She'd probably love it."

Dylan's eyes lit up, though he hesitated for a moment. "She doesn't have a saddle or bridle," he pointed out cautiously. But then, excitement quickly took over. "But I don't mind, if she doesn't."

Dawn gave him a reassuring smile. "Oh, she won't mind at all," she said, with a touch of feigned confidence. "Come on, I'll give you a leg up."

Dusty stood patiently, grazing on the hedgerow, as Dylan sprung up on to her back like a professional. Settling himself on her back, he held his breath, smiling with exhilaration as he felt the warmth of Dusty's body beneath him. He'd never ridden bareback before; it felt thrilling and a bit nerve-wracking all at once.

Prince, clearly excited by the scene, started jumping up and barking.

"No, Prince. Stop!" Dylan called, laughing. But Dusty, startled, turned sharply and kicked her left leg in Prince's direction – a gentle warning rather than an actual attempt to kick him. Prince immediately backed off, cowering a little but with his tail still wagging.

"Good boy, Prince," Dylan said lovingly. "You just walk along with us, alright?"

"Look at you, Dyl! You're a natural," Dawn declared, "I would've fallen off then for sure!"

Dylan grinned with pride. He felt on top of the world. Dawn took the end of the lead rope and tied it to both sides of Dusty's head collar to create makeshift reins. "There you go, Dyl. Now you can ride her on your own."

Dylan felt like a superhero. Dusty walked with purpose, following Prince, almost like she was enjoying the adventure.

The forest looked freshly painted with all the autumnal colours. The beautiful sound of Dusty's little hooves was only spoilt by the sound of Dawn, a few steps behind them, munching on a packet of pickled onion Space Raiders.

As they walked, they chatted about their lives. Dawn told Dylan about her large Catholic family, how she had seven siblings and how they all had to attend church every Sunday, without fail. Dylan listened intently, fascinated by the difference in their worlds. Just as they rounded a corner on the forestry path, the peaceful morning was abruptly interrupted by the distant roar of an engine.

A white van appeared, speeding down the path towards them, kicking up mud as it drew closer. Dusty halted, her ears pricked forward, alert. The van came to a sudden stop just before them and a man in camouflage gear jumped out, his face shadowed under a cap. He walked towards them with a stern expression.

"Are you Barry's lad?" he asked, his eyes fixed on Dylan.

Dylan's stomach dropped. "Erm…" he stammered, uncertain. "Why?"

Dawn stepped in, her voice stronger. "Why do you want to know?" she asked, her tone guarded. Dawn was streetwise and knew better than to hand out information to strangers.

The man's expression softened slightly as he forced a smile. "I'm a friend of Barry's," he replied, nodding towards Prince. "Is this Prince?"

"Yes," Dylan replied quietly, glancing down at Prince.

On hearing his name, Prince trotted over to the man, tail wagging, eager for a scratch. "Hiya boi," the man said, bending down to give Prince a pat. "Your dad told me I could borrow Prince to go shooting today." And without waiting for a response, the man looped a rope lead around Prince's neck.

Dylan's heart skipped a beat as he jumped off Dusty.

"Erm…" Dylan said hesitantly, jumping off Dusty. "I don't really want you to take him now. Let me take him home first."

The man had already loaded Prince in to the back of the van and was getting back in to the driving seat, as he shouted, "Don't worry, I'll look after him. I've heard he's good at getting the pheasants!"

Dylan reached out instinctively, but before he could say anything else, the man closed the door, giving him a dismissive wave.

As the van turned and drove off, Dylan watched in disbelief, a sinking feeling in his stomach. He caught a glimpse of Prince's face in the back window, his eyes wide with confusion as he watched Dylan grow smaller in the distance.

For a moment, the joy of the morning faded, leaving a quiet emptiness in its place. Dusty nuzzled him gently, as if sensing his sadness. Dylan reached out, stroking her nose, but his mind was far away, fixated on Prince's vanishing face.

Dawn placed a comforting hand on his shoulder. "He'll be alright, Dyl. Come on, we're not too far from the lake."

But Dylan couldn't shake the lingering unease. He forced a smile, hoping Dawn wouldn't see the tears in his eyes.

They continued on their walk, the autumn colours still vibrant around them, but somehow, the forest suddenly lost its brightness. Dylan kept glancing back down the path, half-expecting to see Prince bounding back towards him. Dusty gave a gentle snort, nudging him back to the moment.

Dylan's sadness was palpable but the next conversation was about to change Dylan's life. Arriving at the lake, Dawn had an announcement to make that was about to lift Dylan's mood.

"Dyl, I didn't want to tell you this morning, as I didn't want to worry you." She said hesitantly, pulling out a carrot out of her Kwik Save bag for Dusty.

Dylan slid off Dusty and landed gently next to her side. Giving Dusty a hug, he waited for Dawn to continue with her speech.

Dawn took a deep breath, carefully choosing her words. "Sooo," she began slowly, "my cousin's mam and dad are getting a divorce and because of that, my cousin can't keep Dusty any more. Dusty's not going back to England." She paused, watching Dylan's face closely. "My mam and dad have said we can't keep her either, since we can't afford it… but they suggested we give her to you."

Dylan let out a laugh of disbelief. "What?" he asked, his eyes wide as he stared at her, frozen in surprise.

Dawn continued, her tone gentle. "Do you want her? If you can promise to look after her, then she's yours."

For a moment, Dylan was speechless, his mind racing. "Are you serious?" he finally managed, feeling a mix of shock and excitement.

Dawn nodded, smiling at his reaction. "Yes, I'm serious. But don't tell anyone yet," she cautioned, "because my family doesn't want my cousin to find out just yet."

Dylan's face lit up with joy as he processed the news. "Of course, I'll look after her! And I won't tell a soul." He let out a loud cheer, almost unable to contain himself. "My own pony? Yes! DUSTY!" He laughed, looking at Dusty with wonder. "Is this real? Am I dreaming?"

Dusty seemed to sense his excitement. She lifted her hoof and splashed it in the lake, sending little ripples across the water, then bent down to take a drink after their long walk through the hills.

Dawn chuckled, watching them. "Well, then she's yours now," she said, smiling warmly. "Just look after her, alright?"

Dylan couldn't contain his happiness. Throwing his arms around Dusty's neck, he hugged her tightly, forgetting everything else for a moment. Whispering into her ear, he said, "You're about to have the best life, Dusty. I'm going to love you forever."

Dawn watched them with a soft smile. "So, as she's officially your pony now… and you seem pretty capable of handling her on your own," she continued, "I'm going to step back and let you two bond without me after today."

Dylan nodded eagerly, confidence radiating from him. "That's fine," he replied. "I already have plans for how to make some money so I can buy her food and maybe even a nice rug."

Dawn laughed. "You don't need to spoil her too much, Dyl – she's a hardy little pony. Just check on her once a day after school, and she'll be fine. Starting tomorrow, she's all yours."

"Alright," Dylan said, his mind whirling with excitement. Then he hesitated for a moment. "But on Sundays, I go to see my nana. Could you check on her tomorrow, just this once? I'll take over from Monday."

"Of course," Dawn agreed. "And you can keep her head collar and lead rope. They're yours now too."

"Thank you…" Dylan said, his voice almost a whisper. He still couldn't believe it. "This feels like a dream."

Dusty gave a soft snort, turning back towards the path they'd come from, as if signalling she was ready to go. She nudged Dylan gently, almost pulling him forward.

Dawn laughed again, noticing Dusty's impatience. "Looks like Dusty's telling us it's time to move on. Let's head back down to the field, shall we? We can take the bridle path – it'll be softer on her hooves."

Dylan nodded, his heart full of excitement and gratitude as he walked alongside his very own pony, feeling like the luckiest boy in the world.

****

9

Sunday Truths.

On Sundays, Dylan always visited his nana and taid. In his short life, he'd endured many broken promises, but nothing – not even the chaos at home – could keep him from seeing his nana on a Sunday. Her house was a safe haven, where warmth and love were constants in his life.

It was a crisp, bright Sunday morning, and Dylan could barely contain his excitement. Today, he would tell Nana all about Dusty, the horse who had captured his heart. He rushed around the house, eager to leave.

"Quick, Mam, or I'll miss the bus!" he called out, barely able to stand still. "Quiiiick!"

Magi, his mother, shuffled around the kitchen with bleary eyes and a voice thick from the remnants of last night's drinking session. "Hey, don't fuckin' talk to me like that, or you'll get nothing," she muttered, sounding as dry as the Sahara desert. "You'll have to find my purse. I can't remember where I put it."

Dylan was used to this. His mother had a habit of hiding her purse when she came home from the pub, making sure Barry wouldn't help himself to money from it and leave her penniless. To Dylan, it was just part of the routine – another survival tactic in their turbulent household.

He searched quickly and triumphantly called out, "Found it! It was in the fridge."

Magi gave him 50p, the bus fare he needed. "Oi, give me a kiss before you go," she added. "And don't be telling Nana about any rows that have gone on here, ok? You'll only worry her and make her ill."

Dylan gave her a quick peck on the cheek, trying to stay away from the smell of her wine breath, but his mind was already elsewhere. He darted out the door, not bothering to reply. His feet pounded the pavement as he raced through town, his small legs moving as fast as they could carry him.

At the top of the street, he could see a line of people boarding the Number 19 bus. He got into the queue, out of breath but grinning as he reached the door.

"Half return to Bryn Morfa, please," he said, polite but eager.

The bus driver, Larry, gave him a friendly wink. "Just get on, boy," he said cheerfully. "Buy yourself some sweets with that fare. And if a conductor gets on, tell him you lost your ticket, alright?"

Dylan grinned back. Larry was everyone's favourite driver. Known for his good humour, he would belt out Elvis Presley tunes at full volume while speeding through the winding country roads. The usual 20-minute ride from Llanrwst to Dolgarrog always took Larry just 15 minutes, and Dylan marvelled at how fast he could fly through the narrow, hilly lanes. It was almost as if Larry had been a Formula One driver in a past life.

As the bus roared to life and pulled away from the curb, Dylan leaned back in his seat, his excitement bubbling over. He couldn't wait to see Nana, to feel her warm hug and to tell her about Dusty. For now, though, he'd sit back, listen to Larry crooning "All Shook Up," and let his mind drift to the adventures ahead.

The big old Crossville bus pulled up abruptly at the bottom of Bryn Morfa, a neat little line of council houses that created a community reminiscent of Henryd. Dylan knew everyone in the 18 terraced houses and they all knew him.

Dylan ran up the steep hill and his heart raced with excitement as he spotted his nana waiting for him at the garden gate. Wrapped in her usual cosy cardigan and apron, her little brown eyes sparkled as she saw him approach.

"Nanaaaaaaaaaaa" squealed Dylan with delight, wrapping his arms around her. "I've missed you."

Annie, or "Annie Bach," as everyone in the village called her, chuckled, her arms gently squeezing him back. "Ahhh, I've missed you too, my boy," she said warmly, her voice soft but strong, full of love. "A whole week without seeing you!" she added with a playful tone of mock shock. There was a hint of loving sarcasm in her words, but Dylan, too caught up in his excitement, didn't notice.

"Have you been a good boy?" Annie asked, pulling back slightly to look at him with a knowing smile.

"Always!" Dylan replied immediately, his voice full of sincerity. And it was mostly true. For all that he had been through, Dylan was, at heart, a good-natured boy. Life had thrown challenges his way, but here, with his nana, he could still be the little boy he longed to be – safe, loved, and protected in her care.

Annie smiled and stroked his curly hair affectionately. "Go on then," she said, giving him a gentle nudge, "there's a Kit Kat waiting for you in the kitchen. Taid's gone down to the farm, but we'll go for a walk down the track to see him after, alright?"

The mention of the Kit Kat sent Dylan racing into the house, his feet barely touching the floor.

Annie was the heart of their family, the one who kept everything together. She might have been small in stature, but she was strong – strong enough to keep everyone in line with a balance of kindness and firmness. Dylan always felt like the most important person in the world when he was with her.

Moments later, Dylan skipped into the living room, the chocolate already half-eaten. He plopped down onto the big, soft sofa next to Annie, his legs dangling over the edge. He wriggled closer to her, his head resting against her warm side. The familiar comfort of her presence calmed him, and he closed his eyes, savouring the moment.

"So then," Annie began, her voice full of enthusiasm as she settled into the cushions, "what stories have you got for me this week? I'm sure you've been up to something exciting!"

Dylan's eyes welled-up.

"A man has taken Prince away." Dylan said tearily. "He said that Dad said he could borrow him to go shooting. But he hasn't brought him back yet. I was cold in bed last night without him."

"Oh no," Annie responded, giving him a cwtch, "well, I'm sure he's just gone on a holiday for a day. I bet you he will be in your house waiting for you when you get home." she said reassuringly. "What else have you been up to?" she continued, trying to change the subject.

Dylan's eyes lit up. "Weeeeeeeell," he started, sitting up a little straighter, "I'm helping a girl called Dawn, look after a pony called Dusty." And without coming up for air, he explained… "Basically, I was feeling miserable, yeah, and looking out of the window… and I saw a little black pony in the flats. I thought I was dreaming, Nana… and I ran outside, yeah, and basically, made friends with Dawn… and I've been helping her look after Dusty."

Annie listened intently, her eyes twinkling as she heard the joy in his voice. "Well, that sounds like quite the adventure," she said, nodding approvingly. "I know you've missed the horses since Henryd, haven't you?"

Dylan's face softened for a moment. "Yeah," he said quietly. "It's made me really sad, Nana. But being with Dusty… it's made me happy again. Really happy. Can I tell you a secret?"

"Of course you can, my boy." Annie said gently.

"Dawn has actually given Dusty to me, for free." Dylan continued, with his eyes full of excitement, "Basically, I've rescued her. Because her owner can't keep her any more. So they've given her to me!"

Annie smiled gently, not really believing his story, but reaching over to ruffle his hair. "Well, I'm glad you're happy, Dyl. That's all I want for you, is for you to be happy." She paused for a moment, taking a sip of her tea. "And how's school? You've been settling in alright?"

Dylan shrugged but smiled. "I hated it at first, but now it's ok. I've been doing some singing, and that's been fun. But looking after Dusty, well, that's made everything better. It's like… everything in my life is good now because of her."

Annie chuckled, her laughter a soft melody that filled the room. "In your life, eh?" she teased. "You sound like a little old man sometimes, Dylan." She reached for her cup of tea again, settling back comfortably into the sofa.

Dylan hesitated for a moment, his mind wandering to a question he had been too nervous to ask anyone else. He rested his head on her warm stomach. Listening to the tea gurgling around in her belly, he hesitated before speaking, his voice barely above a whisper. "Can I ask you something?"

"Of course you can," Annie replied, smiling down at him. "Always. You can always ask me anything you want, you know that."

Dylan shifted uncomfortably before blurting out, "Is Dad my real dad?"

Annie froze, mid-sip, her cup trembling as she nearly choked on her tea. Her eyes widened in surprise as she glanced at Dylan, taken aback by the bluntness of the question. "What are you on about, Dylan?" she stammered, her voice suddenly unsteady. "Oh God…" she struggled for words…" you shouldn't be asking me things like that."

"Why not?" Dylan pressed, his voice innocent but insistent. "Is Mam my real mam?"

Annie's answer came quickly, almost too quickly. "Of course she is!" she said, her tone firm. But there was something in her voice – something unsure – when she added, "Where's all this coming from, Dyl?"

Dylan looked at her with a puzzled expression. "Well, you said mam is my real mam straight away," he pointed out, "but why didn't you say that dad is my real dad?"

Annie's face softened, her eyes clouding with a mixture of concern and tenderness. She sighed deeply, unsure how to respond. She could see that Dylan was far too clever to be brushed off with an easy explanation. She reached out and gently stroked his unruly curls, her heart aching as she realised how much this boy had already figured out on his own.

"I'm not going to tell you anything, Dyl," she whispered, her voice soft but pained.

"What do you mean, Nana?" Dylan pressed, his tone now rising with frustration. "Nana? Tell me. He's not, is he? I *knew* he wasn't. He's horrible to me all the time. And anyway, I hate him." The words tumbled out, raw and full of the emotions he'd been holding in.

"Now, now, you shouldn't say 'hate,' Dylan," Annie said gently but firmly. "That's not a nice word, and you don't really mean it. But listen, boy, it's not for me to answer these questions. You need to ask your mam."

Dylan's teary eyes lit up with sudden realisation. "So he's not," he said, half laughing. "If he was, you would've just said 'of course he is.'"

Annie's face turned serious, but she didn't interrupt. She watched as Dylan continued, as if finally piecing together a puzzle. "Nana, I just want to know." Dylan went on to explain, "Last Easter, my friend in Henryd made a card for her mam, and she wrote 'To Mam and John, Pasg Hapus, Love from Jenny,' because John wasn't her real dad. So, I copied her and wrote 'To Mam and Barry…' on my card, and mam went *mad*. She yelled at me and asked why I'd written Barry's name like that."

Annie exhaled slowly, her arms pulling Dylan closer into a tight embrace. "I think we've talked enough about this now, Dyl," she said, stroking his hair with care. "This should stay between us, okay? If you ask your mam, it's going to upset her. So let's just keep this as our little secret. Agreed?"

Dylan nodded, though the look in his eyes revealed a different resolve. "OK, Nana..." he muttered, a new determination stirring inside him. At nine years old, Dylan had just discovered a secret mission – a quest that only he could undertake. He was going to find out who his real father was.

Annie's hand gently continued to smooth his curls, though her thoughts were far away. She felt a twinge of guilt for not being entirely honest with him, but she had made a promise to herself a long time ago. She would never lie to him about who he was. But the truth – she knew – would have to wait a little longer.

"Right, let's go for a walk down the track, shall we?" Annie announced with a burst of energy that belied her usual calm demeanour. She stood up from her spot on the couch, brushing the crumbs from her apron, her cheeks flushed with a determined glow. "And let's take a bag with us. We can pick up some nuts if the squirrels haven't had them all already!"

Dylan, still curled up next to her, perked up at the suggestion. A walk with Nana down the track was always an adventure. But before he could think about anything else, he instinctively asked, "Have you had your Solpadeine, Nana?" His voice carried the authority of someone far older, with the precision of a school teacher checking on a student.

Annie smiled down at him, her eyes softening as she saw the seriousness on his little face. "Yes, thank you, boy. I've only just had one," she reassured him with a touch of humour in her voice.

For Dylan, time in his nana's house seemed to move differently. Hours slipped away like minutes. He didn't need a clock to know how the day was going; he measured it by the number of Solpadeine his nana took. The routine was as familiar to him as the weather in their little village. He knew she had to take one every four hours because of her headaches – headaches that had become part of her life after the brain haemorrhage she'd had when Dylan was still a baby. It was a story told so often that it had become family folklore – how Dylan had taken his very first steps in Walton Hospital while Annie was recovering.

Dylan, in his young mind, liked to think he played a special part in his nana's healing process, even if it was just fetching her water and measuring out the perfect amount to dissolve the two tablets. There was something comforting about the ritual, the way the tablets would sizzle in the water, and how he felt a certain grown-up responsibility in preparing them for her. By the time the third serving of the fizzy healer was made, he knew the day was nearing its end. That usually meant it wouldn't be long before he'd have to catch the bus back home – a reality that always dampened his spirits.

The walk, however, was enough to lift his mood again. Dylan leapt off the sofa, grabbing the old shopping bag Annie kept hanging behind the door, eager to go for a walk with his nana.

Dolgarrog in late autumn was a sight to behold. The little village, nestled deep in the valley beside a looming mountain, seemed to glow under the golden light of the season. The trees covered the mountain in shades of orange, red and gold, and the crisp air filled Dylan's lungs, making him feel alive. Even though Dolgarrog didn't get much sunshine – being tucked in so close to the mountain meant the sun only reached the village for a few hours each day – the warmth came from the people. The community was tight-knit, the kind of place where everyone knew everyone, and most were related in one way or another. There was a 'distinctive Watkins nose' and 'rather large, signature chin' in all of Dylan's family on his mam's side. Dylan had inherited both, of course, and it gave him a strange sense of belonging. As Dylan was growing up, he could see who he was related to from a mile off… and also those to whom he wasn't.

The cool autumn breeze rustled the colourful leaves, which crunched softly beneath their feet. Annie walked a few steps ahead, the bag in her hand swinging gently at her side as they wandered down the familiar path. This year, the squirrels had been extra busy, and they had to search a bit harder for the hazelnuts that usually lined the trail. Annie turned it into a game, pretending to chase the squirrels, which made Dylan laugh, his earlier worries fading with each step.

"Do you think Taid's still at the farm?" Dylan asked, hinting that he was ready to move on from their nut-hunting adventure.

Annie smiled warmly, sensing his restlessness. "Let's go and see, shall we?" she said, eyes twinkling. "I think we've gathered enough nuts to last us a week!"

Dylan eagerly took hold of the carrier bag, now filled with hazelnuts. With his other hand, he reached out for Annie's hand, which she took with a playful chuckle. "You are such a gentleman," she teased him gently.

Dylan beamed at her, feeling the warmth of the moment. As the pair walked down the muddy track – a tradition with a lot of local families on a Sunday – a dirty little poodle came bounding towards them, a stick clutched in its mouth.

"Hello Madonna," Annie said, kneeling to take the stick. "And where's Geoffrey?"

"Moooooorniiiiiiing," came Geoffrey's chirpy voice from behind a nearby bush.

Annie laughed and nudged Dylan. "Looks like we interrupted Uncle Geoffrey watering the flowers," she teased as Geoffrey emerged, pulling up the zip on his jeans. Dylan was momentarily distracted by Madonna, who barked impatiently, urging him to throw the stick. "Ooooh, hello Dylan!" Geoffrey called, winking at Annie. "Look at you, you've grown so much since I last saw you."

"Hi, Uncle Geoffrey. Yes, I have grown," Dylan replied proudly, rising onto his tiptoes. "I've only got one more year until I start top school."

In reality, Dylan was short for his age, which is why he had dreams of being a jockey. Also, in reality, Geoffrey wasn't Dylan's uncle, he was his second cousin. But in Dolgarrog, like in so many other Welsh villages and towns, any elders in the family, or even neighbours for that matter, were always given the titles of *aunties* and *uncles*. (So it's not really as inbred as one would be led to believe.)

"Are you coming down to see your nana next Sunday?" Geoffrey asked, smiling.

"Of course," Dylan said, flashing a grin at his nana.

"Well, bring your schoolbooks so you can show me your work, I'll pop down to see you." Geoffrey added, throwing a playful wink at Annie. "Right, I'd best get Madonna home to give her a bath."

He ruffled Dylan's hair, gave Annie a quick cwtch, and trotted off, using his rainbow-coloured umbrella as a walking stick.

Dylan watched him go with a smile, amused by the sight of Geoffrey's brisk power-walking, the bright umbrella bobbing along with every step.

"Nana," Dylan asked, turning to Annie with a curious frown, "why doesn't uncle Geoffrey have a wife?"

Annie paused, considering her words. "Weeeeeeell," she said slowly, "he's what you'd call a… career man."

Dylan's confusion deepened. "What do you mean, nana?"

Annie smiled, bending down to meet his gaze. "Well… some people choose a career over having a wife." Annie explained warmly. "Geoffrey went away to work and… chose a career."

Dylan went quiet and thought about this.

"Do you think I'll be a career man, nana?" he asked earnestly, his wide eyes full of sincerity.

Annie's expression softened, and she chuckled quietly. "I don't know Dyl," Annie smiled, "but do you know what the most important thing is?"

"What?" Dylan asked, his eyes bulging with curiosity.

Annie's smile grew as she leaned closer. "The most important thing is that you're happy, and…" she paused, "Uncle Geoffrey is happy being a career man." She smiled knowingly at Dylan. "That's all that matters."

Dylan nodded, as if letting the idea sink in, his young mind turning over the concept of happiness and choices. Annie watched him for a moment, a knowing smile on her face. "Now," she said, standing up and taking his hand, "let's go find your taid. He'll have some fresh milk from the cows for us."

****

10

An Angel in the Making…

Monday morning.

As Dylan opened his eyes, he thought it had all been a bad dream… but it was all real; Prince hadn't been brought home. A dull ache hit Dylan's stomach. Dylan's little brain was awash with emotions – sadness from not having Prince in bed with him, alongside the excitement of seeing Dusty after school. The juxtaposition of emotions had kept him awake for much of the night, but the thought of him having his own little black pony made him bounce out of bed, and he was dressed and ready for school before 7am. His two siblings eagerly following him down the stairs.

Barry and Magi were still fast asleep, their hangovers pinning them to bed, leaving Dylan to handle the morning routine on his own.

In the kitchen, Dylan opened the fridge and pulled out a big plastic bottle filled with fresh milk from the farm. Taid had poured it out for him specially, knowing how much the little ones loved their milk. Carefully, he filled a small bottle for Baby J and then made Ela her favourite strawberry milkshake. But when he brought it to her, she wrinkled her nose in hesitation.

"I don't like this milk, Dylan," Ela moaned, looking at the milkshake with a mix of curiosity and distrust. "Can I have the normal milk instead?"

Dylan sighed, trying to stay patient. "It *is* normal milk, Ela," he explained gently, with a little smile. "It's fresh, straight from Taidy's cow!"

He took a sip himself and understood why Ela wasn't thrilled – it was thicker and creamier than the store-bought milk from Kwik Save. Even he found the taste a bit strong, but he didn't want to let Ela see his doubt.

"Please, Dyl…" Ela's voice softened as her eyes began to fill with tears, her little face crumpling with disappointment.

Dylan's heart melted. He knelt down beside her and gave her a gentle kiss on the forehead. "Okaaaay, ok… don't cry," he said softly. "Let me check the fridge and see if there's any of the milk you like, alright?"

After a quick search, he found a small carton with just enough left for one last shake. He quickly whipped it up, pouring the milkshake into her favourite cup. Ela's face lit up, her earlier disappointment forgotten.

"There you go," he said with a grin. "Now, drink up before it gets warm."

As she sipped contentedly, Dylan remembered the surprises he had hidden in his school bag. He rummaged through it, feeling the excitement of his plan bubbling up inside him. He pulled out the little glow-in-the-dark toys he'd bought over the weekend, treasures he knew would brighten their morning.

"Alright, you two! Close your eyes!" he announced with a mischievous glint in his eye. "Dylan's got a surprise for you."

Ela and Baby J, still in their cosy pyjamas, squeezed their eyes shut, trying not to giggle as they wriggled with excitement. Dylan placed the tiny toys in their little hands, watching their faces as they opened their eyes.

"Wooooooow!" Ela shrieked with delight, her voice filling the quiet kitchen. She held the toy up to the light, watching it glow faintly, her eyes wide with wonder. "I've always wanted one of these! Thank you, Dyl!" She threw her arms around him in a tight hug, her gratitude as warm as the morning sun.

Baby J, on the other hand, glanced at his toy with mild interest before tossing it aside, more focused on trying to grab Ela's milkshake. Dylan couldn't help but laugh at the little one's determination.

"Can I have this one too?" Ela asked, her voice soft with hope as she eyed Baby J's discarded toy. "He doesn't want his."

Dylan chuckled and gave her an exaggerated nod. "Yes, I suppose you can," he said, watching as she clutched both toys to her chest, her happiness evident in every inch of her little frame.

"Dyyyy-laaaaan," came the hoarse, hungover wail of Magi's voice from upstairs. "Can you get Ela dressed for school, please, boy…"

Dylan rolled his eyes but then looked at Ela with a smile. "Yes, Mam."

"Good boy. I'll be down in a minute," Magi muttered, her voice muffled by her pillow.

Thankfully, Dylan had thought ahead and laid out Ela's uniform the night before, so getting her ready wasn't too much of a struggle. With the promise that she could take her new toys to school, Ela happily complied with his instructions. The "three musketeers" then sat together, watching a cartoon on TV until Dylan announced that he was leaving for school.

"Mam, you need to get up now. I'm going," he called out.

"Can you take Ela with you, please, and drop her off?" Magi replied, though it sounded more like a command than a question.

"Maaaaam, I don't want to take Ela. I'm supposed to walk with Jamie," Dylan protested, his voice full of frustration.

"Dylan, you'll take your fuckin' sister to school now, or I'll stop you from going to see that little pony!" Magi snapped.

Dylan let out a frustrated sigh as he put on his shoes. But even at just ten years old, he knew it wasn't Ela's fault. Kneeling down, he gently helped her into her shoes and coat, then grabbed her school bag. Before they left, he picked up Baby J and ran him upstairs. As he opened the bedroom door, the smell of stale alcohol hit him like a wave.

"We're off to school now, Mam. You need to look after Baby J. See you later – I'm going to see Dusty after school, so I won't be home until later," Dylan said.

Magi responded with a half-hearted grunt. Dylan kissed his little brother on the forehead. "Bye Baby J. Be a good boy."

Back downstairs, Ela waited patiently by the door, clutching her new toys. She looked up at him with a small, trusting smile.

"Right, let's go, Ela," Dylan said, taking her hand.

He decided against knocking for Jamie that morning – showing up with his little sister in tow wouldn't exactly be 'cool.' Instead, he hatched a plan. With 70p still in his pocket, he decided he'd expand his tuck shop business by adding a fresh variety of sweets. He'd stop at The Green Shop on the way to keep his customers interested.

"Helloooooo, wee Dylan! And how are you today?" came the cheerful, lilting voice of Mary as they entered the shop. "Hello, Ela! Don't you look posh in your school uniform!"

Mary, who had recently moved to town to take over The Green Shop, made it her mission to know everyone's name. To Dylan, Mary seemed exotic with her Scottish accent – something he'd only ever heard on TV. It fascinated him that she'd seen the world beyond the Conwy Valley yet had chosen to settle in Llanrwst. And he was grateful, too, as she had brought in a whole selection of unique sweets that none of the other shops carried.

"Could I have seven bags of the 10p mix, please?" Dylan asked politely.

"Oooh, seven bags!" Mary chuckled. "Someone's got a sweet tooth! Now make sure you're brushing those teeth, or they'll be dropping out with all that sugar!"

Dylan gave a polite laugh, handed over the money, and grinned at the thought of the profit he'd make from these sweets. With his bag of treasures in hand, he walked Ela over to the door of the infants' school.

He helped her take off her coat, carefully hanging it up for her. Then he bent down and gave her a kiss on her head. "There you go. Have fun today!"

"And another *sws*…" Ela asked sweetly, using the Welsh word for "kiss."

Dylan's heart softened as he leaned down to kiss her cheek one more time. "Right, be a good girl," he said, watching her trot off happily to join her classmates.

Dylan made his way to class, a spring in his step as he thought about his growing tuck shop business. The morning flew by with spelling tests and maths tests, both of which he breezed through easily. Still, his mind wandered – flitting between thoughts of Prince, Dusty, and the excitement of possibly getting in a ride after school, if he could reach the field before it got too dark.

When break time arrived, he barely had time to set up before a small crowd gathered around him. The kids from the farms were lining up, eager to buy sweets, their eyes gleaming with anticipation as Dylan presented his selection.

"These bags have chewing gum in them too," he announced, holding up a bag with pride. "But I'm still selling them at the bargain price of 20p!"

Dylan was busy counting the coins piling up in his hand when Jamie appeared, a grin on his face despite the bruises darkening his cheek.

"Selling sweets again, are you?" Jamie laughed, looking impressed.

"Yes!" Dylan said proudly. "I've already made another pound to put in your gambling machine, or you can give it straight to your dad if you want."

Jamie shook his head, his smile fading slightly. "Nah, don't worry about it. My dad's had his mates round, and they've filled it up again. He's happy now. Besides, I don't want to play it any more."

Sensing Jamie's lingering sadness, Dylan thought for a moment, then came up with an idea. "Why don't you take this 40p and start selling sweets too?" he suggested with a grin. "We can be business partners! Here, I'll give you a head start."

Handing Jamie the 40p, Dylan added, "Look, these lot don't even care that I'm charging 20p a bag – they don't know how much the sweets really cost!"

Jamie's face lit up, visibly cheered by Dylan's generosity and infectious enthusiasm. Inspired by his friend's entrepreneurial spirit, he gave a nod. "Alright, I'll give it a go tomorrow. And if you run out of sweets, just send your customers over to me," he joked.

Before they could talk more, the loud, commanding ring of the school bell echoed through the playground, calling everyone back to class.

"Right, Dosbarth 5," Mrs. Jones greeted them cheerfully as they settled into their seats. "This Christmas, we're putting on 'The Nativity,' and we've assigned the roles today. A list will be posted on the board at lunchtime."

A few whispers of excitement rippled through the class, followed by a cheeky voice from the back.

"Miss, can Dylan be Mary?" Iwan quipped, smirking.

Without missing a beat, Dylan shot back, "Miss, can Iwan be the donkey? He's already got the ears for it!"

The class erupted in laughter, and even Mrs. Jones had to bite back a smile as she regained control. "Byddwch yn ddistaw!" she hushed them in Welsh, gesturing for silence.

In most years, the Year 6 students automatically got the lead roles, but this year the teachers had decided to open up the casting to Year 5 as well, since there wasn't much talent among the older students. Still, there was one student who had always been a "star" in school productions – Melvin Stevens.

Melvin, a Year 6 pupil, stood taller than everyone else in his year. With his tan that somehow stayed even in winter and his broad shoulders that filled out his school shirt, he looked more like an actor from Grange Hill than a typical schoolboy.

Every year, apparently, Melvin managed to snag the lead roles, and everyone knew he'd be cast as Joseph or the Angel Gabriel this year too.

Dylan's eyes glazed over as he zoned out of the classroom noise. The dulcet tones of Mrs Jones teaching Religious Education were blurred out by happy thoughts of Dusty. A flashback of Prince's face in the back of the white van smashed into Dylan's mind. He could feel his eyes starting to water.

"Dylan, I will ask you once more…" came the voice of Mrs Jones, interrupting Dylan's daydream nightmare. "Do your family go to chapel?"

"Erm…" stuttered Dylan, trying to reconnect his brain with being in class, "No, not really. I do go to Catholic church, but only because the old ladies give me money at the end of mass." replied Dylan truthfully.

The other children laughed at Dylan's brazen honesty.

"Well, that's not a reason to go to the Lord's house" responded Mrs Jones, who was an avid chapel-goer.

The lesson ended, and Dylan found himself in the big hallway outside the headmaster's office, standing before the freshly posted casting list for the Christmas play. His heart pounded as he scanned the paper, searching for his name among the sea of Year 5 and Year 6 students listed.

The list was long, with roles ranging from shepherds to wise men. His eyes drifted down, and there, bold as anything, was *Melvin Stevens – Herod.* Just below that, he saw it: *Dylan Evans – Angel Gabriel.*

Dylan's face broke into a huge grin, and his heart soared. He'd done it – he'd been cast as one of the leads! Not just any role, but the Angel Gabriel, the messenger, the one with the big lines. He felt a rush of pride wash over him. Caroline had landed the role of Mary, her absolute dream part, and Eirian, with her wild, curly hair, was cast as one of the lead sheep – a fitting choice, Dylan thought, as he pictured her bouncing around in costume. Only four students from Year 5 had been chosen for lead roles, and he was one of them.

As he stood there beaming at the list, basking in his success, a low, gruff voice interrupted his thoughts.

"You've done hell of a good, ynai?" Melvin's voice was loud and held a note of authority, as if he were acknowledging Dylan's achievement with a kind of approval reserved for people he deemed worthy. Dylan turned around to find Melvin Stevens standing behind him, looking every bit the school star. He wore a tight denim jacket and had a football tucked under his arm. Next to Melvin's well developed frame, Dylan looked like a walking mop with malnutrition.

"Getting the role of Gabriel, eh?" Melvin continued, nodding towards the list. "Means we get out of class now for extra rehearsals ynai? That's the best part, yeah." He grinned, giving Dylan a nudge.

Dylan's excitement doubled. Not only had he landed a part, but Melvin – *the* Melvin Stevens – was actually talking to him, as if they were equals.

"Yeah… it's good," Dylan managed to say, feeling both nervous and thrilled under Melvin's gaze.

Melvin gave him a friendly nod. "You're from the flats, yeah? My mam knows your mam, ynai?"

"Yes," Dylan replied, his voice a bit quieter now, feeling a little awestruck.

"My mam said that you belong to me ynai… like, my uncle is going out with your aunty. So we're probably cousins, ynai?" Melvin explained with enthusiasm.

Dylan had never heard this kind of talk before. He soon came to learn that 'belonging' to someone, in Llanrwst, was a way of saying that you were related to them. He was also soon to learn that, in one way or another, most of the town 'belonged' to each other.

Melvin bounced his football against his knee and caught it smoothly. "I live in George street. It's a bit posher than the flats, yeah. Do you like football?" he asked. "I support Man U."

Dylan hesitated. He knew how popular Man U was, especially around here, but he couldn't bring himself to lie. "Erm… not really. I support Liverpool," he said, bracing himself for a disappointed reaction. Supporting any team but Man U his dad's team, was practically an act of rebellion.

But Melvin didn't seem bothered. He shrugged and moved on. "What about Shakin' Stevens?" he asked, as if going through a mental checklist of interests, trying to find some common ground.

Dylan's face went blank. He didn't know who Shakin' Stevens was, and he felt a pang of disappointment, wishing he could say yes. "Ermmm, I don't know him," he admitted, feeling like he'd missed a chance to connect.

"No worries," Melvin said, smiling as he bounced the football again. "I'll bring my tape to school tomorrow. You can have a listen. He's helluva good."

Dylan's eyes lit up. "Yeah, that'd be cool!"

As Melvin turned to leave, he gave Dylan a 'thumbs up'. "T'ra, boy!" he called over his shoulder, striding down the hall with the easy confidence that came so naturally to him.

Dylan was mesmerised by the star of the school and couldn't wait to start rehearsals to be able to spend more time in his company.

****

11

Gone Without Goodbye.

"Mam, where's Prince?" Dylan asked. Covered in mud and horse hair after visiting Dusty, he had been hoping to find his loyal little dog waiting for him when he got home, but the flat felt strangely empty.

Magi barely looked up, focused on melting lard in a pan to make chips for the family. The heavy smell of fish fingers hung in the air, mingling with the grease. "He's gone, Dyl," she replied flatly, her tone distant, almost dismissive.

Dylan felt a chill ripple through him, a hollow ache forming in his chest. "What?" he whispered, disbelieving, his voice barely audible. "Gone where?"

"The farmer's got him now," she replied, still not meeting his gaze. "He's gone to live in Conwy." She gestured to the table, her tone emotionless. "Pass me my drink, will you?"

Dylan's heart seemed to stop. His mind struggled to catch up with her words, but a slow, creeping sense of loss settled over him, heavy and suffocating. He could feel the tears building, pressing against his control. "Why?" he murmured, his voice breaking as the reality hit him. "Why did you do that?"

Just then, Barry entered the kitchen, a can of lager in his hand, his voice cutting through the tense air as he backed up Magi's explanation. "Because he was a pain in the arse in the flat, Dylan," he said, taking a long sip. "We don't have fuckin' room for a dog here."

Dylan's vision blurred as he tried to hold back the tears. "But he was my dog…" His voice shook with a mix of hurt and anger. "Why did that man just steal him from me in the woods?" he choked out, his hurt now bubbling into raw, desperate rage. "I… I hate you! I fuckin' hate you both!"

Before he could take another breath, Barry's hand came down hard across his cheek, the slap sending him stumbling backward, his face stinging from the blow.

"Don't you fuckin' talk to me like that," Barry snarled, his face flushed with anger. But Dylan was already gone, sprinting out of the kitchen, his footsteps pounding up the stairs as he ran to his room and slammed the door behind him. The house fell silent in his wake.

In his bedroom, Dylan collapsed onto his bed, his whole body trembling as he clutched his pillow. The empty space beside him where Prince should have been felt like a gaping hole. He buried his face in the pillow, his sobs breaking the stillness, each gasping breath hitching in his chest as he cried. The pillow grew damp with tears as he whispered into the silence, his heart heavy with loss and anger.

After a while, a small voice interrupted the quiet. "Dyl, move up. Can I get into bed with you?" It was Ela, her voice soft and full of care. Time had passed, and Dylan had cried himself into an exhausted sleep, not realising the evening had slipped by. "Mam said it's time for bed," Ela continued, climbing onto the bed beside him.

"Of course you can," Dylan said, wiping his face and forcing a small smile for her sake. "Come on, in you get," he said, wrapping an arm around her as she settled beside him.

A moment later, Magi entered the room with Baby J on her hip. "Your food's on the table," she announced, her tone cool. "You're lucky Prince isn't here, or he'd have had it already," she added with a dry tone, laying Baby J down in his cot.

Dylan stared at her, his face streaked with tears, feeling the weight of her words. He wanted to say so much, but the pain of losing Prince tightened in his chest, leaving him silent until she looked at him expectantly.

"Did you want to say anything to me?" Magi questioned, watching him closely.

Dylan's voice trembled as he finally spoke, "Yes." He paused, his voice barely a whisper. "Why, Mam?" The tears flowed freely again, breaking his voice. "Why did you do it like that… and have someone just take him away from me?"

Magi sighed and crossed her arms, but there was a brief flicker of guilt in her eyes. "Your dad was offered good money for him, and we're skint, Dylan," she said, trying to keep her voice steady. "He's gone to a good home now, a proper place. He'll be happier there than he was stuck here in this flat."

She glanced down at Dylan and, for a moment, something softened in her expression. She could see the weight of sadness in his eyes, how deeply this had hurt him, more than she'd expected. The alcohol usually dulled her sense of guilt, masked her sense of responsibility. But tonight, she felt it; she knew she'd broken something in him. "Come here…" she said, holding out her arms. "I'm sorry."

Dylan's heart fluttered with a small glimmer of hope. "Can we get him back, mam?" he asked, his voice desperate, clinging to any chance that his beloved dog could come home.

Magi's face hardened. "Oi, now don't start with that, Dyl. You've got to let it go. And you're going to have to say sorry to your dad for all that swearing. That wasn't very nice."

Dylan looked at her, his mind whirling with confusion and hurt. He was only ten years old, too young to fully grasp the complexity of his family's struggles, but old enough to feel the betrayal searing into his heart. He swallowed back the urge to argue, feeling too exhausted to do anything but nod.

"Right, Dad has gone out and I'm going to play Bingo. I've lost the key again so don't lock the door." Magi instructed. "T'ra. See you in the morning."

As Dylan settled beside Ela, pulling her close, he stared up at the ceiling, his heart heavy with the realisation that Prince wasn't coming back.

Before long, his siblings were gently snoring away, so Dylan gently unpeeled himself from Ela's arms and made his way downstairs to find his cold dinner on the table. Chips with lard solidified around them, and sausage. Dylan grabbed himself two pieces of white bread from the cupboard and made himself a chip sandwich. Putting the sausage in the bin, he welled up at the thought of giving it to Prince. Perhaps mam was right, Prince would be better off on a farm with lots of fields to run in. Hopefully the farmer would feed him better than the leftovers he got at the flat.

After eating his cold chip butty, Dylan grabbed his pencil case from his school bag and sat down with his writing pad. He was about to hatch a new plan.

He drew three neat vertical lines down the page with his ruler and a horizontal line across the top. In the three tabs he wrote 'name, address and amount'. Dylan had created a sponsor form. "That's my job for tomorrow," he said to himself. "This'll get Dusty some food and a new grooming kit. And maybe get myself some new riding boots too, if I can get enough sponsors."

****

12

Knocking on Every Door.

Now that the clocks had firmly gone back, the early darkness of winter evenings made it a real challenge for Dylan to spend much time with Dusty after school. The sun dipped below the horizon shortly after he left the classroom, painting the sky in shades of purple and deep blue over the little market town. With the lack of daylight, navigating a black pony in the dark countryside was difficult and, at times, a bit daunting. But that didn't deter him. Every day, he strode down Gwydir stretch to the field where Dusty grazed, whilst practising his songs for the school nativity, his pockets stuffed with carrots and apples. The cold air nipped at his cheeks, but the moment he saw Dusty's ears perk up at his approach, all the cold and darkness seemed to fade away.

His mission now was clear: he needed to collect sponsorship money to ensure he could feed her throughout the harsh winter months ahead. Dusty depended on him, and he was determined not to let her down.

Dylan had knocked on almost every door in Glanrafon. Most residents had been generous; they always were, especially along the veranda where the neighbours looked out for one another. He knew exactly who would always sponsor him when he set himself a challenge – Mrs. Thomas with her cats, old Mr. Hughes who loved to tell war stories, and the young couple in Flat six who always had a smile for him. He also knew the ones who would grill him with endless questions or shut the door in his face, but this didn't deter him. After all, he had saved Dusty from a potential life of the unknown, and she deserved every bit of effort he could muster.

Arriving at the top level of the flats, Dylan felt a mix of hope and nervousness. Each block had six flats, with two on each of the three levels. On average, he would get three sponsors from each block – a decent success rate, he thought. Clutching his slightly crumpled sponsor form, he approached the first door and knocked.

"Hello, Mr. Talbot, I'm asking people to sponsor me for—" Before he could finish, the door slammed in his face. Mr. Talbot was notorious for his gruff demeanour and lack of interest in the community, but Dylan simply sighed and moved on. It was worth a shot.

He knocked on the door of the adjacent flat. The familiar scent of freshly baked bread wafted through the cracks.

"Hello, Dylan! And what are you up to now?" came the kind voice of Mrs. Goodwin as she opened the door. Her eyes crinkled warmly behind her glasses.

"I'm raising money for a pony called Dusty that I've saved," he explained eagerly. "She was left in a field with no food, and I'm trying to raise sponsorship so I can buy her food, a rug to keep her warm, and maybe a grooming kit. I'm doing a sponsored walk with her to Geirionydd Lake and back."

"Well, that sounds very kind of you, Dylan," Mrs. Goodwin said, her smile widening. "Put me down for 50p. And if you call by on Sunday afternoon, you can have my vegetable cuttings. I'm sure Dusty would love them!"

"Thank you so much!" Dylan beamed. "Dusty *would* love that!"

As he left, Mrs. Goodwin handed him a freshly baked scone wrapped in a napkin. "Here you go, del. Keep up the good work."

Dylan skipped down the stairs, taking a big bite of the warm scone. Moments like these made all his efforts feel worthwhile. Time to make another sponsor form, he thought happily, as he'd filled two A4 pages with sponsorships.

Back in his little bedroom, sat on the edge of his unmade bed, Dylan carefully counted his sponsorship promises. Jamie's dad had even sponsored him £5! That was a surprise. He must have forgiven Dylan for the gambling machine incident with a donation like that.

"And the total sponsorship money so far for Dusty is... £38.50!" Dylan announced to himself, grinning proudly at the numbers scrawled across his crumpled forms. He punched the air in excitement. Nearly £40! That would go a long way towards keeping Dusty fed and warm.

Then an idea sparked in his mind. If the school football team could get sponsored by the local wallpaper shop, maybe he could find a business to sponsor Dusty. He'd seen how the school asked local companies for support, and they were often generous. Perhaps they would be willing to help a pony in need this winter. Determined, Dylan grabbed a fresh sponsor form and headed out.

His first stop was Dalatrek, a local electronics company that had once visited his school to give a talk about technology. The building was modern, like a big caravan on legs, and somewhat out of place among the older stone structures in town.

Dylan took a deep breath and knocked confidently. After a moment, the door opened to reveal a tall, older man with a bald head and thick-rimmed glasses perched on his nose. He wore a crisp white shirt and a navy tie, and his eyes looked down at Dylan over the rims of his glasses.

"Hello, can I help you?" came the stern, posh voice of the Englishman.

"Erm, yes. My name is Dylan, and I'm from the flats," Dylan began, his voice steady. "I have rescued a pony, and I am doing a sponsored walk to raise money to feed her through the winter. Would you like to sponsor me?"

The man's expression shifted from neutral to irritated. "No, thank you," he said firmly, his voice rising slightly. "Please do not call here again." Before Dylan could utter another word, the door was firmly closed, leaving him standing on the doorstep, the chilly wind biting at his cheeks.

For a moment, he felt a sting of disappointment. But he shook it off. Not everyone would understand, and that was okay. Dusty was counting on him, and he wasn't about to give up.

Undeterred, Dylan continued with his mission. He made his way to Siop Bach, the little shop that sold everything from sweets and vegetables, to homemade jams. The bell above the door jingled as he entered.

"Hello, Dylan!" Rose greeted him from behind the counter. Her silver grey hair was coiffed up high at the front, and her eyes sparkled with warmth. "What can I do for you today?"

"I'm collecting sponsorships for a pony I've rescued," he said, holding out his form hopefully. "I'm doing a sponsored walk to raise money for her care."

Rose smiled kindly. "Put me down for 50p," she said, signing her name with a flourish. "But your legs better walk every step of the way!" she added with a playful wink.

"They will, I promise!" Dylan grinned.

As he left the shop, he felt his spirits lifting again.

Walking back towards Glanrafon, Dylan heard a familiar "Yooo-hoooo!" coming from the open door of The Top Chippy.

"You're not going to pass this chippy without popping in to say hello, are you, Dylan?" came the cheerful voice of Charlie, affectionately known as Charlie Chips. He was a tall, jovial man with bright rosy cheeks, his curly hair peeking out from under his grease-stained cap.

"Hi, Charlie!" Dylan replied, stepping inside the chippy. The warmth of the shop and the sizzle of frying batter enveloped him.

"Do you want some batter bits to take home with you?" Charlie offered, scooping some into a paper bag.

"Yes, please!" Dylan nodded eagerly. The batter bits were a rare treat.

"What have you got there, boy?" Charlie asked, noticing the sponsor form in Dylan's hand.

"I've rescued a pony called Dusty," Dylan explained, his eyes brightening. "I'm doing a sponsored walk to raise money to feed her through the winter. Would you like to sponsor me?"

Charlie's face broke into a wide grin. "Put me down for 50p, boy," he said, taking the form and signing it with a flourish. "And I've put some extra chips in there for you, too. Tell your mam they're from Charlie. But shhh," he added, putting a finger to his lips. "Don't tell anyone I'm giving away free chips, alright?"

Dylan laughed. "I won't tell anyone. Thanks, Charlie!"

As he left the chippy, the smell of the greasy food lingering on his clothes, Dylan couldn't help but think about Charlie. On his walk back to the flats, a thought crept into his mind: Could Charlie be his real dad? After all, they both had curly hair, and Charlie was always so kind to him.

But he didn't have a wife or kids, as far as Dylan knew, so maybe Charlie was a 'career man', like Geoffrey.

But he did always ask, "How's your mam?" whenever Dylan stopped by. Maybe that meant something? Maybe Magi and him had split up years ago and Charlie was hoping to get back with her? Dylan's mind was running wild.

Dylan arrived home and kicked his trainers off in the hallway.

"Maaaaaaam" Dylan called as he made his way into the kitchen. "Charlie gave me some chips and some batter bits."

"Ahhhh that's nice of him," Magi replied, "I've made some pie, do you want to have some nice chicken pie with it?"

"No thanks Mam, I'll just have some batter bits and chips. Can I take them upstairs to my room please?" he asked politely.

"Do what you want. The kids are going up in half an hour though so you'll have to come down then." She added.

Up in his room, Dylan munched on his chips and batter bits and pulled out his Fraggle Rock diary. He turned to the back page and he wrote in careful, neat writing "Men Who Might Be My Dad." Underlining it carefully with a big bold line.

Underneath, he listed:

- **Charlie Chips: Curly hair. Kind to me. Always asks, "How's your mam?"**

He tapped his pen against the paper, deep in thought. He remembered the way Charlie's eyes crinkled when he smiled, the way he always slipped him extra batter bits, and how he seemed genuinely interested in Dylan's well-being.

"Maybe it's possible," he whispered to himself. It was nice to imagine. With a satisfied smile, he closed the diary, feeling hopeful that one day he would find his real dad.

That evening, Dylan sat by the kitchen table, learning his lines for the nativity. He could hear the dull sounds of Magi and Barry arguing over money, through the wall.

"You just don't give a shit." Magi shouted. "Christmas is less than four weeks away and you promised me it would be different this year."

"Don't blame me. All you do is fuckin' drink your problems away." Barry retorted.

The arguing continued and little did they know that in the kitchen, Dylan was sat on a gold mine of sponsors – a gold mine that had Dusty's name written on it!

Dylan felt a real sense of accomplishment. Despite the setbacks, he had raised nearly £40 sponsorship money for Dusty, and he had a plan to raise even more. The future felt hopeful.

As he got ready for bed, he glanced out of the window towards the distant fields. The stars were just beginning to dot the sky, and the moon cast a gentle glow over the flats.

"Don't worry, Dusty," he murmured to himself. "I'll make sure you're taken care of."

Climbing into bed, Dylan pulled the covers up to his chin. Thoughts of Dusty, the kindness of his neighbours, and the mystery of his father swirled in his mind. Despite the challenges, he felt content. He closed his eyes, drifting off to sleep with a smile on his face, ready to face whatever tomorrow would bring.

****

13

Decorations.

Magi was always the first on any estate they'd ever lived on to put up her Christmas decorations. But it seemed like the Glanrafon 'flat-rats' had caught on to the festive spirit even earlier than Magi. Dylan noticed that more than a few neighbours had already started decking their windows with lights and tinsel. For families here, struggling with tight budgets, addictions and endless unemployment, Christmas felt like a rare moment of unity and celebration. For a few weeks, at least, the bleakness of everyday life faded behind the sparkle of holiday cheer, and even the hardest days seemed to soften a little under the glow of coloured lights.

"Dylan, pass me that snow spray," Magi called over the sounds of Foster and Allen's rendition of "Hark the Herald Angels Sing," which crackled from their old cassette player. Dylan handed her the can, watching as she carefully leaned over the wide, rickety window to spray each corner with artificial snow. She'd used black tape to create windowpane-like squares, transforming the flat's plain windows into what looked like a festive cottage.

Standing back to admire her work, Magi took a long sip from her glass of wine, her eyes squinting as she evaluated her creation. "It's going to be a lovely Christmas this year, boy," she said with satisfaction, finishing her glass with a single swig before reaching to refill it. "Aunty Fay's coming around next week to bring us some money. And I'm seeing Mr. Lazars tomorrow too, so don't forget to get that Christmas list ready!" she added, a bright smile spreading across her face.

Dylan's mind buzzed with excitement at the mention of his Christmas list. Money was scarce, but in their world, it seemed that 'Aunty' Fay and Mr. Lazars had an endless supply of it. They were like regular Santa Claus figures, stopping by to deliver money to his family and many others in the flats. Every week, without fail, they'd come around again to collect money payments, just like clockwork. Dylan saw it as a bit of a mystery – he wondered why they would give out cash just to ask for it back. It almost felt like a version of his own sweet shop business but on a much bigger scale. To his young mind, it seemed silly, like they were giving gifts and then asking for them back.

But he knew better than to voice his thoughts. Right now, his focus was entirely on making sure his Christmas list was ready. He glanced back at Magi, now humming to the music and filling up another glass, her cheeks flushed from both the wine and the festive spirit. She was determined to make this Christmas one to remember, and seeing her so happy filled him with a rare warmth. He hurried to find a pen and paper, imagining what he'd add to his list this year.

"Dyl, can you entertain Ela and Baby J for a bit?" Magi called out, a hint of impatience in her voice. "I want to get all this decorating finished before tea."

Dylan looked around, grabbing the kitchen scissors, some paper, and the well-loved Walls ice cream box filled with crayons. He felt a little surge of inspiration. "Alright," he announced to Ela and Baby J with a playful grin. "We're going to make some magical snowflakes and colour them in nice and pretty, yeah?"

He pretended he was hosting a kids' show, folding a piece of paper several times and carefully snipping little shapes along the edges. "Now, are you both ready for the magic?" he asked, his voice taking on a dramatic flair.

"Yes!" Ela and Baby J shrieked in excitement, their little faces lit up with anticipation. Dylan held the paper up and slowly unfolded it to reveal a delicate snowflake pattern. His siblings clapped and cheered, their eyes wide with wonder. He made a few more, letting them colour each one in their own unique way, while he admired the bits of cheerful creativity splashed across the paper.

By now, Magi was fully immersed in her decorating – and also in the second bottle of wine she'd opened to help fuel her Christmas spirit. But the living room sparkled, the tree draped in shiny decorations and lights, looking like a festive masterpiece.

"Right then kids," she announced with a grin, swaying a bit as she held out some baubles. "Here's a bauble each. Are you going to help Mam put them on the tree?"

"Yeeeeeeah!" Ela and Baby J squealed with joy, bouncing over to the tree, their little hands reaching for the ornaments.

Magi turned to Dylan with a smile, handing him a tiny, matchstick Santa Claus ornament with a bit of frayed felt for a hat. "And for you, Dyl... look at this. Remember? This little matchstick Father Christmas is what you made when you were small. I've kept it for the tree every single year," she said, her voice soft with nostalgia.

Dylan laughed, rolling his eyes. "It's crap, Mam! Why do you keep it?"

She chuckled, pulling him into a quick hug. "You were only three when you made that and I love it. It's not crap – it's cute, and it reminds me of when you were tiny."

They both laughed, sharing a rare, warm moment amidst the lights and glitter. Magi had done it again, created a room glowing with festive spirit that would keep the kids completely wound up with excitement every day until Christmas day!

****

14.

Behind the Green Door.

December always brought a sense of cheer to Llanrwst, even for families with little money. The promise of Father Christmas visiting with presents filled every child with a spark of hope, including Dylan. The shop windows in town were strung with twinkling fairy lights, each shop window making a special effort to brighten up the market town. The decorations were intended to lure tourists to stop and shop rather than simply passing through on their way to the Winter Wonderland of Betws-y-Coed.

Meanwhile, rehearsals were in full swing for the school's nativity play, though Dylan quickly realised this was nothing like the traditional play he'd been a part of in Henryd. Mr. Tudur, a tall, lanky student-teacher with a small moustache and long black hair pulled into a ponytail, was leading the angels in a rather ambitious tap-dance routine. As Gabriel, Dylan was positioned right at the front, tasked with leading the group through the steps.

"Sir, one of my 2p's has fallen off my shoes! Can you glue it back on, please?" came Leeanne's worried voice.

Few of the children had ever tapped before, and even fewer could afford tap shoes. Mr. Tudur had creatively glued 2p coins to the soles of each angel's shoes to mimic the tapping sound. And while it did create a "tap," there was nothing particularly angelic about it.

"Step, ball-change, step, ball-change, both hands out to present!" Mr. Tudur called out in his high-pitched, enthusiastic voice. "And again…"

The children practised over and over, but there was little that could make Gavin and Michael look graceful. With their boisterous energy, the two bounced around like rugby balls as opposed to the delicate angels they were meant to be.

Mr. Tudur observed the chaos with a pained smile. "I think it might be best for Gavin and Michael to take spots at the back," he suggested gently. "Can we move you both to the back, please?"

"Like full-backs, sir?" Gavin asked proudly, a glint of understanding in his eyes.

"Yeah, we're the full-back angels!" Michael added, puffing out his chest with pride.

"Exactly that…" Mr. Tudur replied, though it was clear he didn't have the faintest idea about rugby positions. He simply clapped his hands, urging them off the stage.

"Right, Gabriel, lead all the angels off stage to the right, please!" Mr. Tudur called out, his voice echoing through the rehearsal hall. "Mrs. Jones, play *This Ole House*, please!"

The angels scrambled together in a noisy huddle, each child trying to be the first to squeeze offstage. Wings bumped, halos tilted, and a few feathers floated to the ground as they giggled and jostled their way through the exit. Mr. Tudur watched the organised chaos with an amused sigh – it might not have been perfectly angelic, but it was certainly lively.

"Melvin Stevens, you need to be on stage…" he started to shout, only to be interrupted by Melvin's grand entrance. In his double-denim outfit and a glittering, hand-crafted gold crown perched proudly on his head, Melvin looked like the love-child of Lady Diana and Shakin' Stevens. His take on King Herod was unique, to say the least, adding some pop star glamour to the nativity story.

Mr. Tudur had decided to add a humorous twist to the play by reimagining Herod as a well-meaning but misguided figure who, rather than hunting down the holy family, wanted to offer 'family allowance' to help with baby Jesus' arrival. This plot twist would be introduced with Melvin's rendition of Shakin' Stevens' hit song, *Green Door*, much to the delight of the young cast.

As Mrs. Jones hit the first notes on the piano, Melvin's eyes sparkled, and he strutted to centre stage, brimming with confidence. His booming voice filled the room as he launched into the song, delivering each line with infectious energy and a touch of rock-and-roll flair.

His voice carried through the hall, each phrase punctuated by dramatic hand gestures and Elvis-style hip swings. The audience of cast members watched, spellbound, caught up in the unexpected charm of Melvin's rock-and-roll Herod.

When he reached the chorus, the entire cast poured onto the stage, joining him in a lively call-and-response. Melvin led with his belting voice, leaning into each note with full theatrical gusto, while the cast echoed him, their voices ringing out in unison. The atmosphere was electric, the rhythm contagious.

Melvin leaned into the final verse, his swagger growing with each word. He swayed his hips and drew out the last note with a dramatic flourish, his voice rich and soulful. The cast, angels, shepherds, and wise men alike, joined in for the grand finale, their collective voices filling the hall with excitement and pride. The final refrain ended in one triumphant, unified shout, leaving the room buzzing with applause and laughter.

As the last note rang out, Melvin took a deep, theatrical bow, pausing for applause that wasn't coming but lingering as if it were. He then bowed again, and then once more, until the other children started giggling.

Mr. Tudur clapped his hands. "Well done, Melvin! And well done to everyone for remembering all the steps and lyrics," he praised, glancing around at the excited, slightly exhausted group. He then noticed Emyr in the shepherds' group, chewing on something conspicuously.

"Emyr, make sure you're not chewing gum, please," Mr. Tudur called out, raising an eyebrow. "The shepherds wouldn't have had *Hubba Bubba* back in those days."

"Sorry, sir," Emyr mumbled, quickly swallowing, his face reddening as he glanced down, hiding a small smile.

The rehearsal moved on, but the children were still buzzing from the thrill of the song, knowing this nativity was one to remember.

"Right, now we move on to the finale" instructed Mr Tudur. "Get into your places."

The final scene was the heart of the nativity. Mary and Joseph, bathed in the glow of soft lights, took centre stage with the baby Jesus cradled between them. Mrs. Jones played a gentle vamp on the piano to help everyone find their places. Dylan, standing tall on a wooden box at the front of the angel choir, took a deep breath as he prepared to sing his solo: *Once in Royal David's City.* His voice rang out, soft and pure, filling the hall as the other angels gathered around him, their white wings glinting under the stage lights.

As Dylan sang, the entire room seemed to fall still; not a single cough or shuffle disturbed the air. You could hear a pin drop as Dylan poured his heart into each note, his voice carrying the timeless melody with such sincerity that the other cast members watched him in quiet awe. With each verse, the rest of the cast joined in, their voices swelling in unison, bringing an unmistakable warmth to the song.

As the final notes faded, Dylan glanced over at Mrs. Jones. She was wiping away a tear with her handkerchief, her eyes glassy with emotion. She caught his gaze and gave him a proud thumbs-up, her face beaming with approval. Dylan's face lit up as he smiled back at her, feeling a mixture of pride and happiness.

Then the school bell rang, shattering the quiet moment, and the students burst into motion, hurrying to gather their bags and coats for the weekend.

"We have our dress rehearsal on Monday!" Mr. Tudur called out over the commotion, struggling to make himself heard. "Don't forget to bring all your costume pieces with you, and have a good weekend!"

Dylan was about to join the rush when he felt a heavy hand on his shoulder. He looked up to see Melvin Stevens standing beside him, an intrigued look on his face. "What are you doing tomorrow, boy?" Melvin asked.

Dylan felt a rush of excitement. "I'm doing a sponsored walk with my pony, Dusty," he said proudly.

Melvin's eyes widened. "You've got a pony?" he asked, clearly surprised. A boy from Glanrafon flats with a pony seemed almost impossible to believe.

"Yeah, I rescued her," Dylan replied, feeling a bit shy, but proud. "I'm trying to raise money so I can keep her fed through the winter."

Melvin looked thoughtful for a moment, then nodded. "Come to my house tomorrow. I'll get my mam to sponsor you," he said with a grin before heading off to join the boys' football team for their Friday practice.

Dylan felt as if he was walking on air. The day had gone better than he ever could have imagined. He'd nailed his solo, and now even Melvin wanted to help him with Dusty. It was more than he'd hoped for, and he could hardly wait to tell Dusty all about it.

As he made his way out of the hall, he noticed Mr. Tudur gathering up the angel wings and packing them into a large box. Dylan hesitated, then walked over, an idea brewing in his mind.

"Sir, I was wondering," he began, feeling a mix of nerves and excitement. "Do you want a donkey in the nativity?"

Mr. Tudur raised an eyebrow, amused. "A donkey? Why, have you got one, Dylan?"

Dylan smiled. "Not exactly, but I do have a pony. I could make her some donkey ears and bring her in. She's really tame – I think she'd be perfect."

Mr. Tudur's eyes lit up at the thought. A real pony in one of his self-written, highly experimental nativity plays? This could be the show of the century! He nodded slowly, already envisioning the excitement Dusty could add to the performance.

"Well, leave it with me, Dylan," he replied, a hint of excitement in his voice. "Let me speak to the Headmaster. I'm not sure we'll be allowed, but I'll ask."

Dylan beamed. "Thank you, sir!" he said, practically bouncing out of the hall with excitement.

Outside, he spotted Jamie by the school gate, waiting with his usual easy-going smile. "Hiya, Dyl," Jamie greeted him. "How's the nativity going?"

"It's really funny," Dylan replied, feeling a surge of pride.

"I can't wait to see it on Tuesday!" Jamie said, grinning. "What're you doing now? Want to come over to mine?"

"Nah, I'm off to check on Dusty and then get an early night," Dylan explained. "We're doing the sponsored walk tomorrow."

"Ah, fair enough," Jamie replied. "I've sold loads of sweets today, by the way. I'm gonna use the money to buy a new cap from *David Cohen Fashion shop* tomorrow!"

Dylan laughed, giving Jamie a quick wave as he set off towards Dusty's field, his heart brimming with excitement for the weekend and all the adventures it promised.

The walk from school to Dusty's field had become second nature to him; if he picked up his pace and ran part of the way, he could make it there in twelve minutes flat, which felt like a small victory in his daily routine.

As he approached the field, Dylan slowed his steps, savouring the anticipation of seeing Dusty. She was already trotting down the hill to meet him, her little frame ploughing through the mud and tufts of grass. Dylan slipped through the gate, pulling a carrot out of his pocket with a grin.

"Just a quick visit today, Dusty," he whispered as he approached, reaching out to stroke her velvety nose. "Just a kiss and a carrot – got to check that you're all good and cosy."

Dusty nuzzled his hand, her warm breath visible in the crisp evening air. Dylan gently scratched her behind the ears, the simple contact filling him with a sense of calm. Although he'd heard that Shetland ponies were hardy and well-suited to cold weather, he often found himself worrying about her on particularly windy nights. Sometimes he'd lie awake, listening to the gusts whistling through the gaps in his bedroom window and he'd wonder if she was warm enough, shielded from the chill by the trees around her field. In truth, Dusty was probably better equipped to handle the elements than he was, her thick coat keeping her snug, but Dylan didn't know this for sure and it didn't stop his concern.

He handed her the carrot, watching with quiet pride as she munched contentedly. "You've got a big day tomorrow too, you know," he murmured, smiling as she nibbled down the treat. "We're going to walk all the way to Geirionydd lake, and everyone's going to see how amazing you are."

Dusty's ears perked up at the sound of his voice, as though she understood every word. Dylan laughed softly, reaching forward to give her a gentle kiss on her furry forehead. She responded with a little snort, sending a puff of warm air towards him as if to say she was ready for whatever adventure he had planned.

"Alright, girl," he whispered, giving her one last pat. "You stay warm tonight. Tomorrow's going to be the best day ever!"

With one last look, Dylan reluctantly turned to make his way home, feeling the weight of responsibility but also the thrill of knowing he was doing his best to care for her. Dusty watched him go, her figure blending into the shadows as he headed back down the Gwydir Stretch towards the bridge.

Walking through the town, he stopped to let 'Calvin Fruit and Veg' – as he was known – pass in front of him to load his van with deliveries.

"Thanks Son," Calvin said smiling to Dylan, appreciative of Dylan's manners.

Dylan stood gawping at Calvin. Broad shouldered with curly black hair and the biggest, bluest eyes, Calvin said "Hey, I've seen you with a little pony. I've got some old carrots here... pop in tomorrow and you can have them."

"Thanks Calvin…." Dylan said, smiling at him.

Calvin nodded his head and climbed into the back of his van to rearrange the fruit and veg boxes.

Dylan raced home but couldn't get Calvin's voice out of his mind. *"Thanks Son…"*

He flew through the door and shot straight upstairs to get his Fraggle Rock diary out. Dylan flipped to the back page where he had made his list of potential dads.

He added to the list in his neat handwriting.

- **Calvin Fruit and Veg. Called me son.**

He paused, before adding,

- **Curly hair. Big blue eyes like mine. Giving me free carrots so he must like horses, just like me. Could be my dad.**

He smiled to himself. The possibilities… If it was Calvin, Dusty would never want for apples and carrots ever again. If it was Charlie, Dylan would have free chips for life! What a conundrum!

****

15

The Sponsored Walk.

The sun had come out, casting a warm glow over the frosty hills, making it feel like the perfect day for Dylan and Dusty's big adventure. Dylan didn't really know how many miles they'd be covering, but he knew the route well enough to feel confident. Walking all the way from Llanrwst to Geirionydd Lake and back was definitely sponsorship-worthy, and he felt proud of every step they took together.

They had been walking for nearly two hours now, and Dylan smiled at Dusty, admiring the way the sun shone on her shiny black coat. As he shrugged off his shell suit jacket, tying it loosely around his waist, he noticed a light sheen of sweat glistening on Dusty's chest. She looked as if she'd just been polished.

"Are you hot, my baby?" he cooed, his voice soft and playful as he gave her neck a gentle pat. "Let's take a little break, shall we?"

They pulled into a small, grassy layby along a quiet lane that Dylan knew was a dead-end. He figured it was the perfect place for a quick rest. Dusty immediately lowered her head to munch on the untouched grass, then took a few sips from a little stream trickling beside the lane. Suddenly, she raised her head, wiggling her nose and baring her teeth, as if the cold water had startled her.

"Ahh, is it cold, Dusty?" Dylan laughed. "Cold water makes my teeth hurt too… you probably have cavities," he joked, giving her a light rub on the nose.

He pulled a packet of *Tangy Toms* from his rucksack, unwrapping them with care, and grabbed a carrot for Dusty. "There you go, girl," he murmured, holding it out for her to nibble on. Dusty crunched it eagerly, and Dylan grinned as he tossed her the occasional crisp. He wasn't entirely sure tomato flavour crisps were the best snack for a pony, but she seemed to enjoy them.

They sat in silence, boy and pony, enjoying their rest in the winter sunshine. Dylan munched his crisps contentedly, and Dusty nibbled at the grass beside him. It was a simple, peaceful moment that felt just right. Dylan's brain was always over active, but around Dusty he found perfect peace, the only place he felt de-stressed.

Suddenly, without any warning, Dusty's head shot up, ears pricked, and her muscles tensed. She let out a loud snort, eyes fixed on something in the distance. Dylan followed her gaze, brow furrowing.

Dylan sat upright. "What is it, Dusty?" he asked, a flicker of alarm in his voice. She was acting strange, her body rigid, nostrils flaring as she looked towards the end of the lane. She pawed the ground, her hooves stamping restlessly.

Dylan gave her lead rope a reassuring tug. "Come on, Dusty, it's probably just a sheep or something," he murmured, though he felt a prickle of unease himself. As he threw his rucksack on and stood up, he began to hear faint sounds – muffled but unusual, like something struggling or maybe even in pain. Dusty was on high alert, her hooves planted firmly, her eyes wide as she snorted, pulling slightly away as if warning him to turn back.

"Hello?" Dylan called out, his voice echoing down the narrow lane. "Is everything alright?"

The faint sounds grew louder as they approached, and Dylan felt his heart beat a little faster. He edged forward, cautiously pulling Dusty along, when he caught sight of a black Range Rover parked at the dead-end. The vehicle was rocking slightly, and Dusty tried to pull back, her eyes fixed warily on the car.

Dylan's mind raced with possibilities. Maybe this was his big moment. What if he'd stumbled across something mysterious, like an alien encounter – an E.T. moment just waiting for him to discover?

He took a few steps closer, peering at the car, when suddenly the back door swung open. A tall man stumbled out, his shirt half open, fumbling with his belt. He stared at Dylan, his face flushed with a mix of shock and alarm.

"Hiya," Dylan said, smiling innocently, oblivious to the man's discomfort. "My pony heard some noises, so I came down to check if everything was okay. It sounded like someone was hurt or something!"

The man's eyes widened as he tried to straighten his clothes, pulling his shirt over his chest while adjusting his trousers. "Oh… erm… yes," he stammered, struggling to find his words. "Yes, we're… fine. Thank you."

Dylan tilted his head, studying the man's face and shiny bald head. Suddenly, recognition dawned on him. "Hey, I know you!" he exclaimed, his voice bright with excitement. "You're the man from Dalatrek! Remember? I came to your office asking you to sponsor me for my walk with Dusty."

The man's face flushed an even deeper shade of red. "Erm… yes. Yes, I remember you," he said, clearing his throat as he looked nervously over his shoulder.

"But you didn't sponsor me," Dylan pointed out, a hint of disappointment in his voice. "What are you doing up here?" he asked innocently, looking between the man and the car.

At that moment, a blonde woman emerged from the car, her hair slightly tangled, cheeks flushed, looking just as startled as the man. Her gaze flickered between Dylan and the man, her eyes wide with surprise and a hint of panic. She seemed uncertain, her expression frozen as she adjusted her coat and gave a polite, flustered smile.

Dylan, unaware of the tension in the air, gave her a friendly wave. As he looked closer, he realised he recognised her too. "Oh! You work at the bank, don't you?" he said with cheerful innocence, as though meeting neighbours on a casual stroll. "I remember seeing you there with my mam. I'm actually in the middle of my sponsored walk now!" he added proudly, beaming at them both.

The woman managed a shaky smile but kept silent, glancing at the man for guidance. The man, still buttoning his shirt, gave a forced cough. "Well… er…" he stammered, clearly trying to compose himself. "I suppose I'd better sponsor you, hadn't I? Why don't you… uh… why don't you come to my office and see me Monday afternoon? I'll sponsor you… let's say… £50."

Dylan's eyes went wide. "£50?!" he repeated, his grin widening in disbelief. "The most anyone has given me is £5! With £50, I could buy Dusty loads of food… maybe even a new bridle!"

"Yes," the man replied, flashing a nervous smile. "Well, best to be generous, right?" He looked towards the lane, clearly eager for Dylan to leave. "Now, you'd better keep going if you want to finish that sponsored walk properly. Can't let too many breaks slow you down!"

"I'm going, don't worry!" Dylan assured him with a proud nod. "Come on, Dusty, let's go!" He tugged on Dusty's lead, but the pony's curious gaze lingered on the pair, her ears flicking forward as if sensing the unusual atmosphere.

"And, er… hey, boy!" the man called after him, causing Dylan to pause and look back. "What's your name again?"

"My name is Dylan," he replied, smiling as he stroked Dusty's nose. "And this is Dusty."

The man nodded. "Dylan, well, I'll see you on Monday. And, uh… let's keep this little meeting between us, alright? A… uh… little secret just for us. Don't you be telling anyone you saw us up here," he added, winking with a forced grin.

Dylan's eyes widened with a conspiratorial excitement. It was like he was being let in on something grown-up and mysterious. "I won't tell anyone! Your secret is safe with me," he promised, feeling like he'd just become part of something big.

With a final wave, Dylan let Dusty lead him away. As they turned the corner back down the lane, he glanced over his shoulder to see the man and woman ducking hurriedly back into the car, their flustered expressions clear even from a distance. Dusty snorted, pulling Dylan back towards the main path.

After a while, they arrived at the lake – their turnaround point. The water was calm, reflecting the surrounding mountains like a giant mirror, and Dylan felt a sense of pride and accomplishment wash over him. They'd made it halfway, and now he just needed to make it back to complete the walk. The sun cast a golden light over the scene, and with nobody else around, Dylan felt a sudden urge to sing. It was like the lake was inviting him to fill the silence with his voice.

Clearing his throat, he began to sing the song he'd been practising for the school nativity. "Once in royal David's city…" His little soprano voice carried over the still water, clear and bright, and he felt a rush of joy as the lake seemed to echo it back to him.

"Mary was that mother mild, Jesus Christ her little child…" He sang each line with careful attention, imagining Mrs. Jones' proud smile as he hit the notes just right. Dusty stood nearby, grazing peacefully, her ears flicking back as if listening to him. He went over the verse a few more times, his voice ringing out in the crisp air, letting each word linger.

After a few more rounds, he smiled, feeling satisfied. His voice, Dusty's calm presence, and the quiet beauty of the lake all came together in a moment that felt… perfect. As he turned to Dusty, he patted her neck fondly.

"Come on, girl," he said softly. "Let's head back home. We've got £50 coming tomorrow, thanks to that strange meeting!" Dusty snorted as if in agreement, and together they began the long walk back.

With Llanrwst finally in sight, Dylan decided he deserved a bit of a rest for the last stretch of the journey.

"Hey, Dusty. How about giving me a lift for the last ten minutes?" he asked with a hopeful grin.

Dusty nuzzled against Dylan's leg, scratching an itch as if to say she didn't mind. Carefully, Dylan looped the lead rope around her neck, tying it to either side of the head collar to create makeshift reins. Taking a deep breath, he gently hopped onto her back, settling in as comfortably as he could. He felt the warmth of her coat through his clothes, and a quiet thrill rippled through him as he thought about how lucky he was to finally have his own pony.

Dusty seemed to sense they were on the home stretch. Her hooves danced excitedly, and she began to jog on the spot, her eagerness bubbling over. She knew exactly where they were, and without warning, she stretched her nose towards the ground, tugging the lead rope out of Dylan's hands.

"Whoa, Dusty!" Dylan laughed, gripping her mane for balance. "Dustyyyyyyy, slow down!"

But Dusty was in her element, her excitement taking control. She broke into a lively trot that quickly became a canter. Dylan adjusted his seat, recalling Wendy's voice from years ago echoing in his mind. "Sit up, Dylan. Hands down."

Repeating the words out loud as if Wendy were right there, he felt a momentary surge of confidence. But Dusty was just warming up. With a spirited flick of her head, she shifted into a gallop, picking up speed as they started down the sloping forestry path.

Dylan's heart raced as he realised they were moving faster than he'd ever gone before. Trees blurred by as Dusty surged forward, her hooves pounding in a powerful, steady rhythm that pulsed through Dylan's whole body. The thrill of it was like nothing he'd experienced before, but as Dusty's pace quickened, a thread of panic started to creep in.

He tugged at the reins, trying to steady her, but Dusty's head was down, her nose almost to her knees as she galloped freely, lost in the thrill of the speed. Dylan had lost all control. He held on tightly, feeling the wind whip past his face as they thundered down the path, the forest a blur around them.

"Dusty, please – slow down!" he called out, but she was having the time of her life, and nothing was going to stop her. The rhythm of her gallop jolted through him, every beat making him feel as if he were part of her powerful stride.

Dylan's fingers clenched Dusty's mane as he leaned forward instinctively, feeling the rush of wind, the rough bounce of the path, and the sheer, exhilarating speed that left him both terrified and thrilled. In that wild, unstoppable moment, pony and boy were as one, charging down the path like a whirlwind through the forest.

Dylan could see that they were finally approaching Dusty's field, the gate just ahead. Dusty let out a loud whinny, her call echoing through the trees, as if announcing their return to her field mates. In response, the other horses perked up, their heads turning to greet her. But Dusty wasn't content to make a simple entrance. She picked up speed again, her powerful little hooves thundering across the ground, and then, without warning, she slammed her front hooves down, skidding through the mud with a suddenness that made Dylan's heart lurch.

He barely had time to react before Dusty dropped her left shoulder, giving an almighty buck. The force was enough to send Dylan sailing through the air. For a moment, all he saw was a blur of green and brown before he landed, with a wet thud, in a soft, mossy ditch. Mud splattered up around him, and he lay there, dazed, trying to catch his breath. The fall had knocked the wind out of him, and he lay still, blinking up at the branches overhead, feeling the cool, damp earth beneath him – the wet soaking through his clothes.

After a moment, he pushed himself up, brushing bits of moss and mud from his face, and checked himself to see if anything hurt. Nothing seemed broken – just a few sore spots and, mostly, a bruised ego. Slowly, a smile spread across his face as he looked over at Dusty, who was now standing by the gate, her chest rising and falling as she exhaled in deep, satisfied breaths as if nothing out of the ordinary had happened. She dipped her head to munch on a patch of grass, totally unfazed.

Dylan shook his head, laughing to himself. "Thanks for making sure I landed somewhere soft Dusty… you cheeky girl!" he called out, still grinning.

Dusty's ears flicked in his direction, but she didn't look up, too busy tearing up mouthfuls of grass. She was home, and Dylan couldn't help but feel grateful that, in her own way, she'd given him a ride he'd never forget.

Dylan grabbed his grooming kit out of his rucksack and set to work, brushing Dusty's coat with gentle, rhythmic strokes.

"I'm so proud of us Dusty – we completed the sponsored walk!" he said, smiling. Dusty closed her eyes, savouring the attention, every so often letting out a soft snort of contentment.

Once her coat was gleaming and free of sweat, Dylan reached into his bag and pulled out a couple of carrots. "Here you go, girl," he said with a grin, holding out the treats. Dusty took them gently, crunching away with happy enthusiasm as Dylan gave her one last affectionate pat on the neck.

Finally, with a reluctant sigh, Dylan opened the gate to the field, leading Dusty back to join her field mates. She gave him a final nuzzle before trotting off, her tail flicking in the breeze.

"Dusty!!" Dylan shouted, laughing as Dusty undid all of Dylan's hard work and rolled in the mud. After a few rolls and face rubs in the mud, Dusty bounced up on to her feet, squealed in delight and galloped off up the hill to join her friends. Dylan leant against the fence feeling a deep sense of satisfaction – another happy day together to add to the memory bank.

Dylan was exhausted, his legs sore from miles of walking, but his heart was full. The sponsorship money they'd raised would make sure Dusty was fed and cared for all winter. Mission complete!

****

16

The Detective.

"Where the bloody hell have you been?" Magi demanded, a mock-angry tone in her voice as Dylan walked in.

Dylan barely had time to answer before his Aunty Jane's cheerful voice cut in. "Hiya, boy!" she greeted him lovingly. "I hear you've been doing a sponsored walk with your pony Dusty? Why haven't you been to see me?" Her smile widened as she took in Dylan's mud-streaked face and dishevelled clothes.

Jane, Magi's sister, was the only other person in the family who shared Dylan's obsession with horses. But horses and kids from council estates were rarely seen together, and Jane hadn't been around horses in years. Her eyes lit up as she approached him. "Ooooooh, come here, let me smell you," she laughed, leaning in as if to catch the scent of the stables. "I haven't had the whiff of horses around me in ages!"

"Stand still, Jane, or I can't measure you," Magi muttered, frustrated as she tried to hold a tape measure to her sister's arm.

Dylan looked between them, amused. "What are you doing?" he asked gently.

"I'm knitting a cardigan for Aunty Jane here, but it's never going to be ready by next Friday!" Magi sighed, shaking her head as if it was the most daunting task in the world.

"It better bloody had be," Jane replied, raising an eyebrow at her sister. "You promised, Magi, and I've got nothing else to wear!"

Dylan watched the sisters dissolve into laughter over the comical struggle with the cardigan's measurements. They clutched each other, giggling uncontrollably as Magi struggled to keep the tape measure in place. "Don't… Magi… I'm going to pee," Jane gasped, crossing her legs as she tried to hold in her laughter.

Dylan, observing the cardigan with a curious expression, remarked innocently, "Is it supposed to be so… fluffy? It's like cat fur!"

Magi put on her best faux-posh accent, patting the fuzzy material. "It's posh, darling – it's mohair. It's proper London fashion ynai!"

"Maybe it is," Jane said, still giggling, "but I bet in London the sleeves are the same length!" She held up her arms, one sleeve trailing well past her hand while the other barely reached her elbow. Both sisters burst into a fresh round of laughter, their voices echoing around the room, while Dylan chuckled along, watching them with a grin.

"So, how much sponsor money have you raised for Dusty then?" Magi asked, her voice light but her eyes betraying a cunning glint.

"Errrrm, in total, I think I'll have around £52," Dylan replied hesitantly, carefully avoiding mentioning the £50 that the man from Dalatrek had promised.

Magi leaned back in her chair, swirling the last drops of wine in her glass. "Well, I've got an idea," she said casually, her tone shifting to one she used when she was about to sweet-talk someone into something. "Why don't you go and collect some of the sponsor money now? And however much you collect, if you let me borrow it, I'll give you back double on Monday when I get my money from the Post Office."

Dylan frowned, suspicion prickling at him. "No thanks," he replied politely but firmly.

Magi's smile tightened, and she pursed her lips in irritation. "Right, well, I'm not asking you," she said sharply, her tone hardening. "I'm *telling* you. Go and collect some sponsor money now, and then you can have chips from the chippy for tea."

"Put me down for a pound, boy, and I'll give it to you on Friday, yeah?" Aunty Jane chimed in, trying to diffuse the tension. She reached over to tousle Dylan's hair affectionately. "Go on, boy."

"Thanks, Aunty Jane," Dylan mumbled, his mind racing as he tried to figure out how to navigate this situation. Pausing for a moment, he looked back at Magi, his voice cautious. "If I go and collect sponsor money now…" he hesitated, "and you borrow it, you'll definitely give it me back tomorrow, won't you?" He looked her in the eye. "It's money to buy Dusty food."

Magi let out a laugh that didn't quite reach her eyes. "Of course, I'll give it you back," she said with exaggerated sincerity. "Go on, see if you can get £20 worth of sponsor money in. I bet you can't collect £20 in an hour," she added with a challenging tone, as if it were all a fun game.

"Right, I'm off," Jane interjected, gathering her belongings and slinging her bag over her shoulder. "I've got a bus to catch – I can't miss this one, there's not another for an hour."

She gave Dylan a quick pat on the head. "Good luck with your sponsors, boy. And don't let her take all your pennies," she added in a whisper, giving Magi a playful wink as she headed for the door. "T'ra now!"

Dylan sighed and grabbed his sponsor form, heading out onto the veranda. The cold air bit at his cheeks as he trudged from door to door, explaining how he'd completed his sponsored walk and still had energy to spare. Some neighbours listened kindly, offering a pound or two, but others slammed the door in his face with curt refusals. It stung a little, but Dylan pressed on, determined to do right by Dusty.

By the time he glanced at his little Casio watch, nearly an hour had passed, and he'd managed to collect £9.50. It wasn't the £20 his mam had set as the challenge, but it was still a good haul – and enough to buy a couple of bags of pony nuts from Gwyn Lewis. He tried to focus on that positive thought as he walked back home, clutching the coins in his hand.

When Dylan returned to the flat, an unusual hush greeted him. The usual chaos of his siblings playing or Magi shouting instructions was absent, leaving the place feeling oddly still. He kicked his shoes off by the door and ran upstairs.

He peeked into Baby J's room to find him fast asleep, his tiny chest rising and falling in a peaceful rhythm. In the corner, Ela was curled up on her bed, quietly flipping through one of her picture books, her lips moving silently as she mimicked reading.

Downstairs, Magi was perched on the armrest of the sofa, nursing the last of her wine. The television played softly in the background, but her attention was elsewhere. She looked up as Dylan entered.

"Well? How did you do?" she asked, her voice carrying a mix of eagerness and impatience.

"£9.50," Dylan replied, holding out the small collection of coins. His tone was subdued, a mix of pride and disappointment. "A lot of people weren't in."

Magi reached out, her hand closing around the money with practiced ease. "That's not bad for an hour's work," she said, jangling the coins in her hand. "There you go," she said, handing Dylan some of the coins, "There's 50p for your bus to nana's tomorrow."

Dylan nodded. "Thank you." he said.

"So, I owe you £9. Don't worry, you'll get it back on Monday." Magi said, taking into account that she'd already given him 50p back.

"You promise?" Dylan pressed, his voice carrying a hint of hope.

Magi paused, her wine glass poised mid-air. "I said I'd give it back, didn't I?" she replied, abruptly, draining the last sip and setting the glass down firmly. She stood and grabbed her coat, pulling it over her shoulders. "The kids are already in bed. Why don't you get the catalogue out and pick something nice from Father Christmas?"

Dylan's eyes lit up at the suggestion. "Where's the catalogue?" he asked, his excitement bubbling up despite himself.

"In the cupboard," Magi replied, tugging on her boots by the door. She glanced back at him, her voice softening. "Pick whatever you like, okay?"

Before he could respond, the door slammed shut behind her, leaving Dylan alone in the quiet flat. With a determined smile, he headed towards the cupboard and grabbed the catalogue and his pen and paper.

Flicking through *Kays* Christmas catalogue was always one of Dylan's favourite traditions. He would start with the toy section, circling the pages filled with brightly coloured possibilities that seemed to jump off the glossy pages. Next came the trainers, where he would fantasize about the coolest pair to show off in school. Finally, he'd make his way to the clothing section, adding a few items to the end of his list – less important, just in case Santa couldn't carry too much in his sleigh.

Dylan always held onto a sense of hope at Christmas, though deep down he knew the gifts he dreamed of often wouldn't materialise. Most years, he found himself crafting little lies to tell his classmates about the presents he'd supposedly received. But this year felt different. Dusty had come into his life, and for the first time, Dylan felt like he already had the best gift he could ask for. Nothing was going to spoil that.

Sitting by the twinkling lights of the Christmas tree, Dylan immersed himself in the catalogue. He'd already circled too many toys, so he began the meticulous process of going back and drawing second circles around the ones he truly wanted. His wish list grew in neat handwriting, each word carrying a secret hope.

When he turned to the clothing section, something caught his eye. He stopped abruptly on the page featuring men's underwear. Dylan's hand hovered over the page, pen poised as he considered circling the Sloggi Tanga pants. But his focus shifted, and he found himself staring at the models. His eyes were locked on the images, unable to move past the bulging fabric and confident poses. His mind raced, struggling to understand why he felt so captivated by the page. He told himself he was just deciding on a colour, but deep down, he knew it was something else – a feeling he couldn't quite explain, leaving him in a strange, frozen moment.

A knock at the front door jolted him from his trance. Flustered, Dylan slammed the catalogue shut and shoved it back into the cupboard, his cheeks flushing red at the thought of being caught.

"Dylan," Jamie whispered through the letterbox.

Relieved, Dylan opened the door to find Jamie standing there in a new shell suit and cap, with a plastic bag filled to the brim with sweets.

"I like your cap." Dylan remarked.

"I bought it from David Cohen's" Jamie said proudly. " Do you like my shell suit?"

"Yeah. It's really nice." Dylan said.

"Do you want one?" Jamie asked.

"Erm…what do you mean?" Dylan asked.

"When I bought this cap, I went and tried on this shell suit on and just put my own clothes back on over it!" Jamie laughed. "Freebie!"

"You stole it?" Dylan asked, in disbelief.

"Borrowed it for a bit." Jamie responded. "I'll take it back next week and swop it for another one." He chuckled.

Dylan couldn't believe what he was hearing.

"I'll get you one if you want. It's easy. I've brought these to share," Jamie said, grinning ear to ear. "My sweets business is booming!" He laughed and added, "How's yours going?"

Dylan chuckled and shrugged. "I've got another business now," he said proudly. "I've been doing a sponsored walk for Dusty!"

As they sat on the living room floor, Dylan launched into the story of his day – recounting every step of the walk, the encounter in the woods, and the promise of a £50 sponsorship from the man in the Range Rover. Jamie hung onto every word, his face lighting up with amusement as Dylan described the events in vivid detail. When Dylan finished, Jamie burst into uncontrollable laughter.

"Dyl, they were definitely doing rudey-nudeys!" Jamie exclaimed between gasps of laughter.

"What?" Dylan replied, his brow furrowing. "What's that mean?"

Jamie wiped a tear from his eye. "You know... shagging!" he said, trying to suppress his giggles.

Dylan's confusion deepened. "What's shagging?" he asked earnestly.

Jamie, suddenly feeling like an all-knowing expert, leaned in conspiratorially. "It's what adults do to make babies."

Dylan's face twisted in disbelief. "So does that mean that woman's going to have a baby now?"

"No, adults sometimes do it for fun." Jamie explained. "When they do it for fun, they don't have babies."

Dylan tried to process this new information, his innocence clashing with Jamie's self-proclaimed wisdom.

"But sometimes, you just get a baby in your belly anyway, even with no shagging. Like Mary and baby Jesus?" Dylan asked his knowledgeable mate.

Jamie looked momentarily stumped but nodded sagely. "Yeah, probably."

The conversation took a turn as Jamie, clearly enjoying the topic, smirked and asked, "So... did you see the woman's titties?"

Dylan's jaw dropped in shock. "Nooooo!" he exclaimed, his laughter bubbling over despite his embarrassment. "I didn't see anything like that! They could've just been having a picnic or something!"

Jamie shook his head, laughing harder. "Dyl, if the car was rocking and the man came out putting his clothes back on, they weren't having a picnic!"

Dylan waved his hand dismissively, eager to move on. "Whatever they were doing, the important thing is he's giving me £50 for Dusty on Monday!"

Their voices and belly laughs filled the quiet flat, echoing through the space like Christmas bells.

"Do you want a sugar butty?" Dylan asked, a mischievous grin spreading across his face.

"Always!" Jamie replied eagerly, his eyes lighting up with excitement, as if they hadn't already consumed enough sugar for the week.

The two boys burst into the kitchen. Dylan opened the cupboard and pulled out a plate and a loaf of bread with a dramatic flourish, as if unveiling fine dining ingredients. "Welcome to Dylan's Kitchen," he announced in a pretend posh voice. "First, you pour some sugar onto a plate," Dylan began, sprinkling a generous mound of sugar and shaking the plate, sugar already going everywhere. Jamie leaned on the kitchen table, laughing at Dylan's antics.

Dylan held up a slice of bread as if it were a prized delicacy. "Next, you take your piece of bread. Usually I like to use Vitalite, but today we are having to work with *No Frills* margarine from *Kwik Save*!"

Spreading the margarine to every corner with exaggerated care, Dylan smiled at his handy work.

"And now, for the best part," Dylan declared, carefully pressing the margarine-covered side of the bread into the plate of sugar. "Roll it, shake it, make sure it's evenly coated… and voilà! Behold zee masterpiece: zee butty sugar!" He held up the finished product like a trophy, his face alight with pride.

Jamie erupted into applause, nearly doubling over with laughter. "And can the chef make one for me please?" he asked.

"Of course! Only the best for my guest," Dylan said with a mock bow, handing the sugar-dusted butty to Jamie before making one for himself.

The boys sat by the kitchen table, munching their creations and giggling between bites. Sugar butties like these were the height of luxury. Jamie licked his fingers clean and looked at Dylan with mock seriousness.

"When you are a grown up you should open a café! Dylan's Sugar butty shop. You'd make a fortune." Jamie laughed.

Dylan grinned. "Only if you're my business partner, Jamie. We'd make the best sugar butties in all of Llanrwst!"

The two boys laughed as they stuffed their faces with the sugar-laden bread, crumbs and granules scattering across the table. But Dylan had something weighing on him, and the laughter started to fade from his face.

"Jamie," Dylan began, his voice dropping to a serious tone. "Can I tell you something?"

"Yeah," Jamie mumbled, still chewing on the last bite of his sugar butty. He barely looked up, preoccupied with wiping the stickiness off his fingers.

Dylan glanced towards the stairs to make sure Ela hadn't sneaked down to eavesdrop. Once he was sure they were alone, he took a deep breath, bracing himself for the reveal.

"I don't think my dad is… my real dad," Dylan said, his voice barely above a whisper.

Jamie froze mid-wipe, his eyes snapping to Dylan. "What?" he asked, half-laughing. "What do you mean?"

"He's not my *real* dad," Dylan repeated, his words a little firmer this time. "And… I think I know who my real dad is."

Jamie snorted, still thinking it was some kind of joke. "You're winding me up, right? Why don't you think he's your dad?"

Dylan hesitated, then leaned forward as if letting Jamie in on a big secret. "Well… back when we lived in Henryd, my friend Samantha didn't have a dad. But sometimes, she'd write cards to her mam and a man called Andy. Then one Easter, she wrote a card to her mam and a man called John."

Jamie tilted his head, trying to follow the story. "Okay… but what's that got to do with you?"

"Well," Dylan continued, his voice lowering even more, "last Easter, I copied Samantha. I wrote my card to 'Mam and Barry,' and when my mam opened it, she went mental. She was shouting at me, saying it wasn't nice to call him Barry like that. She told me to call him Dad. I didn't get why she was so upset. So, I asked my nana if he was really my dad. She said I should ask my mam… but then she told me not to, because it would make her sad."

Jamie blinked, trying to process everything. "That's… weird," he admitted. "Your family is proper weird sometimes."

"And that's not even the worst part," Dylan added, leaning back and crossing his arms. "The other night, my mam and dad were fighting, and I heard him shout, 'You can tell that little bastard who his real dad is…'"

Jamie's mouth fell open. "What? Do you think he meant you?"

"Of course, he meant me!" Dylan said, half-laughing in disbelief. "Who else could he have been talking about?"

Jamie sat back in his chair, his face serious. "Dyl, that's… that's mad. What are you gonna do?"

Dylan straightened up, a determined look in his eye. "I'm on a mission to find out who my real dad is," he said with a confidence that made Jamie shake his head.

"You're always up to something," Jamie said, a touch of worry in his voice. "Why do you wanna go looking for trouble?"

Dylan sighed, his gaze dropping to the table. "It's easy for you to say, Jamie. You've got your mam and dad."

Jamie crossed his arms defensively. "Yeah, the nicest dad ever," he said bitterly.

A silence hung between them, the air heavy with unspoken feelings. Dylan realised he might have hit a nerve. "Sorry, Jamie," he mumbled, breaking the tension. "I didn't mean it like that. It's just… I wished for a new dad once. And now it looks like I might actually have one. And…" Dylan hesitated, glancing at Jamie. "I think I know who it is."

Jamie's curiosity immediately overtook his annoyance. "What?!" he asked, leaning forward, a grin breaking across his face. "You're like Inspector Gadget with all this detective stuff!"

"Do you want to know who I think it is?" Dylan asked, the excitement returning to his voice.

Jamie's eyes lit up. "Let me guess… Mr. Tudur?" he teased, bursting into laughter.

Dylan rolled his eyes, but a small smile tugged at his lips. "If you're just going to mess around, I won't tell you."

"Alright, alright. Go on, then," Jamie said, stifling his laughter and sitting up straighter.

Dylan took a deep breath, as if what he was about to say was the most serious thing in the world. "It's between two men," he began. "Who do you think I look like more… Charlie Chips or Calvin Fruit and Veg?"

Jamie's jaw dropped, and then he burst out laughing so hard he nearly fell off his chair. "WHAT?!" he exclaimed, clutching his stomach.

"I'm serious!" Dylan said, though he couldn't help but laugh a little too.

After catching his breath, Jamie wiped a tear from his eye. "Alright, alright. So, what makes you think it's one of them?"

Dylan explained how Charlie Chips was always nice to him and gave him free batter bits, and how Calvin Fruit and Veg called him 'son'. Jamie listened intently, his grin growing wider with every detail.

"Okay," Jamie said, nodding sagely. "Here's what we'll do. On Monday, we'll walk past the fruit and veg shop on the way to school. I'll have a good look at Calvin and see if he looks like you."

"Ok," Dylan agreed. "But I still think it could be Charlie. He's got curly hair like me."

Jamie shook his head. "Nah, I've seen him in Margaret the hairdresser's with my mam, with rollers in his hair. Those curls aren't real."

Dylan's eyes widened. "What? No way!"

"I swear," Jamie said, laughing. "And anyway, I don't think your mam would be his type."

"What do you mean?" Dylan asked, frowning.

Jamie hesitated, then shrugged. "I dunno. Just… trust me. I reckon it could be Calvin."

Dylan nodded, though he wasn't entirely convinced. "Alright, then. Monday morning, we'll find out."

"Are you going to your nana's tomorrow?" Jamie asked." We're going to Abergele market, I can ask if you can come with us."

"I'm going to my nana's but I'm coming back early so I can collect some more sponsor money in." Dylan responded. He was desperate to get the cash in before his mother could get hold of it.

"Ok, well I better go home now. Hopefully my dad's mates will have gone home now. They're all in my bedroom on my gambling machine!" Jamie shook his head. "I can't believe how thick they are putting all their money in when they never win. My dad is the biggest conman!" Both boys laughed as Jamie made his way out of the door.

"See you Monday morning Dyl." Jamie whispered as he pulled the door behind him to a gentle close.

"Yeah, night Jamie." Dylan looked around the kitchen. *"Shit, there is sugar everywhere!"* he said to himself as he grabbed a cloth to start cleaning up the mess.

At that point the whole flat plunged in to darkness. Dylan fumbled around in the dark and checked the meter for the spare pound. Not there.

"Shit," he said to himself, *"Mam's going to kill me when she sees the mess in the morning."*

****

17

Here's One I Made Earlier...

"Ta-daaaaaa!" Dylan shouted, his voice echoing through the warm, cosy kitchen as he flung open the back door to his nana's house. His cheeks were flushed from the cold, and his excitement lit up the room before he even stepped inside.

"Bloody hell, you nearly gave me a heart attack!" Annie exclaimed, spinning around from the counter where she'd been making Welsh cakes. A dusting of flour covered her hands and apron, and her silver hair glinted under the soft light of the kitchen. For a brief moment, her startled expression gave way to a warm smile, her eyes crinkling at the corners. "What are you doing here so early? I thought you'd be on the next bus! I would've come to meet you if I'd known."

Dylan grinned as he stepped inside, pulling off his woolly hat to reveal his tousled curls. "I came early because I need to make my angel costume, Nana," he explained, his voice tinged with a mix of urgency and hope. "And I need your help. Please?"

Annie's face softened even more, her Grandmotherly instincts instantly kicking in. "Ahhhhh, you're my little angel," she said, as she stepped closer, squinting at him like she was inspecting him for injuries. Her smile turned to a frown of concern. "But where's your coat? You're freezing cold!"

"I'm okay," Dylan replied, stifling a laugh. "My coat's filthy. I fell off Dusty in the forest. She bucked me off, and I landed in a load of mud."

Annie's hands flew to her hips, her mouth twitching as she fought to keep a straight face. "You and that pony!" she scolded, though her fondness for Dusty shone through. "What were you doing to get yourself thrown off?"

"She bolted with me!" he said proudly. "At the end of the sponsored walk, she just galloped off with me." Dylan said with a sheepish grin. "It wasn't her fault, she was just excited to get back to her field."

Annie shook her head, clicking her tongue. "You're as bad as each other, you and Dusty. Come here, you look frozen stiff. Let me warm you up before you catch your death."

Dylan stepped into her open arms, sinking into her cwtch. Her embrace was a cocoon of warmth and comfort, her familiar scent of Lily of the Valley perfume mixed with the comforting aroma of freshly baked Welsh cakes. "Love you, Nana," he murmured into her shoulder, his voice full of adoration.

"Love you too, boy," she replied, giving him an affectionate squeeze. "Right then, you sit down in the living room and I'll make you a nice cup of tea and some jam on toast. I bet you haven't had a proper breakfast yet, have you?"

Dylan hesitated, then admitted, "I haven't." As if on cue, his stomach growled loudly, making both of them laugh. "Can I have the jam with no bits, please?"

"Of course you can," Annie said with a laugh, ruffling his hair. "Now go and put your feet up, I'll bring it in."

Dylan didn't need to be told twice. He dropped his bag by the door and made his way into the living room. The familiar scents of Brasso and Shake n' Vac greeted him, along with the warmth from the fire crackling in the hearth. He sank into his taid's well-worn armchair, the soft fabric moulding to his small frame like it was made just for him. The mantelpiece was lined with family photos – his nana and taid in their younger days, his mam and her siblings as teens, and, pride of place, a photo of him as a toddler with his aunty. His blonde curls and her ginger afro made the picture look like a family comedy act.

Within minutes, Annie appeared carrying a tray with a steaming mug of tea and a plate of golden toast slathered with smooth jam. "Here you go, boy," she said, setting it on the little side table next to him. "Eat up, and then we'll sort this angel costume out for you."

Dylan reached for the toast, his mouth already watering. The first bite was warm and buttery, loaded with just the right amount of jam. He sighed contentedly. "Thanks, Nana. I love your toast."

"So," Annie began, settling onto the sofa opposite him. She crossed her legs, her kind brown eyes fixed on him with a mixture of curiosity and concern. "What exactly do you need for this angel costume? And what have you got so far?"

Dylan swallowed a mouthful of tea and reached for his school bag, which he'd tossed onto the floor. He unzipped it and began pulling out its contents. First came a crumpled bed sheet that looked more grey than white. Then, an almost-empty roll of tinfoil, followed by a tangle of Christmas tinsel that had definitely seen better days. He laid them out on the rug, his cheeks flushing with embarrassment as he realised how pathetic it all looked.

"Mr Tudur has got big angel wings for me, but this is all I've got," he admitted, his voice small. "Mam said we didn't have any proper white sheets at home. She told me to just use this."

Annie pursed her lips, studying the pile of would-be costume materials with a critical eye. "Hmm," she said finally, leaning forward to pick up the sheet. "Well, I can tell you now, my boy, this won't do. Angel Gabriel's got to look the part, hasn't he? You can't go walking onto that stage looking like you've wrapped yourself in a dishcloth."

Dylan laughed, despite himself. "I know," he said, shrugging. "But I didn't have anything better."

Annie's eyes softened, and she reached over to pat his knee reassuringly. "Don't you worry, boy. We'll sort this out together. Finish your toast, and I'll fetch something that'll make you look like the best angel Llanrwst has ever seen."

Dylan watched as she headed upstairs with brisk determination. The sound of drawers opening and closing echoed through the house, along with the occasional muttered, "Where is tha bloody thing…?" After a few minutes, she returned, holding a pristine white sheet folded neatly over her arm.

"This," she said with a flourish, shaking it out, "is what we'll use. Don't tell Taid…" she winked, "It's our best bedding, but an angel needs his costume!"

Dylan's eyes widened. "Nana, you don't have to use your best sheet!"

"Don't be daft," she replied with a wave of her hand. "You've got to look your best!"

She spread the sheet out on the floor and went to fetch her sewing kit. "Right, up you get," she said, motioning for him to stand. "Let's see how this fits."

Dylan stood patiently as Annie began draping the sheet over his shoulders, pinning and folding it with the precision of a seasoned seamstress. She adjusted the fabric here, tucked it there, until the sheet began to take the shape of a flowing angelic robe. Her last touch was to take her gold 'tie-back' from her curtains and wrap it around his waist.

"There now," she said, stepping back to admire her work. "That's looking better already."

Dylan glanced down at the robe, the fabric swishing lightly around his legs.

"Do me a spin." she instructed with a smile.

Dylan spun around, giving his best gypsy turns with the fabric floating effortlessly around him. He couldn't help but grin. "It's brilliant, Nana."

"Not quite finished," Annie said, her voice brimming with determination. "An angel needs a halo, doesn't he?"

Dylan's face lit up. "Oh yeah, but I didn't bring anything for that."

"No problem," Annie said, heading for the cupboard under the stairs. "We'll make you a halo that'll have the whole audience clapping."

She emerged moments later, her arms full of Christmas decorations. She laid them out on the table – a strand of battery-powered fairy lights, some glitter, and a coil of tinfoil.

"Now, let's see," she said, picking up a wire coat hanger. "We'll bend this into a circle and wrap the lights around it. You'll be the brightest angel they've ever seen."

Dylan watched in awe as Annie worked. She twisted the coat hanger into a perfect halo shape, carefully wrapping it in tinfoil for extra shine. Then she wound the fairy lights around it, securing them with bits of tape. Finally, she added a finishing touch of gold tinsel, fluffing it up until it sparkled like the North Star.

"Right, let's see how it looks," Annie said, placing the halo on Dylan's head. She stepped back, her face glowing with pride. "Ta-da! What do you think?"

Dylan turned to look in the mirror, his mouth falling open. The glowing halo, combined with the flowing robe, made him look like a proper angel.

"Nana, it's amazing," he said, his voice filled with wonder.

"You are amazing," Annie replied, giving him a wink. "Gabriel has to shine, doesn't he?"

Dylan nodded, his chest swelling with pride. "Thanks, Nana."

"Anything for my boy," she said, pulling him into a warm hug. "Now, let's test those lights. We don't want them going out halfway through your big moment."

Annie flipped the switch on the fairy lights and the halo lit up with a soft golden glow. Dylan's grin widened as he twirled around the room, the lights casting a warm, magical aura.

"You'll be the star of the show," Annie said, clapping her hands. "No one will forget Gabriel this year."

Dylan stopped spinning and looked at her shyly. "Nana… are you coming to watch me on Tuesday?"

Annie paused, her hands resting on her hips. "Do you want me to come?"

Dylan nodded quickly. "Yeah. Just in case Mam doesn't make it."

Her face softened, and she reached out to cup the cheeks of his face. "Of course, I'll be there, boy. I wouldn't miss it for the world."

Dylan's eyes lit up. "Yes," he said, as he fist-bumped himself in the mirror.

"Right," Annie said firmly, "let's pack this costume up nicely. We don't want any of it getting ruined before your big performance."

Annie insisted on making a few extra touches, sewing a gold trim onto the robe and gluing glitter onto the tinsel for extra sparkle. Dylan stayed by her side the whole time, watching her work with quiet admiration.

"What the hell is all this mess?" Taid shouted with mock anger, entering the living room. It looks like Father Christmas' grotto in here!"

"Hiya Taid," Dylan laughed. "Nana's been making me an angel costume for my nativity on Tuesday. Are you going to come and watch me?"

"Watch you? They've asked *me* to play the Angel Gabriel." mocked Taid. "Unfortunately, I'm busy that day!" he laughed. "Of course I'll be there to watch you. Now then, let me go and get out of these mucky clothes and you can practise your lines with me!"

In Dylan's eyes, his nana and taid were like magicians – they spread happiness everywhere they went.

Dylan looked at his costume and beamed with pride. He couldn't wait to get on stage!

****

18

Chaos in the Wings.

The school hall buzzed with chaos as performers darted about – tugging on costumes, rehearsing their lines, and fretting over last-minute details. Voices rose and fell in a cacophony of excitement, nerves, and barely contained energy. Dylan stood in the middle of it all, clutching his beloved homemade angel costume. His nana's insistence on adding a light-up halo had seemed like a brilliant idea at the time, but now, under the bright lights and surrounded by his classmates, he felt a flicker of embarrassment about standing out so much.

"Dylan, can I have a word with you, please?" Mr. Tudur's voice cut through the din, sounding unusually enthusiastic.

"Erm, yes, sir," Dylan replied, his stomach flipping. He instantly assumed he was about to be told off, though he couldn't think of what he'd done.

Mr. Tudur leaned closer, a grin breaking across his face. "I've spoken with the headmaster," he said, his voice brimming with excitement, "and he's agreed; Dusty can be part of the show!"

Dylan's eyes widened. "Really?!"

"Yes! She'll have to stay outside, of course, but we'll set up a pen with plenty of hay bales around the back to keep her comfortable until her scene," Mr. Tudur explained, nearly bouncing on his heels.

"She'll be happy eating the hay, sir," Dylan said, laughing at the thought of Dusty munching her way through the nativity preparations.

"Well, bring her in with you tomorrow morning. The show starts at ten o'clock, and Aunty Bev has already offered to help look after her until her big entrance."

Dylan couldn't hide his grin. "Ok, sir! I'll make sure she's sparkling for her debut!"

"Good lad," Mr. Tudur said, wiping sweat from his brow. "Now, help me carry these wings backstage, will you?"

Setting his costume down carefully, Dylan rushed to help with the six pairs of angel wings piled up in a corner.

"Dyl!" Jamie's familiar voice rang out, cutting through the commotion. Dylan turned to see his best friend bounding towards him, wearing a silver Kappa tracksuit that he'd *'borrowed'* from David Cohen Fashion Shop. Jamie skidded to a stop, pulling a glittery silver star from his bag, which promptly shed flakes of glitter everywhere.

"Look at this!" Jamie exclaimed, holding it aloft like a trophy. "Lloyd is having his tonsils out, so guess what? Mr. Tudur asked me to be the Star of Bethlehem! I can't believe it – I'm *the star*!" He struck a dramatic pose, waggling his eyebrows and earning a chuckle from Dylan.

"Sorry I didn't knock for you this morning," Jamie added, lowering his voice conspiratorially. "My dad sent me to Siop Bach to get him fags, and I ended up being late for school."

"It's fine," Dylan replied. "I had to go and get milk for the little ones, so I was running late too."

Jamie tilted his head, his eyes narrowing mischievously. "Shall we walk home together later and go past Calvin Fruit and Veg's shop? We can ask if he's your dad."

"We're not going to *ask* him!" Dylan hissed, his face reddening at the very thought. "We're just going to walk past, and you can tell me if you think I look like him."

Jamie rolled his eyes. "I already know what he looks like, and you definitely look like him. Why not just ask and settle it?"

Before Dylan could respond, the hall erupted with laughter as Melvin Stevens strode in, his costume now glittering with additional sequins. He threw his arms out wide and spun dramatically.

"Make way for Shakin' Stevens!" Melvin declared, his voice dripping with theatrical flair. His pompadour was slicked to perfection, and his confidence filled the room.

"Melvin, stop messing around and help with these wings!" Mr. Tudur barked, mopping his forehead with a handkerchief. He was getting sweatier by the minute, his patience fraying under the mounting chaos.

The room buzzed with energy as pupils dashed about, voices blending into a symphony of excitement. There were misplaced props, forgotten lines, cries of "where's my costume?" and bursts of giggles from children barely managing to contain their nerves.

"Right, we're starting the dress rehearsal in five minutes!" Mrs. Jones called as she took her place at the piano. "Everyone, get to your opening positions, please!"

Within moments, the cast scrambled into their places. Dylan adjusted his angel robe and wings nervously, fiddling with the light-up halo his nana had made. Beside him, Jamie struck an exaggerated pose, holding centre stage as the glittering Star of Bethlehem.

The rehearsal began, and Jamie twirled dramatically, scattering glitter in every direction. "Follow me, everyone!" he bellowed, his booming voice drawing chuckles from the teachers watching in the wings. His over-the-top performance delighted everyone, especially since Jamie rarely participated in anything at school.

The angels sang and tap-danced their way through their routine, hitting every step with precision. But as Mary and Joseph made their way to Bethlehem, chaos erupted. The animals stumbled through their lines, one shepherd lost his crook, and the Three Kings were nowhere to be seen – Leeanne had suffered a nosebleed backstage, and the resulting mess had rendered their costumes temporarily unusable.

"Stop! Everybody stop!" Mr. Tudur shouted just as Melvin was preparing to strut onstage for his big solo. "I need your attention for a moment. I just want to let you all know that the wooden donkey, so kindly painted by Mrs Morris, is being replaced. We're going to have a real donkey… Dylan's pony, Dusty!"

The hall erupted into cheers and applause. Dylan found himself clapping along with his classmates, grinning despite his embarrassment at all the attention.

"Can I ride Dusty in?" Melvin asked eagerly. "That would look cool, ynai?"

"No, Melvin," Mr. Tudur replied firmly. "Dusty will carry Mary, as she's meant to."

He turned to Dylan. "What do you think, boy? Should Caroline ride her, or would she prefer to lead her?"

Dylan glanced at Caroline, who looked nervous but nodded. "I'll lead her," she said quietly, blushing. "I think I'm a bit scared of horses."

"Perfect," Mr. Tudur said, clapping his hands. "Dusty will enter here, and she'll stand right here for the scene. Nobody is to mess around near her – understood?"

"Yes, sir!" the class chorused, their excitement palpable.

By the end of the rehearsal, the cast were buzzing with enthusiasm. Melvin had performed his scenes with his usual superstar flair, Eirian's contemporary dance as the magical tree had captivated everyone, and Dylan had taken his place to sing the opening verse of *Once in Royal David's City*. As the piano began to play, Dylan flicked the switch on his halo, lighting it up. Cheers erupted from the cast as Angel Gabriel quite literally shone on stage.

The grand finale brought everyone together for a rousing rendition of *Rocking Around the Christmas Tree*. Melvin led with his larger-than-life performance, belting out the lyrics with the confidence of a seasoned rock star, while Dylan danced beside him, his halo shining and wings glinting in the stage lights. Together, they brought the house down.

"Well done, everyone!" Mr. Tudur exclaimed, clapping, with a smile so wide it threatened to split his face. His eyes glistened with pride.

The caretaker, leaning against the wall with a knowing grin, nudged him. "You know what they say – you can't shine shit, but you can cover it in glitter!" He laughed heartily. "Only joking. That was bloody brilliant!"

As the cast took their bows, Dylan felt a surge of pride and an even bigger surge of excitement that tomorrow Dusty would be the star of the show.

****

19

The Weight of Fifty Pounds.

The afternoon lessons blurred together as Dylan stared out of the window, his mind far from the classroom. Instead of focusing on the blackboard, where Mr. Davies was droning on about percentages, Dylan was daydreaming about Dusty's upcoming debut. In his imagination, she wasn't just any donkey – she was the most famous donkey in the world. The entire school would cheer her on, clapping and gasping as she trotted gracefully across the stage. Dusty's fame would spread beyond the town, and soon she'd be on TV, her name whispered alongside other famous animals like 'Black Beauty'.

Snapping back to reality, Dylan flipped open his maths book and began scribbling, not equations but a list of things he needed to do:

- **Collect sponsorship money from Dalatrek.**
- **Pick up carrots for Dusty.**
- **Check on Dusty.**
- **Buy glitter spray (for me and for Dusty).**

The school bell rang suddenly, jolting him out of his thoughts. Dylan looked down at his math book and realised he hadn't done any of his schoolwork. He glanced at the sums on the page and shrugged. Percentages could wait – Christmas was coming, and there were far more important things to think about than fractions.

He threw his pens and books into his bag, zipped it shut, and made his way outside. The cold air hit his face as he shuffled towards the school gates, falling into step with Jamie, who appeared at his side. The lingering buzz from the dress rehearsal filled the air around them, their conversation brimming with excitement.

"Melvin is really good, isn't he?" Jamie said, swinging his bag over his shoulder. "He was strutting around like he was an actual pop star! Did you see Mr. Tudur's face when he said he wanted to ride Dusty?"

Dylan laughed, the image of Melvin's exaggerated hip movements fresh in his mind.

Jamie twirled dramatically on the pavement, mimicking the way he'd played the Star of Bethlehem. "And what about me, eh? Didn't I sparkle out there?"

Dylan rolled his eyes but couldn't help smiling. "You were alright," he teased. "Though I think your tracksuit blinded half the teachers."

"Good," Jamie said, grinning with bits of glitter still sparkling in his hair. "Maybe they'll let me join in a bit more now. It's been fun hanging out with all the posh kids. You fit in well with them, don't you?"

"They're not posh, Jamie," Dylan replied with a sigh. "They just like acting and singing. That's not posh."

"Well, a lot of them seem posh to me." Jamie laughed. "I mean, who actually likes tap dancing?"

As they walked, their chatter turned to tomorrow's big performance. The thought of Dusty being part of the nativity filled Dylan with equal parts excitement and nervousness.

"I can't believe the headmaster actually agreed to let Dusty be in the nativity," Dylan said, shaking his head. "It's mad, isn't it? I just hope she behaves."

The pair walked up Watling Street, the late afternoon sun casting long shadows over the shops.

"She'll be fine." Jamie said. Then, with a mischievous glint in his eye, he added, "Let's cut through *Critch-Cratch* and walk past Calvin's Fruit and Veg. Sorry, I mean – your dad's shop."

Dylan shot him a warning look. "Jamie, stop it. I wish I hadn't told you now."

"Alright, alright," Jamie said, laughing. "Don't get your halo in a twist."

As they passed the shop, Calvin stood behind the counter, stacking crates of apples with practised ease. He looked up as the boys walked by, his face breaking into a wide grin. "Alright, son?" he called, his tone warm and familiar.

Dylan froze for a second, his heart skipping a beat. He nodded quickly. "Alright," he mumbled, keeping his eyes on the pavement.

Jamie glanced sideways at him, his curiosity bubbling to the surface. "He called you son again," he whispered as they moved out of earshot. "You gonna ask him this time?"

"No!" Dylan hissed, his face flushing red. "I told you, we're not asking anything. Just shut up, alright?"

"Hey, wait a minute…" Calvin called after the boys, "I've got some carrots here for that pony of yours."

Handing Dylan a bag full of carrots, Calvin smiled at the two boys.

"That pony keeping you out of trouble Dyl?" Calvin asked, "I've always liked horses myself. They say it's in the genes. My mam is a good horse rider! Anyone else in your family ride, son?"

"Erm," Dylan stuttered, "My aunty used to ride. Not really much any more."

"Well, I hope the pony enjoys them. Pop in once a week and you can have the ones that are just going out of date." Calvin promised as he walked back inside the shop. "T'ra!"

"T'ra. And thank you." Dylan shouted, staring at him walking out to the back of the shop.

"Thank you, *daddy*!" Jamie giggled under his breath.

"Stop it!" Dylan said through gritted teeth.

Jamie couldn't hide his smirk. "Hey, he does look a bit like you. Same nose."

Dylan smiled. "Same hair too… and eyes… it's in the genes," he said wistfully.

"So, what are you doing now?" Jamie asked, sensing the shift in Dylan's mood. "Want to come round mine?"

Dylan shook his head. "I can't. I've got to go to Dalatrek to pick up the sponsorship money from that man. You know, the one with the Range Rover?"

Jamie's eyes widened. "Ooooooh, the one who was, you know… doing stuff in the woods?"

Dylan glared at him. "Shut up. He's giving me fifty quid for Dusty, so it doesn't matter what he was doing."

"Fair enough," Jamie said, laughing. "You want me to come with you?"

"Nah, it's alright, or he might think I've told you, then he won't give me the money." Dylan replied. "I'll be quick. Then I've got to check on Dusty and make sure she's ready for tomorrow."

Jamie gave him a playful nudge. "You should ask titty woman to give you fifty quid too!"

Dylan rolled his eyes, laughing at Jamie's cheeky chappy attitude. "See you later, Jamie."

They parted ways, and Dylan headed towards Dalatrek, the name of the company still fresh in his mind from the man's promise.

He arrived at the portacabins and could see the man from the woods sitting at a desk, flipping through some paperwork.

Dylan hesitated for a moment before knocking on the door. The man looked out of the window – his expression breaking into recognition – and gestured for Dylan to enter.

"Ah, there you are," the man said, standing up. "I was wondering if you'd come."

Dylan nodded, feeling a little out of place in the sterile office. "Yeah, I came to get the sponsorship money. For Dusty."

"Of course," the man said, reaching into a drawer and pulling out an envelope. "Fifty pounds, as promised. You've done a good job, son."

Dylan's ears pricked up at the word 'son' as he studied the man's face. There were no similarities there, but for some reason the man was being overly generous in giving him £50. Worth an entry in to his Fraggle Rock book, just in case. Dylan took the envelope, his fingers brushing against the crisp notes inside. "Thanks," said quietly, tucking it into his pocket.

The man gave him a knowing look. "And about, you know… what you saw in the woods. We'll keep that between us, right?"

Dylan nodded quickly. "Yeah. I didn't see anything."

The man smiled, but it didn't quite reach his eyes. "Good lad. Now run along and take care of that pony of yours."

Dylan left without another word, clutching the envelope tightly as he walked back towards home. The money felt heavier than it should have, like it carried more than just its monetary value. Still, fifty pounds was fifty pounds, and Dusty would have all the feed she needed.

By the time he reached the gate to Dusty's field, the light was fading fast but Dusty had already heard him. She lifted her head as Dylan approached, her ears twitching at the sound of his voice.

"Hey, girl," Dylan said, climbing over the gate. "You're going to be a star tomorrow. Did you know that?"

Dusty snorted, shaking her mane, and Dylan laughed. "Yeah, I know you don't care about being a donkey, but it's a big deal. Everyone's excited to see you." he said, as he emptied half of the bag of carrots into a bucket.

He put the rest of the carrots in to his school bag and pulled a brush from his bag and started running it over her coat, working out the tangles and bits of mud in the dark. "You've got to look your best tomorrow. Mr. Tudor's trusting you not to make a scene."

Dusty nuzzled his arm, and Dylan felt a swell of affection for the little pony. She wasn't just an animal to him; she was his confidante, his escape from the chaos of home.

When he was done, he gave her a final pat on the neck. "Alright, girl. I'll see you tomorrow morning. Try not to get too dirty again tonight." Giving her a kiss on her forehead, he whispered, "Be good, yeah?"

Dylan ran most of the way home as the sky darkened, remembering he hadn't told his mam of his whereabouts. The envelope of money in his pocket, slightly sweaty against his leg.

As soon as he stepped through the door, the familiar chaos of the flat hit him like a wave. Baby J was crying, Ela was shouting about something, and Magi and Barry were sat at the kitchen table, each with a glass of wine in their hand.

"Here he is," Magi said, her eyes narrowing. "Where the hell have you been?"

"I had to go and check on Dusty." Dylan replied chirpily. "Mr Tudor has said she can perform in the nativity tomorrow."

"What the hell is a pony going to do in a nativity." Barry snorted, as he let out a large exhale of smoke from his tiny rollie.

"She's going to be the donkey." Dylan retorted. "And she's going to be brilliant.

"And... I also had to get my sponsorship money," Dylan added, pulling the envelope from his pocket. "It's for Dusty. To buy her food."

Magi's eyes lit up at the sight of it. "Let me see that."

Dylan hesitated. "It's for Dusty."

Magi snatched the envelope from his hand, her expression hardening. "Fifty quid?! Who the hell gave you this?"

"The man from Dalatrek. He sponsored me and said that I've done a good job, rescuing her!" Dylan stammered, starting to get upset at the sight of the envelope in Magi's hand.

"What have I fucking told you about talking to strangers?" Magi shouted, "And especially taking money from strangers. I'll keep hold of this!"

"What? But—"

"No buts," Magi snapped, standing up and grabbing her coat. "I'm going to Kwiks'. I'll be back in a minute."

Dylan watched helplessly as she stuffed the envelope into her pocket and walked out the door, leaving him standing there – a hollow feeling settling in his chest.

"Get me some tobacco and some Rizlas." Barry shouted after her, filling his wine glass with the home brew that Dylan knew would make him witness to late night fighting.

Dylan turned away, eyes glassy with tears but determined not to let Barry see him upset. He made his way up to his bedroom and shut the door behind him. Flicking the light switch on, he discovered the light bulb had gone. Lying on his bed in the dark, he stared at the shadows on the ceiling; the excitement of the day drained away in an instant. He tried to focus on tomorrow, on Dusty's big moment and his own chance to shine as Gabriel. But the knot in his stomach wouldn't loosen, no matter how hard he tried.

Tomorrow, he told himself. Tomorrow would be better.

****

20

A Spark in the Dark.

The sound of heavy footsteps coming up the stairs made Dylan's heart sink further. He knew that tread all too well – the uneven, lumbering stomp of Barry after he'd had one too many drinks. Dylan braced himself as Barry pushed open the bedroom door, the smell of stale beer and cigarettes wafting in ahead of him.

"Oi, Dylan," Barry slurred, a silhouette of him leaning heavily on the door frame, "get downstairs and look after the kids now. I'm going to look for your mam."

Dylan sat up, "Where is she?"

Dylan could see the shadow of Barry as he waved a dismissive hand. "Probably at the pub. I'm going to find her."

"Ok, I'll be down now." Dylan replied quietly.

Barry snorted, his breath reeking of alcohol. "Get the little ones ready for bed. And another thing – taking money from strangers?" He jabbed a finger in Dylan's direction, his voice rising. "Why the fuck would you do that? Are you thick or something?"

Dylan bit his lip, his fists clenched tightly at his sides. He didn't dare argue back. Instead, he gave a small nod, knowing there was no point in reasoning with Barry in this state.

And with that, Barry turned and stumbled back down the stairs, the front door slamming behind him moments later.

Dylan sat frozen for a moment, the weight of responsibility settling heavily on his shoulders. With a deep breath, he pulled on his dressing gown and made his way downstairs.

In the living room, Baby J was already fussing, his tiny fists rubbing at his tired eyes. Ela sat cross-legged on the carpet, staring blankly at the TV, her thumb in her mouth.

"Alright, you two," Dylan said, forcing a smile onto his face. "Let's get you ready for bed, yeah?"

Ela looked up at him, her eyes wide and questioning. "Where's Mam?"

"She'll be back soon," Dylan lied, his voice light and reassuring. "But for now, we're '*The Three Musketeers*' yeah?"

He scooped Baby J into his arms, carrying him upstairs to change his nappy and get him into his pyjamas. Ela followed behind, clutching her favourite blanket. Dylan was always so proud of how quickly he could change both his siblings with a steady stream of chatter and silly songs.

Once they were in their pyjamas, he brought them back downstairs and sat them both on the sofa. "How about some hot chocolate before bed?" he asked, ruffling Ela's hair.

Her face lit up. "With fluff on top?"

"If we've got any," Dylan replied smiling, heading into the kitchen. After rummaging through the cupboards, he found a near empty bag of mini marshmallows – just enough to sprinkle on top for Ela and Baby J – and set to work heating the milk on the hob. Within minutes, he returned with their plastic cups full of hot chocolate, handing them carefully to the little ones.

They sipped their hot chocolate happily as Dylan flicked through the channels, settling on *The Snowman* that was halfway through. For a brief moment, everything felt peaceful.

But then, with a loud *pop*, the TV went black, and the room plunged into darkness. Dylan froze, a groan escaping his lips. "Not again," he muttered, fumbling for the matches.

The electricity meter had run out. Mam had forgotten to top it up again, and there were no spare pounds in the house. Dylan struck a match, lighting both of the decorative candles on the mantelpiece. *"These are only for show,"* he heard his Mam's voice ringing in his mind *"don't ever use them in an emergency!"*

But for Dylan, this was an emergency. It was still too early for them all to go to bed. The warm glow of the Christmas candles flickered across the room, casting long shadows on the walls.

"It's okay," he said, turning back to Ela and Baby J. "Sometimes this happens when Father Christmas uses his magic powers to turn the lights off so he can look into the houses without being seen!"

He pulled the curtains back slightly, revealing the frost-covered window. The fake snow spray Mam had painted along the edges still clung stubbornly to the glass, creating a wintry frame. Dylan set Baby J and Ela on the windowsill, their noses pressed against the cold glass as they peered out into the night.

"Right." Dylan began, his voice taking on a conspiratorial tone. "Keep very still and let me see if I can find him in the sky ."

Ela's eyes widened. "Really?"

"Really," Dylan said, nodding solemnly. "He doesn't just come on Christmas Eve, you know. Sometimes he flies around early to see who's behaving and who's not. If you're really quiet, you might even see him."

Ela gasped, her thumb slipping out of her mouth. "What does he look like?"

"Well," Dylan said, stroking his chin as if deep in thought. "He's got a big red sleigh, of course, and reindeer with bells on their harnesses. You'll hear the jingling before you see him. And his coat is so bright, it glows in the dark."

"And Rudolph will be at the front?" Ela cheered.

Baby J let out a small giggle, clapping his chubby hands together. Ela pressed her face closer to the glass, her breath fogging up the window. "Do you think he'll come here tonight?"

"He might," Dylan said, settling into the armchair behind them. "But only if you're really, really quiet. He doesn't like being seen, you know."

At ten years old, Dylan still believed in Father Christmas. Looking up into the sky was as much for him as it was for his siblings. Dylan wished that he'd see *the* Father Christmas so that he could reassure him that he had been a good boy and was worthy of getting the same amount of presents as some of his classmates, who indeed hadn't behaved for most of the year. But for the last few years, it had been difficult to believe that Father Christmas was real. If he was real, then he needed to up his game with his success rate of matching up the gifts on Dylan's Christmas wish list.

For a while, the room was silent except for the sound of Baby J's contented gurgles and Ela's whispered questions about reindeer. Dylan leaned back, feeling a rare sense of calm. The flickering candlelight and the soft hum of their voices made the small, shabby living room feel almost magical.

The spell was broken by the sound of someone shouting through the letterbox. "Hello? Magi? Anyone in? Dylan?"

Dylan jumped to his feet, hurrying to the door. He opened it to find Aunty Jane standing on the step, bundled up in her coat and scarf. "Why are you sitting in the dark?" she asked, peering past him into the dimly-lit room.

"The electric's gone," Dylan admitted, his cheeks flushing. "There's no spare pound for the meter. Mam and dad have gone out."

Jane tutted, reaching into her handbag. "They are bloody useless sometimes, honestly." She pulled out a pound coin and handed it to Dylan. "Go on, spin this through the meter. And you can keep it afterwards."

Dylan's face lit up. "Thanks, Aunty Jane!" He said, running to the meter, slotting the pound in and twisting it with a satisfying click. Moments later, the lights flickered back on, and the TV whirred to life.

Jane made her way into the living room to find Ela crying. "Has he gone now?"

"What's wrong Ela?" Jane asked, as she put her arms around Ela to comfort her.

"Father Christmas turned our lights off to check on us and we were trying to see him" Ela cried, still looking out of the window.

Dylan winked at Aunty Jane, "We were looking for Father Christmas in the sky. He turned our lights off for a bit to check on us. But Ela and Baby J have been soooooo good, haven't you?"

"Yes, I've been a good girl, all the time." Ela replied, wiping away her snot.

Baby J smiled at Aunty Jane and went in for a big hug.

"Ahhhh, that's better," Jane said, shedding her coat and picking Baby J up. She ruffled Dylan's hair affectionately. "You're a good boy, Dylan. Always looking after everyone."

Dylan smiled shyly, the warmth of her praise filling him with a quiet pride. As he settled back into the armchair, Ela climbed into his lap, clutching her mug of hot chocolate.

"Do you think Father Christmas saw us being good?" she asked, her voice sleepy.

"I'm sure he did," Dylan said, "right, drink up now, it's time for bed for you two now."

"Let me help you Dyl," Jane said, picking up Baby J, whose eyes were rolling to the back of his head. "This one will be straight off to sleep for you."

With Aunty Jane's encouragement, teeth were brushed and the two little cherubs fell fast asleep as soon as their heads hit their pillows.

"Well, I only popped in to see if your Mam had finished my cardigan. I'll see you Thursday, boy." Jane smiled. "Emma is coming to stay with you on Thursday afternoon cos your mam and me are going to get our last few bits; it's late night Christmas shopping in Llandudno."

"Ahhh, can you ask Emma to bring her horse magazines?" Dylan smiled.

"I'm sure she will, Dyl."

Dylan added, "Tell Mam I *really* want a new riding hat for Christmas – a jockey skull cap. In case Mam forgets. They do them in the saddlery shop in Llandudno."

"You'll have to ask Father Christmas," Jane smiled.

"Hmmmm…" Dylan sighed. "If only he'd listen."

Jane cocked her head to one side and looked lovingly at Dylan. "You're a good boy Dyl. T'ra boy."

Dylan gazed out through the window at the frosty night, the candlelight still dancing in the reflection of the window. *Shit I better put those out now; Mam'll kill me!* He thought.

Jane turned around to see Dylan smiling at her through the window and blowing a kiss. With a lump in her throat, Jane smiled and waved back at Dylan, catching his kiss in her hand and blowing him one back.

Wiping a tear away from her eye, Jane turned on her heels and walked decisively towards the pubs to go and scream at her sister.

****

21.

Dusty Steals the Show.

The sky was still cloaked in darkness when Dylan slipped out of bed. The faint glow of dawn was just beginning to creep through his thin bedroom curtains, but it wasn't enough to brighten the room. He dressed quickly in the chilly air, fumbling with his jumper and tugging on his trainers. The day he'd been waiting for was finally here – nativity show day. Today, Dusty would make her debut, and for once, Dylan felt like he had something to be proud of. He grabbed his school bag that still had carrots and his dandy brush inside and threw his wellies into a plastic bag, his breath already quickening with excitement.

Glanrafon was eerily quiet as Dylan stepped outside; the twinkling of the Christmas lights in all of the windows warmed Dylan's insides. A thin mist hung in the air, curling around the lamp-posts and swallowing the edges of the pavement. The world felt still, as though it was holding its breath for something magical. Dylan shoved his hands into his pockets, his footsteps crunching against the frost-speckled ground.

As he reached the field, his heart raced with anticipation.

"Dusty... Duuuuuustyyyyyy" he sang in his little soprano voice.

But as he peered through the mist towards Dusty's usual spot, his excitement turned to confusion. The field looked empty. He squinted, blinking against the grey mist, but there was no sign of her familiar silhouette.

"Dusty!" he called out, his voice slicing through the cold morning air. Silence greeted him. He tried again, louder this time, his heart beginning to pound. "Dusty! Where are you, girl?"

Dylan climbed over the gate, the frost on the metal biting at his fingers. His trainers sank into the muddy ground as he scanned the field. He quickly changed into his wellies to climb up the field. The mist clung stubbornly to the earth, obscuring his view. His calls became more frantic as he trudged across the field, his voice cracking with panic.

"Dusty! Please, where are you?"

The icy grip of fear tightened around his chest. He couldn't lose her – not today, not ever. Tears stung his eyes as he searched every corner of the field, slipping and stumbling in the mud. His imagination ran wild. What if someone had stolen her? What if she'd escaped and was hurt somewhere? The thought was too much to bear, and his voice broke as he called out again.

"Dusty! Come on, girl! Please!"

Just as he sank to his knees, despair threatening to overwhelm him, a faint sound reached his ears. It was soft, almost drowned out by the wind – a faint whinny. Dylan's head shot up, tears falling down his face but hope igniting in his chest.

"Dusty?" he called, scrambling to his feet. The whinny came again, a little louder this time, guiding him through the mist. He ran towards the sound, his heart pounding in his chest, until he spotted her.

She was standing in the far corner of the field, her head down as she chewed lazily on some grass. Relief flooded through him – until he saw the problem. Dusty's legs were caught up in the fence. The wire had wrapped itself around her hooves, pinning her in place.

"Oh no," Dylan whispered, racing towards her. "Dusty, what have you done?"

Dusty looked up at him, her big brown eyes calm and trusting, as if nothing was wrong. Dylan dropped to his knees, wiping tears away from his eyes, his hands trembling as he assessed the situation. The wire was tangled tightly around her legs, but Dusty didn't seem to mind. She just kept munching on the grass, blissfully unaware of the drama unfolding.

"It's okay, girl," Dylan said, his voice shaking. "I'll get you out of this."

He tried to loosen the wire with his hands, but it was too tight. The cold metal bit into his fingers, and the mud made it even harder to get a grip. Panic began to creep back in as Dusty shifted her weight, making the wire dig deeper.

"Stay still, Dusty. Please," Dylan begged, tears welling up again. He leaned his forehead against her shoulder, drawing comfort from her steady warmth. "I'll figure this out. Just give me a minute."

He took a deep breath, his mind racing. Then, an idea struck him. Carefully, he leaned against Dusty, using his weight to encourage her to shift slightly. She obliged, leaning back just enough for Dylan to lift one of her hooves and untangle the wire. He talked to her the whole time, his voice soft and soothing.

"You're such a good girl," he whispered. "I'm just trying to help you, ok? Just one more leg to go."

It felt like an eternity, but finally, Dusty was free. Dylan sank back onto his heels, his hands coated in mud and his clothes streaked with dirt and horse hair. Dusty, of course, didn't seem fazed in the slightest. She nuzzled his arm, then went back to eating grass as if nothing had happened.

Dylan let out a shaky laugh, wiping his face with his sleeve. "You're amazing Dusty, you know that? I love you so much"

After brushing Dusty down and cleaning her hooves, Dylan stood back to admire his handiwork. She looked as perfect as she was going to get, her coat gleaming even in the weak morning light.

"Right, girl," Dylan said, giving her a gentle tug on the lead rope, "Let's get you to school. We've got a big day ahead."

Dusty picked her head up straight away and followed the muddy little boy, knowing that by following him they were surely up for another adventure!

****

The school yard was buzzing with energy when Dylan and Dusty arrived. Children shrieked with excitement, pointing and running to the gate as Dusty trotted in beside Dylan. The frosty air seemed to sparkle with the magic of Christmas, and the laughter and chatter of the pupils filled the space with warmth.

"Look, it's Dusty!" someone shouted.

"She's so cute!" cried another.

Dylan felt a swell of pride as he led Dusty through the crowd, her ears flicking in response to the noise. For the first time in his life, he felt like a celebrity. He wasn't just Dylan, the council estate kid, he was Dylan, the boy with the star donkey.

Around the back of the school, Mr. Tudur was waiting with a grin on his face. He had outdone himself, setting up a makeshift pen out of hay bales and even hanging a hay net for Dusty to snack on. Dusty whinnied in approval as she stepped into the pen, immediately burying her nose in the hay.

"She's a beauty," Mr. Tudur said, patting Dylan on the shoulder. "You've done a cracking job, Dylan. How exciting!"

"Thanks, sir," Dylan replied, his chest puffing with pride. "She's ready for her big moment."

As Dylan tied Dusty's lead rope to a drainpipe, the other kids gathered around, their eyes wide with awe. Parents were already queuing up outside the hall, some of them holding steaming cups of tea as they braved the cold. The excitement was palpable.

Jamie appeared at Dylan's side, his face lit up with mischief. "Dyl, you're covered in mud," he said, laughing. "You look like you've been wrestling pigs."

"I had a bit of a morning," Dylan replied with a sheepish grin.

"Forgot your glitter spray too, didn't you?" Jamie said, pulling a can out of his bag. "Good job I've got you some. Can't have Angel Gabriel looking like he's been dragged through a hedge."

Dylan laughed, accepting the can gratefully. "Thanks, Jamie. You're a lifesaver."

The final touch came when Mr. Tudur revealed a pair of oversized donkey ears he'd made for Dusty's head collar. The big fluffy ears were a work of art, and the kids roared with laughter as Dylan attached them.

"Perfect," Mr. Tudur said, stepping back to admire the sight. "Right, everyone inside. It's showtime!"

****

Inside the hall, the atmosphere was electric. The stage was set, the lights casting a warm glow over the decorations. Dylan and Jamie took their places at the front, ready to open the show. The curtains opened and as Jamie launched into his monologue as the Star of Bethlehem, Dylan quickly scanned the audience looking for his mam; his heart sank as he realised she wasn't there. He sighed, forcing himself to focus on the performance.

But then, out of the corner of his eye, he saw them – his nana and taid, sitting proudly in the second row. Dylan's face lit up, and he gave them a small wave, his spirits lifting instantly.

The performance went off without a hitch. Everyone remembered their lines, each song orchestrated beautifully and every dance step performed with precision.

Dusty's grand entrance was met with a collective "awwww" from the audience, her handmade donkey ears and calm demeanour stealing the show. She stood perfectly still, creating a picture-perfect nativity scene. Dylan held her lead rope tightly, a proud smile spreading across his face.

The final number began, the piano playing the opening notes of *Once in Royal David's City*. Dylan stepped forward and flicked the switch to the lights on his halo which made the audience audibly "awww". Dylan sang in perfect tune, his voice clear and steady throughout the first verse.

He started the second verse and Dusty nudged him which distracted him for a second. He smiled at Dusty and then looked back out into the audience, lifting his gaze to the middle rows of the audience to share his voice with them all.

Just as he was belting the high notes he locked eyes with... his mam – his heart stopped. She'd been sat there the whole time! She smiled and winked at him, wiping away a tear and smudging her bright blue eye liner. Dylan belted out the rest of the song with gusto, pinging every soprano note to perfection.

When the song finished, the audience erupted and leapt to their feet. There wasn't a dry eye in the house.

Dylan smiled at his mam, who stood there crying and waving. His nana and taid were also on their feet waving and cheering.

The show ended with a rousing rendition of *Rocking Around the Christmas Tree* led by Melvin, who had the audience clapping and cheering along. Dusty, ever the professional, nodded her head in time with the music, letting out a triumphant whinny as the song came to an end.

The audience erupted into applause, the cheers and whoops filling the hall. Dylan stood beside Dusty, his heart swelling with pride as he soaked in the moment.

****

22

Chaos Before Christmas.

Wednesday, 20th December – 5 more sleeps!

Dylan was jolted awake by Ela's shrill voice echoing up the stairs. "Maaaaaaam, you need to come downstairs!" she yelled, urgency dripping from her tone. Dylan rubbed his eyes groggily, barely registering her words, the nativity and all the adrenaline had obviously knocked him out. He hadn't heard them get up at all. For a moment, he hoped it was nothing serious – maybe Ela had dropped her breakfast or got into some minor mischief. But as her voice echoed again, he heard a note of something else. Was that laughter?

"Maaaaaaam," Ela shouted, laughing, "You need to see Baby J!" Something about her urgency made Dylan sit upright. Baby J's giggles floated up next, a sure sign that whatever had happened downstairs, was probably bad.

Throwing on his dressing gown, Dylan padded down the stairs quickly, his pulse quickening with every step. The closer he got to the living room, the louder the giggles grew. What had those two got into now?

As he turned the corner into the living room, the sight that greeted him made his jaw drop. It was chaos – pure, sticky, powdery chaos. The living room was a disaster zone – a scene straight out of a festive apocalypse. The presents that had been neatly stacked under the Christmas tree the night before were gone. Wrapping paper was scattered everywhere – crumpled into balls, shredded into ribbons, and thrown into corners like confetti at a party. Baby J was sitting smack in the middle of the mess with a cigar in his mouth, clutching a crushed box of Turkish delight, his hands and face smeared with icing sugar. Next to him was Ela, covered head to toe in talcum powder, her hair now a comical shade of white.

The sofa was dusted with a mix of talc and icing sugar, empty boxes and toys were strewn across the floor.

"Ela! Baby J!" Dylan exclaimed, his voice cracking with disbelief. "What the hell have you done?"

Ela looked up at him, wide-eyed and unapologetic. "He's been. It's Christmas," she said excitedly, her hands clutching a bright pink doll still tied to its plastic casing.

"It's not Christmas for another five days!" Dylan groaned, running his hands through his hair. "Mam's going to kill you. No, actually – she's going to kill me."

Baby J giggled and threw a handful of Turkish delight at Dylan, hitting him square in the face. Dylan pulled the sticky lump away from his forehead, then sighed. He couldn't even be properly angry. They were just kids, after all.

Before he could even muster a response, he heard the heavy stomp of footsteps approaching.

"What the hell have you been doing?" Magi screamed at the kids as she entered the Christmas tsunami that had hit her living room.

Magi sat on the sofa in complete shock and started to cry.

"I try my best here and you little bastards fuckin' ruin it all." Shaking her head, she wiped away her tears. "Barry, get down here and see what these fuckin' kids have done."

Dylan stood frozen, unsure whether to console her or retreat before she directed her wrath at him.

"I'll help clear it up, Mam." Dylan offered quietly.

"Me too." Ela said, sheepishly.

But Magi wasn't having any of it.

"You are a naughty girl." Magi hissed. "Take Baby J upstairs now, until I've cleaned all this mess up."

Oblivious to the razor sharp atmosphere, Baby J smiled at Magi, cigar still in his mouth and clapping clouds of icing sugar to make himself laugh.

"Get these two out of my sight, Dyl." Magi shouted venomously. "Now!"

Dylan picked up Baby J and took both kids into the kitchen and sat them both down with some cereal. "Right, you two eat your breakfast and be quiet here, while Dyl goes and cleans up the mess."

"See, I was a good girl. Father Christmas really did come didn't he?" Ela smiled.

"Hmmmmm… kind of." Dylan laughed. It was impossible for him to be angry with them.

Dylan heard laughing coming from the living room – it was Barry.

"Lighten up Magi, Christ. It's only a few presents." Barry quipped, until he saw four packets of Golden Virginia strewn out all around the Christmas tree. Unsalvageable, white from talcum powder and covered in the stickiness of Turkish Delight! His laughter turned to anger.

"What the fuuuuuuuuck…..?" he raged.

"Oh, not fuckin' funny now is it?" Magi spat.

"Where the hell were you Dylan? Why weren't you downstairs with them?" Barry shouted.

Dylan decided not the answer the question. For now, instead of leaving for school, he had to help clean up this mess – and fast, before the argument brewed over into something else.

Armed with a damp cloth, a dustpan, and a lot of patience, he tackled the talc-and-icing-sugar mountain on the sofa.

Magi, wiping away her tears, tried to salvage what was left of the presents that hadn't been fully played with. Ties, socks, perfume. The presents that were meant for the Kwik Save Ethiopian shoe box campaign.

"If you're not going to help, fuck off upstairs." Magi hissed at Barry. "It's not too late for you to go to work."

Barry lit his rollie and took himself upstairs in a huff.

Every sweep of the dustpan sent puffs of white into the air, making Dylan cough. The shredded wrapping paper took ages to gather, and by the time he'd restored some semblance of order to the room, he was already late for school.

"Right," Dylan said, pulling on his coat and grabbing his bag. "I have to go, alright Mam?"

"Alright boy, you go. Thanks for helping me." Magi said, placing the final bits on the sofa. "It's not too bad," she laughed. "Little buggers, it was mainly talc everywhere."

Dylan paused and smiled at his mam. "Erm… Mam…" he asked cautiously, "Is there any way I can have some of my sponsor money back now please?"

"Fuck off Dylan, now is not the time to be getting on my nerves." Magi sniped.

Dylan stared at her, expressionless.

She did say she'd give it back on Friday, and it was only Wednesday, he thought. He was determined to get his money back off of her.

Dylan popped his head into the kitchen. "I guess you're not going to school today Ela." Dylan said, as he gave his siblings a kiss on their heads. "Dyl will see you both later, make sure you behave and no more opening presents until Christmas day!"

Ela nodded solemnly, but Baby J just giggled, clearly unbothered by the destruction he'd caused.

****

By the time he'd reached school, Dylan was out of breath and twenty minutes late. He'd not had time to check on Dusty before leaving, which made him feel a pang of guilt, but the thought of her happily munching grass back in her field reassured him enough to push the worry aside.

The moment he walked into school, the atmosphere shifted. The pupils were still in *Gwasanaeth* – the Welsh word for daily morning assembly. There was a celebratory atmosphere as Dylan stood outside the hall waiting for the communal singing to finish. Dylan tried to sneak in and make his way to sit on the benches by Jamie. Heads turned, whispers spread, and a few younger kids actually pointed at him as the Headmaster congratulated the school on the success of the nativity.

"The show was absolutely fantastic and I am so grateful to all the teachers who worked so hard to get the show to such professional standards." he praised.

Dylan continued to try to remain inconspicuous, until the Headmaster announced to the school "I will overlook the fact he is late today, but there is one person I wanted to thank… sneaking in at the back there. Dylan Evans!"

Dylan froze and went bright red, with the whole school looking at him.

"A big round of applause for Dylan please!" the Headmaster boomed. "And, of course, Dusty, for making this year's show unforgettable!"

The whole school went berserk with clapping, whoops and cheers. Dylan's face turned to a smile.

The Headmaster continued, "And don't forget – The Daily Post will be here this afternoon to interview Dylan and do a feature on him and Dusty in the paper. A big round of applause again, please, for Dylan and Dusty!"

Dylan blinked, his cheeks still flushing red. He couldn't believe it.

As the excited children walked down the corridor to their classrooms, Jamie ran over to him.

"Here he is!" he declared loudly with a smile, throwing an arm around Dylan's shoulders. "The legend himself! Dusty is officially the most famous pony in Wales!"

"Shut up!" Dylan said, laughing.

"Dyl, you're like a pop star!" Jamie said, gesturing around them. "Everyone's been talking about the nativity. Dusty stole the show, and you… well, you were alright too." He winked, nudging Dylan playfully. "Not one person has mentioned me – saving the day – the shining star of Bethlehem."

"Not even your mam?" Dylan asked, innocently.

"Yeah, but she doesn't count." Jamie laughed.

As they walked down the corridor, students called out to him.

"Well done yesterday, Dylan!"

"Dusty was amazing!"

Even the teachers seemed to be in a particularly good mood towards him. Mrs. Jones stopped him in the corridor to say, "That was the best nativity we've had in years, Dylan. You should be very proud." A passing Mr. Tudur gave him a big thumbs-up, and even the usually grumpy caretaker managed a smile.

By the time he reached his classroom, Dylan was grinning from ear to ear. It was nice, for once, to feel like he wasn't invisible. He wasn't just another kid from Glanrafon – he was Dylan, the boy with the superstar pony who made the nativity shine brighter. And, they were going to be in *The Daily Post*! Like celebrities!

****

The last day of school before Christmas was always more about fun than lessons. The morning flew by in a blur of Christmas crafts, board games, and a slightly chaotic talent show that had Melvin Stevens performing his own rendition of *Jingle Bell Rock*.

Dylan was then ushered out of the classroom to be interviewed by the journalist from *The Daily Post*, a flamboyant man named Lloyd Floyd, who arrived wearing a scarf so long it seemed to double as a coat. His enthusiastic energy immediately put Dylan at ease.

"So," Lloyd began, his pen poised. "Tell me about Dusty. She's the real star, isn't she?"

Dylan beamed, nodding his head.

After answering all the questions like a pro, Dylan asked when his moment of fame would occur.

"The article will be out just before Christmas – I'll try to make sure you get the centrefold!" Lloyd smiled. "I absolutely love this story, Dylan. What an amazing bond you have with your pony – she must really trust you to have stood in the middle of the whole show quietly."

Dylan felt like he was dreaming. For the first time in a long while, he felt truly proud of himself.

****

By lunchtime, Dylan and Jamie were sitting together in the canteen, laughing about the morning's events.

"Right," Jamie said, leaning forward conspiratorially. "I've got an idea."

Dylan raised an eyebrow. "What kind of idea?"

"A money-making idea," Jamie said, grinning. "We should go carol singing tomorrow."

Dylan wrinkled his nose. "Carol singing? You're joking, you can't even sing."

"I can't but you can!" Jamie said, his grin widening. "Think about it. We take Dusty with us – stick some reindeer antlers on her, maybe a Santa hat – and go round the houses. People will love it. You can be a singing Santa and I'll be an elf and hold the money bucket!"

Dylan considered it, his mind already picturing Dusty dressed up in tinsel and flashing reindeer antlers. It was ridiculous, but it could work. "And what do we sing?" he asked.

"Anything," Jamie said with a shrug. "*Jingle Bells, Silent Night*, some Welsh songs. Sing the one you sang in the show. Doesn't matter, as long as we look Christmassy."

Dylan smirked. "Alright. But only if you wear an elf hat with ears."

Jamie groaned but laughed. "Fine. I'll wear the hat, as long as we split the takings."

"It's a deal!." Dylan laughed

****

The final bell rang and the school erupted into cheers as students poured out of the classrooms their bags bulging with handmade Christmas cards and leftover crackers. Dylan walked home with Jamie, the cold December air nipping at their cheeks.

"Are you going to check on Dusty now?" Jamie asked as they reached Dylan's street.

"Yeah," Dylan replied. "Make sure she's ok after all the treats she had yesterday!"

Jamie grinned. "Alright. See you tomorrow, then. I'll make myself an elf hat tonight."

Dylan waved him off and headed towards Dusty's field, feeling a little spark of excitement. The nativity had been a success, and now he had something to look forward to tomorrow.

When Dylan reached Dusty's field, the sight of her galloping towards the gate brought a big smile to his face. He climbed over the gate, scratching her neck as she nuzzled his pocket for carrots.

"Hey, girl," he said softly. "Shall we go carol singing tomorrow? Jamie thinks it'll make us rich."

Dusty snorted, flicking her ears, and Dylan laughed. "I'll take that as a yes."

He spent the next half hour brushing her coat and picking out the mud and stones from her hooves, humming *We Wish You a Merry Christmas* under his breath. The cold wind bit at his fingers, but he didn't care. Dusty was warm and steady, her presence soothing him after the chaos of the morning.

Time passed so quickly when he was with Dusty. It had somehow turned dark quickly so it was time for him to leave.

"Love you Dusty. See you tomorrow!" he said, giving her a kiss on neck.

As he slowly walked back home, Dylan felt a flicker of something he hadn't felt in a long time hope. Christmas was just around the corner, and for once, it felt like it might actually be something worth looking forward to.

****

23

Dusty's Secret.

Thursday, 21st December – 4 more sleeps!

The flat was unusually quiet, a silence so rare that Dylan almost didn't trust it. However, Magi and Barry had taken Ela and Baby J to see Father Christmas in Betws y Coed, leaving Dylan home alone. The stillness felt like a gift which he knew wouldn't last long, but an idea had been brewing in his mind ever since Jamie suggested their carol-singing scheme and this was the perfect chance to set his plan in motion.

He glanced out of the window up towards the fields where Dusty would be basking in the winter sunshine. The thought of taking Dusty carol singing, spreading cheer around the town, filled him with excitement.

Dylan threw on his coat, grabbed the head collar and lead rope from out of his school bag, and made his way to Dusty's field.

"Alright, girl," Dylan called softly as he reached the field. Dusty's ears pricked forward, and she whinnied in recognition. Dylan grinned, scratching her neck affectionately. "You ready for an adventure?" Dusty nudged him with her muzzle, her way of saying yes.

The pony's energy was contagious. As soon as Dylan opened the gate, she surged forward, practically dragging him down the path – yanking the lead rope out of his hand.

Crossing the road, Dusty veered towards a patch of fresh grass on the other side.

"Dusty," Dylan yelled, "Be careful. There are cars that might come down here." He said, as if she understood the meaning and danger of the road.

After a while, Dusty settled, walking calmly beside him and occasionally nudging his pocket in search of treats. Dylan fished out a carrot stub and handed it to her. She crunched it eagerly, her tail flicking with satisfaction.

When they reached Glanrafon, Dylan walked proudly with Dusty through the flats. He led her to the far right-hand side of the estate where there was a long ramp for disability access up to the first floor maisonettes.

"Come on, Dusty," he whispered, giving the rope a gentle tug. "Up we go!"

Dusty followed obediently, her hooves clopping on the concrete ramp. "I bet you've never been so high up, have you girl?" Dylan teased, laughing.

Dusty wasn't bothered in the slightest, she was as confident as he was.

Leading Dusty through the flats felt surreal, and he couldn't help but grin at the curious faces peeking out of windows.

Dylan reached his flat and shouted up to Jamie's window next door.

"What the hell are you doing with Dusty up there?" Jamie called down, laughing.

"I'm giving her a wash in the kitchen," Dylan replied, barely containing his giggles. "Come and help me!"

"Help you?" Jamie barked, "I'll come and laugh at you!"

"Come down then," he said as he turned Dusty around and opened the door to his flat.

"Welcome to my home, Dusty!" Dylan said with mock grandeur, leading the pony into the little kitchen.

Jamie joined them both as Dusty stood calmly, sizing up the small kitchen, her ears swivelling as she took in her surroundings.

"Have you cleaned Dyl? It smells nice in here?" Jamie asked.

"No, my mam must have cleaned – which means she is in a good mood." Dylan laughed.

The kitchen smelled faintly of cigarette smoke and cleaning spray, but Dusty didn't seem to mind. She snorted and blinked curiously at her new surroundings.

"Alright, let's get you cleaned up," Dylan said, his voice a mix of excitement and nerves.

"Your mam is going to kill you if she finds out." Jamie laughed.

'She's gone out with the kids to see Father Christmas." Dylan said confidently, grabbing a bottle of *Vosene* shampoo. "Pass me that sponge."

Together, they manoeuvred Dusty around the little kitchen. Dylan filled a bucket with warm water while Jamie found an old sponge under the sink. Dusty sniffed the bucket curiously, her lips brushing the surface of the water. She gave it a tentative slurp, only to jerk her head back, her ears flicking in surprise as the taste of soap hit her tongue.

"She's trying to drink it!" Jamie laughed, doubling over as Dusty coughed dramatically, spraying tiny bubbles from her mouth.

"Alright, no more tasting," Dylan said, chuckling as he wiped her muzzle with a cloth.

The small kitchen quickly turned into a sea of bubbles. The *Vosene* foamed up as they scrubbed Dusty's coat, leaving a shiny sheen beneath the mess. Dusty seemed to enjoy it, leaning into their touch and occasionally flicking her tail in approval.

The boys, giggling away, towel-dried her and stood back to admire their work.

"We might as well give her the full works," Dylan said plugging in the hairdryer.

Dusty stood like a dream, enjoying her pampering session as the warm air fluffed up her coat. By the time they were finished, she looked spotless and shiny, her winter coat gleaming in the light.

Dylan then went to fetch Ela's light-up reindeer antlers headband from her bedroom. He carefully placed the headband on Dusty's head, laughing as the antlers lit up with little blinking bulbs.

"Perfect!" he declared, pulling on his own Santa hat.

Jamie had brought an elf hat he'd 'borrowed' from the Log Cabin shop. "Good old five-finger-discount" Jamie laughed "They won't miss an elf hat!" Jamie said when Dylan shot him a disapproving look.

"Just make sure you take it back after we've been carol singing" Dylan grumbled, "At least then you were only borrowing it for a bit. It's not stealing if you take it back!"

****

By mid-afternoon, the boys were making their way through the streets with Dusty, who now looked like a reindeer straight out of a Christmas card. Her antlers blinked merrily, and her coat gleamed from the washing.

People stopped in their tracks to admire her, recognizing her instantly as the pony from the nativity.

"That's Dusty!" one elderly woman exclaimed, clapping her hands. "She was amazing in the show!"

Children crowded around, eager to pet Dusty and take pictures. Dylan's singing voice carried through the crisp winter air as they performed carols on the doorsteps of the posh estates, Dusty by his side. Jamie held out a bucket for donations, his elf hat slightly askew.

Everywhere they went, people greeted them with smiles and spare change. Dylan felt a surge of pride – not just for Dusty but for himself – for bringing Christmas cheer to the town.

By the time the sun dipped below the horizon, the boys found themselves sitting on the bench by the Pen y Bont bridge, counting their money.

"Eighteen pounds ninety!" Jamie announced, his face beaming.

"That's nine pounds forty-five each," Dylan said with a grin.

"Lucky you know maths," Jamie teased, nudging him.

Dylan pulled a handful of carrots from his bag and handed one to Dusty, who crunched it contentedly. "I should take her back to the field now," he said, rising to his feet. "Can I borrow your torch?"

"Yeah, sure," Jamie said, passing it over. "Want me to come with you? My Dad will go mad if I'm not home by half past five though."

"No, it's ok. I'll take her back on my own." Dylan responded.

"Call for me after then," Jamie said, "We can go and get batter bits from the chippy and see your other dad!"

"Maybe," Dylan laughed, "I'll call for you later."

Dylan made his way back to the field, the torchlight cutting through the darkness. Dusty walked beside him, her antlers still blinking faintly in the gloom.

As they reached the gate, the beam of headlights swept across the field. A red Land Rover was parked nearby, a trailer hitched to its back.

A posh looking lady with bouncy red hair, wearing tight *Ron Hill* leggings and a Barbour jacket, stepped out of the Land Rover, her expression thunderous.

"What the hell are you doing with my pony?" she demanded, her voice sharp enough to cut through the cold night air.

Dylan froze, his heart hammering in his chest.

"What do you mean, your pony?" he stammered, throwing his arms around Dusty's neck, "Dusty is mine!"

Carol's eyes narrowed. "That pony is called Jill" the woman snapped, "and she belongs to me. I've a good mind to tell the police. What the hell are you doing with her? What's your name?"

Dylan stood silent for a second, before whispering "Dylan…"

Carol continued in her anger.

"Well, Dylan. This pony is an old lady." She explained, "She's retired and is from my riding stables. This field is for retired horses – ponies on holiday. You have been stealing her from my field!"

Dylan's stomach twisted. The truth hit him like a punch to the gut. Dusty – *his* Dusty – wasn't his at all.

"I-I didn't know," he whispered, his voice barely audible. "Please don't tell the police."

Carol's anger softened as she took in the boy's stricken expression. "Why have you been taking her from this field? Who gave her to you?"

Dylan looked at the ground, shame flooding his cheeks. "Someone… a girl…" He stammered, "She told me that Dusty belonged to her and then she gave her to me because she couldn't afford to keep her any more." Dylan started to sob uncontrollably into Dusty's neck. "I thought she was mine."

Carol sighed, her tone gentler now. "Well…" Carol said, looking for words to try to console the young boy. "You've been looking after her well, I can see that."

Carol bent down to meet Dylan's gaze.

'I'm so sorry but this pony is not yours. She's mine. Her name is Jill and I've come to take her back home."

Dylan clung to Dusty's neck, tears spilling down his cheeks. "Please don't take her," he begged.

Tears pricked Dylan's eyes as Carol took Jill and led her into the trailer. He stood frozen, watching as Carol tied up his beloved pony, squashing her in between two tight partitions.

Lifting the ramp of the trailer to secure the locks, Carol announced, "I need to speak to your parents, Dylan."

Dylan begged her not to. "Please," he said, his voice breaking. "Don't tell my mam. She'll kill me."

Carol hesitated for quite some time, staring at the distraught little boy. "Alright," she said finally, "but on one condition. You come to work at my stables. That way, you can still see Jill all the time and help take care of her." Smiling and holding out her hand, she asked Dylan. "Have we got a deal?"

Dylan nodded and shook Carol's hand, tears streaming down his face.

'Come on," Carol said, gesturing to the Land Rover. "I'll give you a lift back into town. It's too dark for you to walk."

Dylan climbed into the passenger seat of the big warm Land Rover, his heart heavy but grateful for the small kindness.

As they drove back towards town, Dylan looked out of the window, silently promising himself that he would make it up to Dusty – no, Jill. Somehow.

Carol dropped Dylan off by *Jones & Bebb*, the local shop where Dylan had bought Dusty's feed buckets.

'You can get the bus up to Penmachno from Llanrwst on Saturday morning. I will pick you up at the bus stop – there will be some other kids waiting there too." Carol explained. "See you on Saturday!"

And with that, the Land Rover and trailer pulled off leaving a big puff of diesel smoke, almost choking Dylan. As the trailer faded in to the distance, Dusty's whinny echoed faintly, tugging at Dylan's heart, as if she knew, as if she could sense, almost, that Dylan was left behind in an emotional state.

Dylan ran home, his chest tight and tears streaming down his face – the loud, bright Christmas lights in all the flat windows stinging his eyes.

The flat was empty – nobody was home. Dylan stared at the mess in the kitchen. *Shit* he thought, *How the hell did we make this much mess?*

After 20 minutes, he had the whole kitchen sparkling, hiding the evidence of Dusty's impromptu grooming session.

He was just finishing drying his hands when he heard the familiar sound of voices echoing up the stairwell outside.

The door burst open, and a wave of noise flooded the flat. Magi walked in first, her arms laden with shopping bags, followed closely by Barry, who carried Baby J on his hip. The toddler's sticky fingers were clutched around a half-eaten sausage, his face lit up with excitement. Behind them came Aunty Jane and Emma, their chatter filling the air as the smell of salt-and-vinegar drenched chips wafted in with them.

"Ah, he's a good boy. Aren't you Dyl?" Magi said, rubbing Dylan on the head.

Dylan smirked, ducking away from her hand. "Hiya, Mam."

"Hiya Dylan," Emma chimed, her face bright with a mischievous smile. "Guess what? I'm sleeping over tonight!"

"Wooooohooooooo" Dylan shouted, "Are you going out, Mam?"

"No, boy," Magi replied, barely stopping for breath. "Aunty Jane and me are going Christmas shopping in Llandudno. We won't be too late." Her words came out in a hurried stream as she bustled about the flat. "Barry's going out too, so you're in charge. Can you do me a favour and feed the kids with some chips? We're going to miss the bus otherwise."

"I just need to go for a quick pee, Magi," Jane called out from the hallway. "No way am I getting on the number 19 through Rowen and all those bouncy roads without going first!"

"We've got chips and sausage!" Emma added excitedly, holding up a bag like it was the Holy Grail. "Can we have a drink of something please Aunty Magi?"

"Don't touch the fuckin' Babycham, that's for your mam and me tomorrow." Magi warned. "You can have a little bit of Cinzano if you want, but don't drink it all!"

Emma's eyes lit up!

The whirlwind energy of the whole family hit Dylan like a tornado, but for once, he didn't mind. The chaos was familiar, comforting even, and it was just what he needed to distract him from the lingering ache of losing Dusty.

"Right, let's get you fed, shall we?" Dylan winked at Ela and Baby J as he took plates out of the cupboard, trying to put Dusty to the back of his mind.

"Can I stay up and play games with you and Emma?" Ela begged.

"If you're a good girl, you can stay up for an extra half an hour," Dylan replied, his tone soft but firm.

Ela grinned, clapping her hands in delight.

Barry appeared in the doorway, his coat half-on, shouting over the noise. "Behave tonight, no trouble please… and leave the presents alone!" He waved and was gone before anyone could respond.

The flat buzzed with warmth and laughter. Fay and Mr. Lazars had delivered the payday loan money a day early, leaving the adults in high spirits, and Magi and Jane seemed determined to make this the best Christmas ever.

For once, Dylan didn't care that he had to babysit. Emma was here, and the promise of a fun evening lifted his mood.

The kids scrambled to the window to watch as Magi and Jane ran to catch the bus. They waved frantically, blowing kisses as the women rushed through the estate, their laughter echoing faintly in the cold night air.

"Alright," Dylan said, clapping his hands to get their attention. "Chips first, then we'll see about playing a game. Yeah?"

With Emma's help, it was a quick affair to get the kids fed and ready for bed. Emma entertained the kids with a game of Kerplunk, while Dylan cleared up the mess.

"Right, I'll take you both upstairs and read you a story." Emma said confidently. Emma was a year younger than Dylan but had the same maturity around the younger children.

"Come on, you can choose the story." Emma offered as she shepherded the little ones upstairs.

Dylan was just finishing off tidying the kitchen, when Jamie knocked and entered the flat.

"Hiya, I saw your mam and dad go out." Jamie said, taking his shoes off and getting ready to make himself at home.

"Yeah, my cousin Emma is having a sleep over. She's just putting the little ones to bed. You can stay though," he assured Jamie, "you'll like Emma, she's fun."

"Shall we play the *Faints* game?" Jamie asked, laughing at the thought of it.

Faints was a typical council estate game. Using what you have, to create fun. In this case, it was using each other as scientific experiments on breath control.

Jamie cleared some space in the living room and greeted Emma as she said to Dylan, "Right, they've both gone off to sleep. That didn't take long at all."

"Emma, you know Jamie, don't you?" Dylan checked.

"Yeah, not properly. Hiya." Emma said, introducing herself confidently.

"Hiya," Jamie responded, equally self-assured. "We're going to play Faints…"

He went on to explain the rules of the game. One person lifts and squeezes another person tightly around the chest, while the person being squeezed holds their breath for as long as they can. The person will then faint and then we time them to see how long they faint for.

"Want to play?" Jamie asked Emma, with a big smile.

"Erm, yeah." Emma said, hesitantly, "but I'm not going first!"

"It's fine, I'll go first," Dylan said confidently, wanting to reassure Emma it would be ok.

Jamie placed his arms around Dylan and squeezed the breath out of him. True to the rules, Dylan fainted and Jamie lowered him slowly to the floor. Counting loudly, like a boxing ring judge, Jamie shouted, "14, 15, 16, 17", at which point Dylan opened up his eyes.

"17 seconds Dyl. Not bad!" Jamie exclaimed. "Gonna have a go, Emma?"

"Yeah, go on then." Emma said, with a mock confidence. "So I just hold my breath, yeah?"

"Yeah," Jamie said, as he wrapped his arms around her.

Within a very short space of time, Emma's body went limp. Jamie lowered her to the floor carefully and started counting.

"8, 9, 10, 11, 12…."

Emma lay lifeless on the floor, looking an unusual shade of grey.

"19,20,21,22,23…."

"She's doing well!" Dylan said, with a slight panic in his voice.

"35, 36, 37, 38, 39…"

"Jamie, I'm getting a bit worried." Dylan whispered as he nudged Emma's lifeless body.

"46, 47, 48, 49, 50…"

"Fuck, Jaaaaamie… We've killed her." Dylan panicked. "Emma, Emma…" Dylan started crying. "EMMA!!!!" he shouted.

Emma's eyes flickered as she gently stirred and then woke up in an instant. "What was my time? Did I win?"

"59 seconds!!!!" Jamie shrieked. "Fuckin' hell, nobody has ever done it for that long!"

Dylan sat in a heap next to his cousin.

"Why are you crying?" Emma asked, laughing at Dylan.

"It's been a long day." He said, wiping tears away from his cheeks, "I thought you were dead!"

The three of them started laughing!

"I don't know anyone who has been out for that long!" Jamie championed. "You're really good at fainting Emma!"

The three of them laughed some more. Council estate games always provided laughter!

****

24

Black Friday.

Friday, 22nd December – 3 more sleeps!

Dylan woke up with Emma's foot squarely in his face. Sharing a bed, head-to-toe, was always their thing, but last night it had taken them a while to fall asleep. As soon as Dylan's head had hit the pillow, the vision of Dusty being taken away in the trailer played over and over in his mind, the scene replaying in a cruel loop, making him cry. He'd tried his best to cry quietly, burying his face into his pillow so Emma wouldn't hear, but Emma always noticed.

"You're crying, aren't you?" she whispered, her voice soft in the dark.

"No," Dylan lied, though his sniffles betrayed him.

Emma didn't press him. Instead, she did what she always did best – made him laugh.

Emma always knew how to cheer him up and had made him see that there *was* a happy ending to this story, that Dusty, or *Jill* as was her name, would still be very much in Dylan's life. And Emma pointed out that Dylan would eventually grow and then there would be loads of bigger horses in the stables for him to ride too.

The giggling went on much longer than usual as Emma felt she really needed to pick him up this time.

"Imagine if I'd have died last night?" Emma said, her voice full of mock seriousness, "What would you have done?"

"I'd have asked your mam if I could have your copies of *Horse Sense* magazine!" Dylan laughed, before pausing for a second to admit, "No, I was really scared."

"I'm a good fainter!" Emma rejoiced. "I'm better than you at fainting." She laughed.

"You are!" Dylan agreed, but his attention was elsewhere.

The two cousins lay in bed, in silence.

"Would you have been sad if I'd died?" Emma asked, full of morbidity.

"Shut up!" Dylan muttered, smiling at her. But Dylan's thoughts drifted straight back to Dusty.

Emma could sense that Dylan wasn't right. "Did you sleep ok?" Emma asked, caringly.

"Yeah," Dylan paused. "I just wish it was all a dream and that Dusty was still here. I need to go to her field today." Dylan said, as he pulled the bobbly orange blanket up to his chin to keep himself warm.

"Want me to come with you?" Emma offered.

"No, I'll be ok. Your mam is picking you up this morning. I think you have to go to work with her." Dylan replied.

"Yeah, I've got to help her feed the old people in the nursing home." She replied. "I like Coed Mawr at Christmas though. All the little old ladies give me loads of chocolate!" Emma laughed.

The smell of bacon wafted up from the kitchen, tempting Dylan and Emma out of bed.

The giggly pair went downstairs to find Magi in the kitchen making bacon butties.

"Well, you two have slept in today, haven't you?" Magi smiled, "Were you awake all night giggling? I've been shouting you for the last half an hour!"

"Sorry, Aunty Magi." Emma replied. "We haven't seen each other for ages so we kept making each other laugh! Plus, Dylan kept farting!"

At which point Emma and Dylan started laughing for no reason.

"You two… you're so bloody stupid together," Magi said, as she handed them both a bacon sandwich. "Eat up, Em. Your mam will be here in a bit to pick you up."

Silence fell up on the kitchen, except for the sound of Magi washing dishes and the two cousins scoffing bacon sandwiches.

After a minute or two, Emma turned to her aunty Magi.

"Dylan was feeling sad last night, Aunty Magi." Emma said, as she bit into her bacon butty.

"What's wrong boy?" Magi said, her big blue eyes, concerned.

"Dusty had to go to the stables in Penmachno," Dylan stammered, carefully crafting his response.

"Why?" Magi asked, her tone softening, "Is she ok?"

"Yeah, she's fine." Dylan said, swallowing a big bite of his butty. "I'm going to start helping out at the stables to carry on looking after Dusty. I'm catching the bus up there tomorrow and the owner of the stables is picking me up." Dylan stared at his mam, not knowing what her response was going to be.

"Well, that sounds fun." Magi smiled, "As long as you're back in time to babysit! I'm going out tomorrow night."

"You go out every night." Dylan muttered under his breath.

"What was that?" Magi sniped, her eyes narrowing and lips pursing.

Dylan hesitated before deciding to push his luck. He was pissed off with always being walked over. At least with Emma there, Magi wouldn't go full force with her screaming at him.

"Can I have my sponsor money today, please?" Dylan prodded.

Magi pursed her lips tight. "Actually, if you weren't so cheeky, I was going to say that I've got some of your sponsor money here." Magi continued, while she washed up the frying pan. "There's £15 on the side there if you want to go to *Gwyn Lewis* to buy yourself some riding boots."

Dylan stared at her, frustration bubbling to the surface. "You've taken way more than £15 though." Dylan replied, with a helpless tone "That's not fair!"

"You are bloody ungrateful." Magi hissed. "If you don't want it then I'll take it back."

"No, I'll have it. I'll get some riding boots for tomorrow." Dylan said, with a little bit of excitement.

"Yooo-hooooooo… *ding dong merrily on high…*" came the voice of Aunty Jane. "Come on Em, get yourself changed. I'm late for work. Everyone ok?" Jane asked, looking at Dylan.

"Yes thanks Aunty Jane." Dylan replied sheepishly. "I'm going to buy some new riding boots now."

"Good boy. I'm sure Father Christmas will bring you some lovely presents too." Jane smiled. "Emma, hurry up. If I miss this bus then I've got 14 old people who will be starving hungry."

Emma came back to the kitchen with her Kwik Save plastic bag full of clothes and sweets. She gave Dylan an awkward hug and left in a hurry with Aunty Jane.

"I'm going out too, Mam." Dylan said, as he slipped out of the kitchen. "I'm going to get dressed and then I'm going to see if I can get some new boots for the stables tomorrow."

"Please make sure you are back by 5 o'clock at the latest Dyl." Magi shouted after him, "The pop man will be round tonight. I'll make sure you've got plenty of pop and crisps."

Dylan wasn't listening. His sights were set on looking his best for his visit to Dusty, tomorrow.

****

Dylan spent the rest of the day on his own. He wandered up to Dusty's field and sat on the gate, recalling the fun times he and Dusty had experienced together. He couldn't believe Dusty / Jill was retired. He had definitely brought her out of retirement! The places they'd been together, the sponsored walks, she'd even been the star of the school nativity!

Shit Dylan thought, *he was going to be in the Daily Post with Dusty. Her real owner Carol may not let him work in the stables if she finds out.*

Dylan laughed to himself, but then the laughter turned to tears. Thoughts of Prince being taken away… and now Dusty. But Emma was right. There could be a happy ending if he enjoyed working in the stables. He would get to see Dusty every single day.

With this in mind, he wiped his tears and made his way back to the town. He got to Gwyn Lewis and tried on the last pair of size 2 riding boots. They were a little bit tight but they were rubber, so he took a chance that they would stretch.

"It's Black Friday today," The lady on the till said, in Welsh. "I'll knock a fiver off them as they are the last ones. And I'll put some free treats in there for your pony too." She said, as she packed the goodies into a big bag for Dylan.

Dylan beamed.

"Wow, Diolch yn fawr!" Dylan said, thanking the lady in Welsh.

On his way out of the shop, Dylan caught sight of the jockey skull caps. *I'll have to sing a few more carols to get my hands on one of them,* he thought.

Dylan swung his bag backwards and forwards, singing to himself as he walked proudly through the town.

"Alright son," came the familiar voice of Calvin as he was passing the fruit and veg shop. "I've got some carrots here for you for Dusty."

"Ah, thank you Calvin. Dusty has now moved to Penmachno so I'm starting work there tomorrow, helping out." Dylan explained.

"Good lad. I started working when I was your age – didn't do me any harm! Tell your mam I'm asking for her." Calvin said, as he handed Dylan a big bag of carrots. "See you later. T'ra boy."

Dylan walked off smiling. "Bye Dad," Dylan whispered to himself, as though he was practising the word for a later date, when Magi might reveal Calvin as his real father.

By the time Dylan arrived back home, Magi and Aunty Jane were busy applying their make-up and sipping on Babycham. Their mohair cardigans hanging up, ready to be shown off to the town.

"I'll sew that sparkly motif on the side for you now Jane, and then it's finished." Magi said proudly. It was a labour of love knitting something so big but Magi was proud of herself for actually completing it in time, for Jane.

Dylan ran upstairs and found Ela and Baby J were sat quietly looking at the Argos catalogue. They both looked up at him and smiled.

"Hello my babies." Dylan said, kissing them both on the head, as he rummaged around in the drawer for his Fraggle Rock Book. He grabbed a pen and opened up the book to add a new entry -

- **Calvin called me son again. He said he started work young. Gave me more carrots.**

- **Asked me to say hi to my mam.**

Dylan ran back downstairs and casually threw Calvin's name into the room.

"Mam, I've just had some free carrots off Calvin fruit and veg." Dylan said, nonchalantly. "He said to tell you he's asking for you."

"Ah, I like Calvin." Jane said, smiling. "Didn't you used to have a thing with him in school?" Jane laughed.

Dylan's ears pricked up.

"Oh shut up, Jane." Magi responded, topping up their wine glasses. "Let's not start that game – we've got little ears listening here" she said, referring to Dylan.

Dylan ignored them both and sat watching Blockbusters – pretending to be engrossed. But not one word went unmissed!

"I've laid a buffet out for you on the table for tea, Dyl." Magi said as she added the final stitches to the sequin motif on Jane's cardigan. "The little ones have had food, and there's loads of sweets and crisps here. Help yourself to whatever you want, ok?"

"Can we have some Viennetta later?" Dylan pressed.

"It's meant to be for Christmas day, but yes… help yourself. I can pick up another one tomorrow." Magi responded.

Jane stood up and tried the cardigan on. She started to well up with tears.

"Ah, it's beautiful Magi." Jane gushed, "I feel like Joan Collins!"

"You look like Joan Collins." Magi said, grinning at her handiwork. "It's taken me bloody ages!"

Jane went to pick her handbag up and noticed that one of the sleeves stayed up by her elbow.

"Magi?" she questioned, "This sleeve is shorter than the other one!"

"Well, I can't do anything about that now." Magi said, trying to hide her smile. "Just roll the other one up for now. I'll add some more stitches to it in the new year."

Jane did a turn and swished the black, shiny, floor-length mohair cardigan around the room.

"Yeah, fuck it – you can't tell if I roll it up!" Jane announced. "Thank you so much Magi. I love it!"

Ela and Baby J entered the room and their eyes lit up at the sight of Aunty Jane.

"You look like a beautiful princess Aunty Jane." Ela declared.

"Ah thank you, Ela. You're my little princess aren't you." Jane said, picking her up for a cwtch.

"Right, let me get my handbag." Magi said, making her way to the hallway. "Come on Jane. We need to get going."

Kisses and cuddles were given and the two women made their way out for the biggest night out of the year – Black Friday in Llanrwst.

The sweet smell of Lily of the Valley perfume lingered in the living room as Dylan switched all the lamps and Christmas lights on, making the living room cosy to settle down for the evening.

Flicking the television on, ET was the film for the evening so the three kids cosied up together on the sofa and watched the film, for the umpteenth time. It wasn't long before Dylan's siblings were snoring away and he was able to deliver them to their beds, quietly laying them down and tucking them in – being sure not to wake them. At ten years old, Dylan was a pro at making sure they didn't wake. He could even change Baby J's nappy and Babygro, in the dark, without waking him – not an easy feat!

Dylan packed his bag ready for his big day tomorrow. He laid out his new riding boots next to his old riding hat and filled his bag with crisps and sweets. He dry-heaved as he made some cheap meat spread – or paté as his mam would call it – sandwiches. He knew that if push came to shove and he ended up really hungry, he would be able to force them down.

Dylan tucked himself up in bed, ready for his big day and drifted off to sleep with a gentle smile on his face.

****

A blood-curdling scream jolted Dylan awake. He sat bolt upright, his heart pounding.

Checking his watch, it was 1:05 a.m. He could hear his mam's voice echoing through the estate, slurring and furious—

"You are not fuckin' ruining Christmas again this year!"

Dylan ran to the window, pressing his nose against the cold glass. His siblings were still snoring away, blissfully unaware of what was about to unfold.

It all seemed to happen quite quickly. The screaming and shouting got louder and lights started to flicker on in the neighbouring flats. This wasn't unusual on a Saturday night in Glanrafon – in fact it was entertainment for some people. Black Friday usually ended in chaos, but this felt different.

Dylan felt helpless, as the crowds gathered outside his flat trying to stop whatever was going on.

"Open the fuckin' door!" Magi wailed through the letter box, to which Dylan ran downstairs and let her in. Dylan did as he was told. "Quick, lock it again." She instructed as she fell through the doorway.

On locking the door, Dylan turned to see his mam, her cardigan ripped and blood on her lip. A graze on her forehead completed the disastrous depiction of the festive season in Glanrafon.

Within seconds, Barry was banging on the door.

"Open this fuckin' door now, I'm warning you Magi." Barry shouted. He was like a wild animal.

"Where's Aunty Jane?" Dylan whispered.

"Get upstairs Dyl." Magi replied. "NOW!"

Magi ran upstairs with Dylan, as the banging on the door became more ferocious.

"You fuckin' wait…" Barry sneered through the letter box as he started kicking the door, trying to force it open.

Magi hung out of the window.

"You need to fuck off to your mam's now and leave us alone. It's over. I'm not doing this any more. It's not fair on the kids." Magi cried. "You promised me things would be different."

Barry kicked the door again, sending a thunderous bang throughout the flat.

"Are you ok there Magi?" came the drunken voice of Mark, one of the local town lads.

"You can fuck off," Barry shouted at Mark, "or I'll break your fuckin' face."

Mark was only nineteen, but was known for being one of the hardest lads in the town. He turned to his two mates and laughed – "Who does this one think he is? What an embarrassment!"

Dylan looked on as the argument began to unfold.

"Listen here, you little prick – fuck off now, before I do you some damage." Barry snarled.

"Come on then… old man… if you think you're hard enough." Mark challenged.

What happened next was a blur. Aunty Gwen was obviously not home, or she would have maintained control over everything.

It all happened so quickly. Punches were thrown. Mark finally held a defeated Barry up against the wall and called up to Dylan, "Hey, do you want to come and give him a smack, boy?" Mark said, covered in blood and smiling like some sort of demented hyena.

Dylan hid back behind the curtains, shaking.

"Stop now!" Magi screamed, crying uncontrollably as she ran down the stairs. "STOP!"

By now, a crowd had gathered. Mark dropped Barry to the floor, hitting his head on the wall as he fell in a heap.

Dylan watched from the window as Magi threw her arms around Barry, screaming-crying and checking where the blood was coming from.

It felt like time passed so slowly at this point, but suddenly the whole estate lit up with blue flashing lights. One of the Glanrafon angels – usually Mrs Owen in number 24 – must have called for an ambulance. Dylan watched as the medics guided Barry and Magi into the ambulance and drove off at full speed.

Within minutes, the crowd had dispersed and the flat was silent.

Dylan sneaked a peak out of the window and saw blood-spattered stains on the floor outside.

Running downstairs to quickly check the front door was locked, he noticed the handle hanging off. This meant he wasn't able to fully lock the door, so he dragged a chair from the kitchen to do his best to jam it behind the door. The Christmas tree lights twinkled in the living room, pulling Dylan out of his sadness.

His watch flashed up – it was 2 a.m.! Dylan needed to be up at 7 o'clock. Nothing was going to ruin his big day with Dusty. A final check on his siblings made him feel at ease that they hadn't had to witness the awful events earlier. Dylan took himself to bed and tried to erase the bloody massacre out of his mind. His mind started to run away with him as thoughts of a stranger breaking in to his house kept him awake for a little while. Dreams of Dusty eventually filled his mind and took him to the safe space of his dreams.

****

25

Finding Home in the Mountains.

Saturday, 23rd December – 2 more sleeps!

Dylan stirred at the sound of his alarm, its high-pitched ring cutting through the haze of sleep. He groaned, pulling the blanket tighter around him. Somewhere in his half-conscious mind, he registered that today was important – *very* important – but his body was heavy with exhaustion.

He squinted at his watch on his bedside table. His heart nearly stopped.

"Seven-thirteen!" Dylan shouted, bolting upright. His bus was due to leave at 7:30 a.m., and he was nowhere near ready.

In a frantic blur, Dylan threw on his clothes and made his way to the bathroom for a pee. *The longest wee ever, he didn't have time for this!* Peeking through the crack in his mam's bedroom door, he could see his mam and Barry lying motionless in bed. *Oh well, he wasn't that badly hurt then. At least they're here to look after the kids,* he thought.

Dylan tugged his new riding boots on, and made himself some cornflakes. Spying his mam's open handbag on the side, he considered his options as he rushed to eat his cereal.

On looking inside the handbag, Dylan saw a folded piece of paper – yellow in colour. It had *For Dylan* written on it. He opened the piece of paper and started shaking. On the inside it had *Dad* written on it, followed by a Llandudno phone number. Dylan gasped at the thought. This bombshell blew Calvin completely out of the water as a prospective father figure.

Dylan slipped the piece of paper into his pocket, helped himself to a fiver from his mam's purse, slurped the rest of the milk from the cereal and grabbed the bag he'd packed the night before.

He kicked aside a bundle of blood-stained clothes that lay strewn by the front door, determined not to let the mess distract him. The cold December air hit him like a slap as he flew out the door, adrenaline and excitement driving him forward. His little legs pumped furiously, the urgency of catching the bus spurring him on. Just as the bus rolled into sight, he skidded to a halt at the stop, arriving just in time.

Dylan had never been to Penmachno before – the village where the riding stables were situated – and as the bus began its ascent into the mountains, he was struck by how different the world outside his window looked. Llanrwst, with its rows of terraced houses and bustling streets, gave way to winding roads lined with frost-kissed trees.

It was like stepping into a winter wonderland. The fields glistened under a thin blanket of snow, and icicles hung from hedgerows like nature's Christmas decorations. Dylan pressed his forehead against the cold glass, his eyes wide as the scenery grew more dramatic with every turn, his stomach churning with nervous excitement.

The bus climbed higher, the mountains looming closer with every passing mile. The world seemed quieter here, more peaceful, as if the bus were carrying him into a completely different realm.

Dylan pulled the yellow piece of paper out of his pocket to examine the hand writing again. It was neat and stylish. Was this a hint towards what his dad might be like? The journey passed by quickly while Dylan day-dreamed about his dad possibly liking horses and the pair of them riding on their horses together, when he noticed the sign for the village destination.

Penmachno was a small, sleepy village nestled in the shadow of the mountains. The bus came to a halt at a stop near the centre of the village. Dylan stepped off, his boots crunching on the frozen ground.

Waiting nearby were two girls, both around his age, bundled up in thick coats and scarves. One had red, curly hair tied into a messy ponytail, while the other wore her brown hair loose, her cheeks red from the cold.

"Are you Dylan?" the red-haired girl asked, her breath visible in the chilly air.

"Yeah," Dylan replied, shifting his bag on his shoulder. "I'm starting at the stables today."

"We work there already!" the brown-haired girl chimed in. "I'm Anita, and this is Mary."

Before Dylan could respond, the sound of a sputtering engine drew their attention. A battered little red van rattled to a stop in front of them.

"Good morning you lot!" came Carol's familiar voice from the driver's seat.

The back of the van was open, revealing a couple of hay bales and a makeshift bench. Dylan and the girls climbed in, laughing as they jostled for space.

In the passenger seat sat an older woman with a cigarette dangling from her lips. She barely glanced at them as she rolled down the window, exhaling a stream of smoke.

"That's Shirley," Carol called over her shoulder. "She's been with us for years. Don't let her scare you."

Shirley turned her head slightly, her cigarette bobbing as she muttered in a scouse accent, "Behave yourselves, and we'll get along just fine."

Dylan grinned nervously, unsure if she was joking.

As the van rumbled out of the village, the road quickly became steeper. It felt as though they were climbing a vertical hill, the engine groaning with the effort. Dylan's ears popped, the sensation making him feel like he was on his way to the heavens.

The frost thickened as they climbed higher, coating the fence posts and trees in sparkling white. The girls chatted excitedly, but Dylan was too mesmerised by the view to join in.

After what felt like an eternity, the van crested the hill, and the landscape opened up before them. A light dusting of snow covered the peaks, glinting under the pale winter sun. Frosted gates lined the winding road, and the air felt crisper, cleaner.

Dylan could hardly believe his eyes. It was as if they'd stepped into a postcard.

"We're almost there," Carol announced, her voice pulling Dylan from his thoughts.

In the distance, nestled in the middle of the mountains, was the stables. Smoke curled from the chimney of a small stone building, and horses dotted the fields, their warm breath visible in the icy air.

The van rattled to a stop in the yard, and the three new friends climbed out, their boots crunching on the frozen ground. Carol stepped out too, clapping her gloved hands together.

"Welcome to Tŷ Coch," she said with a grin.

Dylan took a moment to take it all in. With a tack room and feed room at the entrance, the stables were larger than he'd expected, with rows and rows of stalls built from weathered wood in the main block and three big stables to the right of the main block. It was never ending. Out the back, there were more stables, a hay-barn and a huge muck heap! It reminded him of Bwlch Mawr. The horses looked well-fed and content, their coats gleaming in the soft light.

"This place is amazing," Dylan said, his voice full of awe.

At the sound of Dylan's voice, a loud whinny came from behind the stable door.

"I know who that is," Dylan beamed. "DUSTY!" Dylan shouted as he hung over the stable door to stroke her face.

"Sorry, I mean *Jill...*" Dylan spluttered, turning a shade of crimson. "Look at you. I've missed you."

"Go inside and give her a hug if you want to." Carol offered. "I bet she's missed you."

"I've missed her... SO much!" Dylan replied, his eyes getting glassy.

Dylan opened the stable door and gave her the biggest hug, taking a step back to rub her favourite spot. Dusty's head shot up in the air, her top lip curling with satisfaction as Dylan worked his magic.

"She likes you Dylan." Carol said with a smile. "Right, let's get these horses mucked out, shall we?"

The morning flew by in a blur of activity. Carol paired Dylan with Anita and she showed him how to muck out stalls, fill hay nets, and groom the horses. Dylan's hands quickly grew numb from the cold, but he didn't care. Being surrounded by the animals, hearing their gentle snorts and the rustle of straw, made him feel at home.

"Can you bring Jill in to the stalls now please, Dylan?" Carol asked, as she tied up a small hay net. "She can stand in here while we muck her stable out."

Jill was soon munching contentedly on the hay net, snorting the dust out of her nostrils every now and then. Dylan felt a pang of longing as he watched her, but seeing her happy and well-cared-for eased some of the ache in his chest.

"Dylan!" Carol called, snapping him out of his thoughts. "Come help me with the feed."

He hurried over, eager to prove himself. Carol handed him a bucket of pony nuts and showed him how to mix it with chaff and supplements.

"You've done this before," she said, watching him work.

"Kind of," Dylan replied. "I've looked after a pony before, but not like this."

"Well, you're a natural," Carol said with a nod of approval.

****

After lunch, Carol surprised everyone with a treat: a ride up the mountain. Dylan's heart soared as he was paired with a little black Dartmoor gelding called Kulin. Standing at 13 hands, Kulin was the biggest pony he'd ever ridden.

The group set off, the sound of hooves crunching on snow-covered paths filling the air. The mountains stretched out around them, majestic and timeless. Dylan felt a sense of freedom he hadn't known in weeks, the weight of recent events melting away with each step Kulin took.

"This is incredible," he said to no one in particular, his voice filled with wonder.

"You need to be careful with Kulin," Shirley warned. "He likes to bolt. If he goes, just try to enjoy it. The more you pull, the stronger he will get!"

The five of them were riding towards a big hill and the horses started to jog. It was evident that they knew where they were and wanted to release some of their energy.

"Hold tight Dylan… Kulin is going to gooooooo" Shirley warned.

Dylan felt like he was on a rocket ship on the way to space. Kulin pulled his head right in between his knees and was going like the clappers. Dylan was petrified but excited at the same time.

"It's ok," said Carol, who had caught him up and was galloping alongside side him on her black beauty, Solitaire. "Just enjoy it, it's a dead end at the end of this track so he can't go far. Stand up in your stirrups and lean forward a little!"

With that, Dylan did as he was told and stood up in his stirrups. It felt like Dylan had just inserted Duracell batteries in Kulin as he changed up the gears a bit faster again.

The dead-end was in sight and all the horses came skidding to a halt.

Horses and riders were sweating and out of breath, but nobody had fallen off.

"Well done Dylan," Shirley said, lighting up a cigarette. "You did bloody well there."

When they got back to the stables, the girls took it in turns to allow Dylan to learn some new skills. Removing more complex tack and martingales from the bigger horses, rugging up to keep the horses from getting a chill and making up sugar beet for the next day.

By the time the day ended, Dylan was exhausted but happy. His boots were covered in mud, his cheeks flushed from the cold, and his heart full of hope. He ran round to the back of the stables to give Dusty a kiss goodnight. The sound of the horses munching on the hay filled Dylan's soul, as the stable lights were switched off for the night.

The drive back to the village felt quite scary in the dark, but Carol knew the windy roads like the back of her hand.

Dropping Dylan off back at the bus stop, Carol offered, "You're very welcome to come up tomorrow if you want to Dylan?"

"Yes please," Dylan said. "Thank you so much for today. I've had the best day!"

Dylan stood waving as the little red van disappeared down the road.

As Dylan boarded the bus home, he couldn't stop smiling. For the first time in a long while, he felt like he belonged somewhere. Tŷ Coch felt like his new home.

Tomorrow was Christmas Eve, and no matter all the shit that he'd experienced the past few months, Tŷ Coch was already proving to be a gift that would make this the best Christmas ever!

****

26

Rearing into Christmas.

Sunday, 24th December – Christmas Eve. 1 more sleep!

The sun barely peeked over the frosted hills as Dylan trudged up the path toward the stables. Every step was an effort – his muscles ached from the previous day's work, and his hands were already numb despite the gloves he wore.

The morning at the stables had started in chaos. Every tap was frozen solid, leaving them to haul water up the hill by the bucket. Dylan had made trip after trip, his arms straining under the weight of the heavy pails, slipping occasionally on patches of black ice. By the time the horses had their first drink of the day, Dylan was exhausted and shivering, his face red from the cold.

The horses, too, were on edge. They stomped and snorted in their stalls, eager to be let out after being cooped up for hours. The frost-covered ground made turning them out a risky business, and Dylan was quickly learning just how unpredictable bigger horses could be.

Shirley, cigarette in hand as usual, seemed to find the chaos amusing. She barked orders at everyone, her scouse accent carrying over the clatter of hooves and the rustling of hay.

"Dylan, take Bow to the stream," she instructed, pointing towards the towering ex-racehorse.

Dylan hesitated. Bow stood over 17 hands high, his sleek black coat glinting in the pale winter sun. He was a far cry from Jill, whose small stature and gentle demeanour had made her feel manageable. Bow, on the other hand, was a giant with a mind of his own.

Swallowing his nerves, Dylan clipped the lead rope to Bow's halter and began leading him down the icy path. Almost immediately, the horse decided he had his own agenda. With a powerful tug, Bow yanked the rope from Dylan's hands and bolted towards the stream.

"Bow!" Dylan yelled, scrambling to keep up.

The racehorse had no intention of stopping. Dylan held onto the rope for dear life as Bow dragged him down the hill, slipping and sliding over the ice. His boots skidded across the frozen ground, and he barely managed to stay on his feet. By the time they reached the water, Dylan was covered in mud and sweat, his heart pounding like a drum.

Bow snorted triumphantly, dipping his head to drink from the icy stream. Dylan took a moment to catch his breath, his hands trembling as he gripped the lead rope.

The return journey wasn't much better. Bow pulled and pranced the entire way back to the stable, his energy unrelenting. By the time they reached the yard, Dylan looked thoroughly dishevelled – his coat streaked with mud, his hair plastered to his forehead, and his gloves soaked through.

Shirley, leaning against the stable door with her ever-present cigarette, let out a low chuckle as Dylan stumbled into view.

"You alright, lad?" she asked, a teasing glint in her eye.

"Yes," Dylan panted, trying to muster some dignity. "Just getting used to the bigger ones."

"If you can handle a Shetland – or as I like to call them, a Shitland," Shirley said with a laugh, "then you can handle anything. They're the worst!" She winked at Dylan, adding, "Well done, you're doing a good job."

Her words, though gruff, gave Dylan a small sense of pride. He might have been out of his depth, but he was holding his own.

By mid-morning, Dylan's stomach was growling. The icy air and physical labour had left him ravenous, and he was starting to wonder if he'd packed enough food to last the day.

"I've got two Pot Noodles if you want one," Mary, one of the older stable hands, offered as they sat on overturned buckets in the feed room.

Pot Noodles and Cuppa Soups, Dylan was quickly learning, were the staples of survival at Tŷ Coch.

"Thank you," Dylan said, accepting her offer gratefully.

As the hot, salty noodles warmed him from the inside, Dylan knew instantly that Mary was going to be a friend for life. The stables were tough, chaotic, and freezing, but there was something about the shared struggle that made it all feel worthwhile.

As the day wore on, Dylan found himself growing more confident. The work was hard, but it was rewarding. He learned how to fill hay nets with greater efficiency, how to scrub feed buckets until they gleamed, and how to navigate the sometimes-tempestuous personalities of the horses.

Jill – his Dusty – was a constant source of comfort. She greeted him with a soft whinny every time he passed her stall, and Dylan couldn't resist stopping to give her a quick scratch behind the ears.

"You've got a way with her," Carol remarked as she watched Dylan interact with the pony. "Not everyone gets that kind of reaction from Jill."

Dylan beamed at the compliment.

"We've got a hack going out this afternoon and you can go along with them if you want to? Just to start getting used to the forestry tracks. Would you like that?" Carol asked.

"Yes please," Dylan said, smiling. "Will I ride Kulin?"

"I think you're ready for something a little bigger, so you can extend your leg." Carol remarked. "Launcelot hasn't been out to stretch his legs for a few days. You can take him."

Dylan couldn't believe it. Two different horses in two days. He felt like he'd ended up in Disneyland!

Mary grinned as she led Bow into the open yard. A few customers had gathered, their breaths visible as they watched with a mix of awe and trepidation.

"Now, if you can pay attention," Mary said, her voice carrying authority.

Dylan watched as Mary demonstrated how to get on, landing gently on Bow's back. She gave a confident and well-rehearsed presentation on how to get the best from your horse.

"If in doubt, keep your hands down, this will keep you balanced. And pull back to stop!" she concluded.

Dylan smiled at Mary, filing away every word that came from her mouth.

Carol had brought Launcelot out for Dylan.

"Now be careful Dylan, he does rear when he gets excited." Carol warned. "Just sit forward, smile and don't panic. Ok? Up you get."

Launcelot was a bright chestnut… or ginger, as Mary would say. He was the biggest horse Dylan had ever sat on. 14.2 hands high. Dylan smiled to hide his fear.

The six riders made their way up the hill at a speedy walk, avoiding any icy patches. There was a tangible excitement in the air.

The hour ride flew by and Launcelot behaved like a dream. The customers were novice riders so the speed had remained calm.

Towards the end of the ride Dylan decided to ask Launcelot to halt to join Mary at the back. And then it happened! Launcelot flew up into the air. Like a missile launching into space.

Then he came back down as if nothing had happened. Dylan's stomach flipped, but he liked it. He maintained a gentle contact with Launcelot's mouth again and pulled gently, giving a little squeeze from both legs. Launcelot shot up again, like a circus horse.

"Holy shit!" Dylan shouted, laughing. "I made him do that!"

"Do it again," Mary laughed, encouraging the naughtiness.

Dylan gave the commands and Launcelot performed his rearing trick again.

"Come on, it's Christmas tomorrow, I need to get home!" Mary laughed.

The two of them pushed their horses into a trot to catch up with the rest of the ride.

Back at the stables, the pace didn't let up. There were still horses to be untacked, stables to be bedded down, and tack to clean. The radio played Christmas carols and Dylan worked alongside Anita and Mary, the three of them falling into an easy rhythm as they swapped stories and jokes.

As the day wound down, Dylan snuck around to Jill's stall to say goodnight. She was munching contentedly on her hay, her ears flicking forward as she noticed him approach.

"Hey, girl," Dylan whispered, stroking her soft nose. "I'll see you tomorrow, okay?"

Jill nuzzled his shoulder, and Dylan felt a lump rise in his throat.

"Thank you Jill – you'll always be *Dusty* to me – thank you for bringing me to your real home. I love it here." Dylan said, hugging his little friend. "I love you Dusty, Happy Christmas."

As Dylan boarded the bus back to Llanrwst, he couldn't stop smiling. The weight of the last few months seemed to have lifted, replaced by a growing sense of purpose. Tŷ Coch felt like home in a way only Henryd had before.

By the time he reached the flats, the familiar chaos of home greeted him: the sound of Baby J crying, Magi yelling at Ela to get ready for bed, and the faint smell of freshly baked mince pies in the air, calming everything down.

He slipped upstairs quietly, stripping out of his dirty clothes and making a quick note in his Fraggle Rock book:

- **Found a note in Mam's bag with my real dad's phone number.**

And for the first time ever, Dylan wrote notes about his life that consisted of more than just entries about searching for his Dad.

- **Kulin bolted with me yesterday and I stayed on! Best ride ever.**
- **Rode a huge horse called Launcelot today. I made him rear and I stayed on! It was fun. Mary and Anita are my new friends. I really like them.**
- **I love Tŷ Coch riding stables.**
- **Dusty's happy. That makes me happy too.**

The words on the page filled Dylan with a quiet sense of pride. He read them over a few times, smiling to himself. These were the kinds of days he wanted to remember.

Satisfied, Dylan tucked the notebook away under his pillow and stretched his arms above his head. His muscles protested, sore from the day's exertion, but it was a good kind of ache from riding horses – a reminder of what he'd accomplished.

He felt a sudden tug of obligation and excitement as he remembered the warm smell of mince pies downstairs. Magi might still be in a mood, but it was Christmas eve, and tonight he needed to show that he could be a good boy.

He made his way down the stairs, the familiar creak of the wooden steps grounding him as he passed Baby J's room. Peeking in, he saw his baby brother finally asleep, his tiny chest rising and falling with each breath. Ela's door was slightly ajar, and Dylan caught sight of her curled up in bed, the Argos catalogue still clutched in her hand. Christmas stockings placed neatly at the ends of their beds.

Downstairs, the kitchen was a scene of domestic chaos. Crumbs littered the counters, a rolling pin lay haphazardly on the table, and a half-empty glass of sherry stood next to a plate of mince pies cooling on a wire rack. Magi was sitting at the table with her head in her hands, a glass of wine sat next to her.

"Hiya, Mam," Dylan said softly, stepping into the room.

Magi looked up, her eyes tired but warm. Pulling her hands away from her cheeks, she revealed a graze down one side of her face and a swollen lip.

"Oh, it's you, boy. You alright? Have you had a nice day at the stables?" Magi pushed the plate of mince pies toward him. "Here. Try one before the kids scoff the lot tomorrow."

Dylan took one, biting into the flaky pastry. The warmth and sweetness filled him with a sudden wave of comfort, and for a moment, all the noise and tension of the past few weeks faded into the background.

"Thanks, Mam," he said, his voice quiet but sincere.

Magi smiled faintly, taking a sip of her wine. "I'm proud of you, you know," she said after a moment. "You've been a good boy these past few days, helping out with the little ones, working at the stables. You're a good boy, Dylan."

Dylan felt his cheeks flush with surprise. Compliments from Magi were rare, and he clung to her words like a lifeline.

"Thanks," he murmured, not trusting himself to say more.

The two of them sat in silence for a while, the sound of the clock ticking softly in the background. The warmth of the kitchen, the sweet smell of mince pies, and the quiet presence of his mam made Dylan feel at ease.

"Where's Dad?" Dylan asked, breaking the silence.

"He's asleep on the sofa. Leave him be for now so we can both have some peace." Magi pleaded.

Dylan tip-toed in to the living room to get his colouring pencils and was delighted to see a huge pile of freshly-wrapped presents by the tree. He turned to see Barry in a Santa hat, snoring on the sofa, with a big black eye and a bruised cheek.

If that's what Santa looks like, then I hope he doesn't come here tonight. Dylan thought.

Dylan went back in to the kitchen to sit with his mam. He paused.

"Please don't drink any more wine tonight Mam… please?" Dylan asked, gently.

Magi looked up at him.

"Do you want a cup of tea, Mam?"

Magi stared at her glass of wine. "Aye, go on then." She replied. "Pour that down that sink for me boy." She said, handing him the glass of wine.

Dylan filled the kettle and clicked it on.

"Shall we play Connect-4?" Dylan asked, presenting the boxed game, hopefully.

"Yes, go on then." Maggie said, smiling at the excitement radiating from her son.

A few more hours and Santa would, hopefully, be paying them a visit.

****

27

Christmas Day.

Dylan woke up to the faint glow of the street lamps filtering through the curtains, it was still dark outside. He squinted at his watch. **6:58 a.m.**

The flat was silent apart from the faint murmur of Baby J's steady breathing and Ela's occasional sleepy mumbles. At the end of their bed, their Christmas stockings were full to the brim, the bulging shapes of gifts wrapped in shiny paper barely contained within the fabric. Dylan glanced towards the foot of his own bed and smiled. His stocking was stuffed too.

He's been, Dylan thought to himself with a small smile.

Unfortunately, he also knew the truth. He'd been awake when *pissed-Santa* – otherwise known as Barry – had stumbled around their bedroom in the dead of night, trying to locate the stockings to fill them. He'd watched silently, pretending to sleep as Barry cursed under his breath about the Sellotape getting stuck to his fingers and tripping over Baby J's discarded toy truck.

Oh well, Dylan thought, *I can still live out the fantasy through Ela and Baby J.*

Truth be told, Dylan had always struggled with the concept of Father Christmas. Every year, he would carefully write his wish list, handing it in with a hopeful heart, and yet, the most important items never seemed to materialise. He'd watch the 'naughty kids' on the estate – kids who bullied others or broke windows – brag about the expensive gifts they'd received. Sometimes, he'd even recognise their presents as stolen goods, courtesy of the council estate dealers like Bill. It didn't seem fair.

Still, Christmas morning had a magic of its own, and Dylan wasn't about to let it slip away.

He leaned over and shook his siblings awake.

"Come on, you two…" he said with a grin, his voice teasing. "He's been!"

Ela shot upright, her curls bouncing, her eyes wide with excitement. Baby J, slower to stir, rubbed his sleepy eyes before breaking into a toothy smile.

"Really?" Ela gasped. "He's been?"

"Of course he has!" Dylan replied, laughing.

The three of them scrambled out of bed, grabbing their stockings and pulling out gifts with unrestrained glee. The sounds of laughter and crinkling paper filled the room as Ela gasped over a new dolly and Baby J clutched a set of toy cars. Dylan watched them, his heart warm. Whatever he thought about Santa, seeing their joy made it all worth it.

The smell of toast wafted up the stairs, and Dylan led his siblings down to the freshly-cleaned kitchen, where Magi was already bustling about, uncharacteristically cheerful.

"Good morning, you lot!" she said, her blue eyes sparkling, "I've been waiting for you to wake! Come on, he's been – let's go and see!"

Her excitement was contagious. She led the children into the living room like the Pied Piper, her dressing gown trailing behind her, toast and tea carefully placed on the side table.

The sight that greeted them was nothing short of magical. The Christmas tree lights twinkled softly, reflecting off the shiny wrapping paper of neatly arranged presents. Each pile had a name tag, and Ela gasped, running to hers.

"He's been again!" she cried. "I must have been a very good girl!"

Dylan exchanged a smile with Magi. Despite the struggles, she'd managed to pull it off. No doubt Fay and Mr. Lazars would be at her door demanding payment come January, but for now, Magi had created a moment of wonder. Today wasn't the day to worry about next year's debt. Today was about the kids.

Barry shuffled into the room, bleary-eyed but smiling. "Is one of those cuppas for me?" he asked, scratching his head.

"Yes," Magi replied brightly, doing her best to keep the morning on track. "Right, let's get opening!"

For the next half hour, the living room was filled with the sound of tearing paper, excited gasps, and shouts of "thank you!" from Ela and Baby J. Dylan quietly helped Baby J open a big box containing a car garage, watching as his little brother's face lit up.

Dylan got to the end of his presents and surveyed his haul: a pair of riding gloves, horse stickers, a Bros tape, new jodhpurs, and a few other bits and pieces. He smiled, grateful for what he'd received.

"Happy, Dyl?" Magi asked, watching him carefully. "Do you like your presents?"

"Yes, thank you," Dylan replied sincerely. But deep down, there was always a part of him that hoped for more – perhaps even the impossible, like a pony of his own. He knew now why Santa never delivered that dream.

Magi disappeared behind the sofa and re-emerged with a box.

"Oh, Dyl," she said with a smile. "There's one here that you forgot about…"

Dylan's heart skipped a beat as she slid the box toward him. It wasn't big enough to hold a pony (obviously), but the element of surprise made his stomach flutter.

"Thanks, Mam," Dylan said, cautiously taking the box.

"And Dad," Magi added gently.

"Yes, thanks, Dad," Dylan said, though less enthusiastically.

Barry chuckled. "I wanted to get you a Man U football kit, but your mam said no!"

Dylan ignored him, his focus on the box. Magi had wrapped it meticulously, using extra paper and tape to create an air of mystery. He tore at the paper, peeling away the layers until he finally reached the contents.

His jaw dropped.

Inside was a brand-new jockey skull cap with a black-and-white silk.

"This is the one I wanted!" Dylan shouted, jumping up and down with delight. "I've wanted this for ages! Thank you so much!"

He immediately placed it on his head, adjusting the fit until it sat snugly. For the rest of the morning, he didn't take it off.

Dressed in his new riding gear, Dylan headed outside, feeling an unexpected rush of pride. For once, he was excited to show his friends what he'd received. He paraded around Glanrafon with his head held high, the skull cap firmly in place, feeling like the luckiest boy in the world.

But there was one more thing he needed to do.

He ran back to the flat, still in his riding clothes, and retrieved the yellow note from his bag. The piece of paper felt heavier than it had before, its significance sinking in. Along with it, he grabbed two shiny ten-pence coins from his pocket and made his way to the phone box near the library.

The walk felt longer than usual, his heart pounding with every step. When he reached the phone box, he stepped inside, the cold metal of the receiver biting against his hand. Taking a deep breath, Dylan dialled the number.

01492...

He added the remaining digits, knowing the number belonged to someone in Llandudno. The phone rang several times, each ring echoing in his ears like a drumbeat.

Finally, a voice answered.

"Hello? Hello, who's speaking please?"

The voice was deep and unfamiliar, but it sent a chill down Dylan's spine. He froze, the words caught in his throat.

Dylan hung up without saying a word, his hands trembling as he stepped out of the phone box. The weight of what had just happened settled over him, a mix of fear, excitement, and uncertainty.

And now, he knew what he had to do.

As he walked back toward the flats, the crisp Christmas air filled his lungs. The sound of laughter and Christmas carols drifted from the open windows, mingling with the faint smell of roasting turkey. Dylan's heart felt lighter than it had in months.

This Christmas wasn't about what he didn't have – it was about what he was beginning to find. For the first time in his life, Dylan felt like he was on the verge of something extraordinary.

At ten years old, Dylan may have discovered on Christmas Eve that Santa wasn't real, but the voice on the other end of the phone confirmed something far more important – his dad was real.

And now, Dylan needed to go and find him…

****

To every person who helped, supported and inspired me along the way and told me 'I could'…

Including -

Bill Kenwright and Jenny Seagrove – for believing in me and giving me the golden opportunity in Windsor.
Cindy Morris – for every hour I spent at Tŷ Coch (except lambing season).
Emma Vaudrey – my constant inspiration to write.
Everyone at Tŷ Coch in the 80s and 90s.
Gill – for the colouring pencils.
Jill Cassy (Dunne) – for introducing me to my lifelong obsession of horses.
Joy Ostle – for all the guidance.
Lesley – for the first lift to Liverpool and the gateway to a new life!
Miss Aelwen Jones – Ysgol Dolgarrog.
Nana – Elin Bach – my best friend.
Pawb yn Henryd yr 80au.
Playful Productions and everyone at the Piccadilly Theatre.
Ruth – for those special packed lunches.
The Real Women – for the laughter.
Wendy Tobias-Jones – For creating a safe space for equine loving kids to be feral in Bwlch Mawr.

And for every pony and horse that has been in my life – thank you for being the kind, non-judgemental teachers, who have brought me so much happiness.

****

A final note from the author –

Thank you very much for purchasing my book.

This book is part of a trilogy.

Please follow me on all socials for more information –

Instagram - @mrcraigryder

Facebook – craigryderactor

www.craigryder.co.uk

Printed in Great Britain
by Amazon